Traitor'

Traitor's Gate

(The Flanders Mare)

by Anne Stevens

Tudor Crimes: Book XIV

This book is copyrighted by TightCircle Publications and the author. © Anne Stevens 2016./2018 Tudor Crimes Series is © the Estate of S Teasdale.2016/17/18

Foreword

Thomas Cromwell, now the 1st Earl of Essex, Knight of the Garter, and leader of the Privy Council, is, after the king, the most powerful man in England. His thoughts on how the English economy, and the new English Church should be run, have come to full fruition, relations with the Holy Roman Empire are the best they have been for years, the Scots are quiet, and the royal treasury is full to overflowing.

England is at peace. Her navy is fast becoming the most powerful military force ever seen, and the country is on the brink of starting a golden age of expansion and exploration. The Draper Company, under the guidance of Lady Miriam, is growing fast, and trade and commerce are now the country's most lucrative forms of income.

Nothing stands in Henry's way, and the only dangerous enemies England has left are all internal. The Holy Roman Empire is almost benign, now the king has taken Anne of Cleves to wife, and the French king, François, knows he is now at a complete military disadvantage.

The future is bright, save for one small flaw. The vanity of man knows no bounds, and it is vanity that makes Thomas

Cromwell blind to his own fallibility, and it is vanity that drives Thomas Howard, the Duke of Norfolk, to one last throw of the dice.

Norfolk is of the most noble blood, and his hatred of Thomas Cromwell, the son of a blacksmith, has grown, until he can contemplate nothing else but his complete destruction. Over the years, he has begrudgingly admired the man, then mistrusted him, and finally… fired him, and his cleverness.

Despite many plots laid against him over the previous decade, Tom Cromwell has been the great survivor, surrounding himself with a loyal entourage of people ready to do their utmost for their master.

Rafe Sadler, once Tom Cromwell's clerk, holds a prominent position at court, and has the king's ear. Richard Cromwell, a forceful young man, now commands the King's Ordinance, and he is highly thought of by Henry, because of his martial prowess, whilst Sir Will Draper, the bastard son of a priest, and soldier of fortune, is Commander in Chief of the King's Examiners. With the young Jew, Mush Draper, in charge of the wall of security about his beloved master, ThomasCromwell, the defensive ring is seemingly unbroken.

Only the casual treachery of an unknown fool cannot be accounted for, and a few ill chosen words, uttered at just the wrong moment, can be enough to bring destruction down on even the most well ordered world.

Great men flourish, and fortunes are made as England moves into a new decade... a decade that promises much in the way of religious freedom, and profitable commerce.

It is in the first few weeks of 1540 that Anne of Cleves arrives in England, and from that moment on, many lives will never be the same again . . . for there is a shadow looming... the dreaded shadow of the Traitor's Gate.

1 The Welcome Feast

Hampton Court Palace sparkles like a jewel, set in a backdrop of early morning mist, and a light, glistening frost. Sir Will Draper, Colonel in Chief of the King's Examiners, smiles as he recalls his first visit to the palace. Since then, he has risen in rank to become a knight of the realm, and commands an elite hundred man cadre, charged with the king's security, and the investigation of crimes touching upon the monarchy.

He pats Moll, his ageing Welsh Cob, on her neck, and mutters encouraging words into her pricked back ears. By his side, Mush is mounted on his latest purchase, a coal black stallion, and regaled in a new doublet, made of fine green velvet, with slit leather sleeves, and silver clasps. Behind them, by no more than a quarter of a mile, comes a well sprung coach of the latest French design, and a half dozen outriders, who are there to protect the ladies within.

Lady Miriam is coming to Hampton Court at the express invitation of His Majesty, Henry Tudor, King of England, Ireland, and France. Apart from providing the kitchen staff, and most of the proposed menu, the elegant Miriam is also thought to be one of the richest women in England. In fact, though Tom Cromwell begs her to keep it a secret from the world, she is, after ten years in the cut throat world of commerce, the second richest woman in Europe.

Beside her is her long time friend, Pru Beckshaw, and opposite sits another lady, Marion Giles, who is fast becoming a good companion to Lady Draper, and a great help to the various enterprises that comprise the growing Draper Company. Next to her is Lady Jane Rochford, the widow of George Boleyn who, for propriety's sake, must arrive at the royal palace apart from her longstanding lover, Richard Cromwell.

"I am sure the seating arrangements will satisfy you, dear Jane," Miriam says, consolingly, to the still beautiful woman. "You will not be long from dear Richard's side."

"Do not fret on my account, Miriam," Lady Rochford responds, rather tartly. "Dick Cromwell is not the only prize on offer this week. He pays me scant regard these days, and I am minded to find myself a new lover… a lover who is rich, and noble enough to marry me. Better a contented wife than an ill used mistress."

"Poor Richard," Pru says. "He is destined never to be happy, no matter how wealthy he becomes."

"You *see* this?" Lady Rochford asks. It is a secret, known to only a few, that Pru Beckshaw can foresee things with uncanny accuracy. Her husband, Major John Beckshaw, now second in command of the King's Examiners, does nothing without consulting her, and heeding her utterances. Her 'sight' has saved his life on at least one occasion, and averted disaster when heeded by others.

"I see a long life for him," Pru says, with some slight hesitation. "This good health, and his eventual wealth, is not enough to make him content. He is destined to break hearts, Lady Jane."

"Horse shit," the Viscountess Rochford snaps. "My heart is not for breaking. The man treats me like a scullery maid, and he can go hang for all I care. What about me though, my dear friend… what does my future hold?" She stretches out her hand, palm upwards, but Pru shrinks back from it, and looks to Miriam for moral support.

"It is not right that Pru uses her power in that way," Miriam says. "It can come to no good. We always pick out the best, and ignore the worst, so anything Pru tells us, personally, is diluted to the point of worthlessness. Now, let us discuss the seating arrangements for tonight, my dear friends."

Pru Beckshaw sighs, and sits back on the well padded seat, content not to have been forced into any disclosure about Lady Rochford's life to come. For some time now, she has seen nothing but darkness about the woman, and senses that a terrible, and fearsome, future awaits her.

*

"Bloody stuck up load of bastards," old Wat Turner moans to his first sauce cook, "deciding to have a welcome feast at three days notice. They best not blame me if it all goes wrong!"

The old man, who was once Cardinal Wolsey's man, and has worked for the Duke of Suffolk, Thomas Cromwell, and the king since, gazes out over the vast kitchens under his command. Over fifty rooms have been knocked into one huge space, and almost one hundred and eighty men, women and children are labouring away at one culinary task or another.

"Nothing too lavish, my dear Wat," Tom Cromwell had said to him. "Let us keep it below twenty courses, and do not be too generous with the king's finer wines. These people are, after all, German… and have no palate to speak of."

"Under twenty dishes at a royal banquet," Wat sneers to himself, and his closest staff. "This new queen in waiting will think that Henry is a pauper. If I do less than twenty four, the poor girl will think she is amongst those barbaric turds, the Scots, rather than English gentlemen. Master Charnos, have the beaver tails been prepared yet?"

Meant as a Friday only delicacy, because of their fish-like associations, grilled beaver tails are being used as a starting dish, purely because of the king's liking for them. Basted with crushed peppercorns in malted vinegar, they are a spicy start to what promises to be a long evening.

Even as this course is finished, the old cook will see that each guest is given a bread charger to rest on his pewter plate, ready to receive a varied selection of spit roasted meats. The bread will soak up the grease and juices, and provide a tasty entrée leading up to the third course. Beside each juicy cut of spit roasted flesh, there is to be a scented bowl of water for the fingers… a *finesse* of manners taken from the fashionable French courts, and introduced by the late Anne Boleyn.

The Hampton Court Palace kitchen staff are well trained in the roasting of meat, and in a typical year, over twelve hundred oxen, eight thousand sheep, more than two thousand deer, seven hundred veal calves, eighteen hundred pigs, and fifty wild boar, pass through the huge kitchens.

Great steaks of whale meat, slow

roasted in a wild berry sauce, will prove a most filling third course, and also keep the costs down, for whales are plentiful in the northern seas, and are amongst the cheapest of fish dishes. To compliment the whale dish, the king's master cook has ordered the royal lakes and rivers to be trawled, and a fine array of broiled carp, poached salmon, stewed eels, dace in vinegar dressing, and brined pike can be had.

At this point, Wat Turner will ensure that everyone's cup is full to the brim of the sweet Portuguese wine that goes so well with fish dishes. The Iberian wine is supplied by Miriam Draper's trading company, at a fair price of course, and it is a serious opponent of the more expensive French Sauternes, or Barsac. There are four hundred gallons standing ready, and most will be drunk before the meal is done with.

The head cook will see that there is a pause in serving at this point, so that those not of a gluttonous nature can ease their stomachs for a while. The privies will be used by the nobles, whilst lesser mortals will defecate on the one of the many flower beds outside. Some, of weak character, might pass out with distended bellies, and many a more robust courtier might wish to tickle his throat with a feather, in order that he can make room for the next delicacies on offer.

Light pastries, made with freshly churned butter, and filled with a delicate egg custard, provided by Miriam Draper's expert staff, will be distributed then, so as to further cleanse the dulled palate for the next, spectacular course. For the wily old head cook has managed to scour the countryside, and round up a veritable flock of magnificent peacocks.

It is traditional that this king amongst birds is roasted whole. The cooked carcass is then bedecked with its own plumage, an array of iridescent blue feathers. … plucked, then replaced after the bird has been cooked. As a nod to the overly ornate French way of presentation, the birds beaks are to be gilded in fine gold leaf, and the whole presented on huge silver salvers, carried by pairs of strong pageboys dressed in the same blue. The breast flesh is light and delicate on the tongue, but the legs and wings are discarded, as being too tough for the human palate.

It is then that Wat Turner will bring forth his culinary masterpiece… his famous *Rôti Sans Pareil.* This amazing 'roast without equal' is his speciality, and consists of a huge roast heron, stuffed with a descending order of other fowl, starting with a bustard, and continuing down through a well larded goose, a pheasant, a chicken, a duck, a woodcock, a partridge, a plover, a lapwing, a quail, and finally, the daintiest little lark. This last, and smallest bird is, of course, the great jest that makes the dish. Upon reaching the centre of the vast dish, some clever wit always cries; "*Ah, but this is a great lark!*"

By this point, most guests should be either fed to absolute perfection, or too drunk to care, but for those who are still eager, there are a bevy of interesting dishes to keep them amused into the small hours of the night. Wat's highly skilled army of culinary experts will bring forth steamed black puddings with mustard dressing, skewers of pan seared pigs offal, beef lungs stuffed with oats, wild garlic and breadcrumbs, steamed suet dumplings, boiled barley and parsley pancakes, sheep udders poached in milk, boar tongues garnished with bay leaves and rosemary, cold soup made from stewed vegetables and onions, rabbit casserole, meat and game pies, hare stew, cream flans, individual spiced fruit cakes, eight varieties of foreign cheeses, and to finish … a speciality of the old cook… marzipan.

This delicacy, like the older *Marchpane* recipe, is made from ground almonds, cinnamon, pepper and sugar , but with the addition of beaten egg whites. It is to be hand sculpted to look like colourful representations of ladies bosoms, gentlemen's private members, and dainty fruits, and will bring a merry end to the meal, along with an array of Flemish, French and Hungarian wine, and vast tankards of mulled and spiced ale to aid the digestion.

So vast is the palace's demand for strong ale that Wat Turner has established a small brewery in a nearby village, whose only purpose is to supply some of the thirty thousand barrels of ale needed every year just to quench the thirst of the six hundred or so courtiers, and the palace's ever growing staff. With each man, woman and working child granted an allowance of six free pints of ale each day, the brewers must work almost around the clock, just to keep up with the demand.

Master Charnos, an olive skinned young man of uncertain birthright, assures the head cook that the beaver tails are being grilled to perfection, and that the salted cod, fish roe, stewed eels and freshly broiled crabs are all well in hand. The huge kitchen is throbbing with activity, and many work stripped to the waist, in the intense heat from the great fireplaces.

"Take your ease, master," young Charnos says. "Your staff all know their part. This Anne of Cleves shall have no cause for complaint where food is concerned. Rather, she will be put off by our lack of German manners, or her husband's bad temper."

"By God, yes," the old cook says, smiling. "The poor girl will have to have an angel's temperament if she is to win out. Now who is this who dares come into my kitchen unbidden?"

"Still blustering, you sly old dog?" Will Draper cries, and slaps the king's cook heartily on the back. The two men have, on a past occasion, intrigued against a common enemy… the now deceased Harry Percy. "I thought you would have been long gone by now, Master Wat. Does not some great emperor wish to purchase your services?"

"Let them wish," the old man cackles. "Why, if it is not *Sir* Will Draper. How are you, you sinful rogue?"

"Well enough, Master Wat," Will says, and sits by the nearest fire. "My wife and her entourage are settling into their chambers, and I am best out of the way. What news have you for me, old friend?"

"Nothing you do not already know," Wat Turner replies, gruffly. "Half of my lads are on your payroll, and spy on us from dawn to dusk. The new queen to be is here. She slipped in, after dark, and stays cloistered away in her private chambers."

"Does she not eat?" Will asks.

"In her rooms," Wat says. "Eggs, boiled hard, smoked bacon, cheese, bread and fresh butter. Lots of fresh butter. My lad says her women cut the bread into thin pieces, and hold them to the fire, until they turn brown. Then they rub butter onto the burnt slices."

"Butter… rubbed onto burnt bread?" Will shakes his head at this, and wonders what other strange customs Anne of Cleves has brought with her. "Have you seen her yet?"

"Not I." The old cook sees where this is heading, and offers what help he can to his old acquaintance. "The lad says they are all most plump looking, and have faces that are not too comely. One is shapely enough, he thinks. That said, he does not exactly know which of them is the lady in question."

"Damn it, but I fear the new queen might not be to Henry's taste at all," Will says. "Let us hope he is wed before the blinkers fall from both their eyes."

*

"Yes… Englishman… *vas* … what is it?" The statuesque lady-in-waiting stands in the portal, as if guarding the portal to Valhalla from invasion.

"I am Thomas Cromwell, madam," Cromwell says, not unkindly, and the woman's face softens from a heavy frown to a gentler smile. "Might I beg a few moments with Lady Anne?" The girl disappears, there is the sound of a flurry of activity, and the door swings open.

"My Lord Cromwell, I am Anne. Please… do come in. I am suitably chaperoned." Tom Cromwell bows, gracefully, and is relieved to see that, whilst no great beauty, Anne of Cleves is not the ugly woman he has been led to expect. He enters, and bows to each lady in turn.

"Welcome to England, Your Royal Highness."

"Are you not acting in a presumptuous manner, sir?" Anne asks the councillor. "I am not yet wed to your king. This makes me still the *common* person, *ja*?"

"The legal papers are all signed and sealed, my dear madam," Cromwell replies. "You and the king are bound together in law, and there remains only a brief religious service. The archbishop will join you in wedlock tomorrow morning."

"So soon married? And I have yet to meet Henry." Anne has taken an immediate liking to Cromwell, and confides in him from the start. "Though some of his gentlemen visited us the other night, and we were not at all amused. Rough old men came into us, with their breath stinking of wine. I fear that they sought to dishonour us by their lewd presence."

"Surely not, Your Majesty," Cromwell says, genuinely shocked at this awful news. "No-one would dare violate the king's intended… on pain of death. Can you describe these felons to me, so that I might have the Attorney General arrest them?"

"You can do this?" Anne asks. If Cromwell has so much power, she thinks, he must be courted, and made into a friend.

"With but one gesture," Cromwell boasts. "The king depends on me in most things, and I am his first minister. Describe these rogues, and they will be taken up, and dealt with to the fullest extent of the law."

"Your English law is well thought of in my country," Anne tells her visitor. "My father says it deals honestly with all."

"Let me but prove it, madam." Cromwell urges her to try and recall their appearance, so he can act.

"One was a pointed faced man with a thin set of whiskers, and eyes like a weasel," she says, after some consideration. It is a perfect description of Sir Richard Rich, the Attorney General of England. "He capered about the chamber like a monkey, and tried to hold the … *titten*… of my poor Helge. She was forced to tweak his nose for him, and box his ears. He only left when their leader became distraught, and ran off."

"Their leader, My Lady?" Thomas Cromwell has a twist of anguish in the pit of his stomach, and is almost too scared to ask the next question. "Was he a big man?"

"*Ja*… you know him?" Anne smiles in triumph. "His face was masked from me, but he was *this* tall … and *this* fat." She gestures with her hands, to show that a man, over six feet tall, and of obese stature was to blame. "Oh, yes, I almost forgot… he had an unkempt red beard too."

"Sweet Christ," Thomas Cromwell mutters. "Was there a fair haired gentleman with them? Quite slenderly built, and somewhat less … forward?"

"*Ja*. He had a well turned calf, and pretty eyes."

"Suffolk," Cromwell mutters, "I shall have your heart on a plate for this foul treachery!"

2   Confessions

"Good day to you, My Lord Suffolk." Mush Draper steps from an alcove, and makes the duke take a step backwards, surprised and a little frightened. He glances about, and sees that they are quite alone in the wide corridor, as most courtiers are busy trying to impress the king with their archery skills. The young Jew is toying with one of his Spanish made daggers, and looks ready to kill.

"Come now Mush… what has happened to you calling me Charles?" the duke asks. "Are we not firm friends… bonded together in our mutual love for Tom Cromwell?"

"Are we?" Mush says, and takes the duke by his elbow. "It seems that our new queen thinks you have pretty eyes, My Lord. I am minded to pluck one out, and have it mounted on a ring for her."

"God alive, Mush… what is it?" Suffolk stutters. "How have I offended you … ever so accidentally?"

"Master Cromwell wishes a word with you," Mush says, and prods the frightened duke in the direction of his master's private chambers. "He is most annoyed over something, and says I need not treat you with undue kindness. Now, move!"

"I am the Duke of Suffolk," Charles Brandon says, as he summons up his last ounce of courage. "You must unhand me, sir!"

"Oh, do shut up, Charles," Mush Draper says, and slaps him hard across the back of his head. "One more ill chosen word, and I will loosen your teeth for you."

"Then I am lost," Suffolk moans. "What is to happen to me… pray speak up, for the sake of friendship."

"It is out of friendship that I come for you," Mush advises the cowed duke. "Had Richard come, he might have killed you out of hand… without bothering to extract a confession."

"But what have I done?" Suffolk protests. He can think of nothing in the recent past, and acts in Thomas Cromwell's best interest at all times. "I am a Cromwell man, and would do him no harm. I am his eyes and ears when with the king, and report faithfully every …oh."

The penny drops, and Charles Brandon, Duke of Suffolk holds his tongue. He sees that it is the mad caper of a few nights before that damns him now. The wild ride to play a trick on the Cleves contingent, and the rather poor outcome, is a cause for embarrassment, and not to be bandied about. Now it comes back to haunt him, as he realises his stupid mistake.

Cromwell did not know of the adventure, and he should have warned him better.

"I sent a boy to find Rafe Sadler," he whimpers in mitigation of his part in the affair.

"Then he did not find him," Mush Draper says with cold disdain. "Master Cromwell must have the story from you now, without further ado. I pray, for your sake, that you are innocent of this thing, or there will be blood spilled this night!"

*

"I like this Lord Cromwell very much," Anne says to her closest friend, and lady-in-waiting. "Did you see the anger in his eyes when I spoke of those sad old men who offended us so?"

"Yes, madam," Helge replies, as she tries to tighten Anne's bodice laces. "Breath in, and I will fasten you tightly. See how it takes in the waist, and pushes the breasts upwards. The king must see something he likes, when first you meet him. I know of no man who would not gaze at a fine pair of dumplings. Henry will stare, and then he will want… *ja*?"

"Cromwell says he is a fine figure of a man," Anne muses. "I hope his age does not affect his manly prowess. I have waited a long time to give myself to a man, and I pray the wait is worth it."

"Then you think of this Henry as

your first man?" Helge says, with a saucy smirk. "What of that ambassadors son, and young Rolf? Both were most attentive you."

"I remained quite virtuous with them… in a legal way," Anne replies with a knowing smile. "For, under English law, the sin is in the fornication… is it not? No man has ever entered me with his member. I soon found out the pleasures of the tongue, and an exploring finger or two. As did you, my friend… yes?"

"Yes, young Rolf is a willing servant," Helge tells her mistress, and they both giggle. The store set by a lady's virginity is greater in England than back home, and both of them have explored the world of heavy sexual petting to its furthest limits.

"You and I have often shared a bed," Anne continues. "Such romantic attachments are most pleasurable, and not condemned in any bible I have read. I wager Lord Cromwell knows how to use a woman in the right way. I wonder if he is married?"

"Hush, madam," Helge says. "I know none of these servants understand our language, but you must be careful. Tomorrow, you will become the Queen of England, but tonight we shall feast."

"I am hungry enough," Anne says.

"I hope they have roast sucking pig, glazed with honey and a caper sauce with it!"

*

"Roast sucking pig, glazed with honey, and served in a caper sauce?" Wat Turner moans. "Are you sure, lad?"

"Yes, master," the young fire tender says. Paulus Weamsley is of mixed English and Flemish blood, can speak five languages with ease, and understands a few more well enough to make a good spy for Thomas Cromwell. "I heard Queen Anne… as she will be, tomorrow, wish for the dish. I thought the knowledge might be of use to you, and earn me a silver penny or two."

"Can you break a shilling?" the cook asks, and young Paulus nods and unfastens his purse. "Here, and give me ten pennies change." The boy effects the transaction, and bows to the cook.

"Serve the lady with her desire," he says, "and she will be a good friend to you, Master Wat." He bows, and retires to his under stairs niche, where he considers what else he has overheard. Poor Anne is in for a rude awakening, he thinks, once she sees the king in the flesh. That, however is not news, and need not be passed up the line to Thomas Cromwell. That the new queen, and her buxom ladies, are not adverse to a dalliance now and then, is news.

Thomas Cromwell must be informed about it. Anne Boleyn went to the block because of her sexual improprieties, and it would cause a stir if the Cleves woman met the same fate. He will tell Rafe Sadler, Richard Cromwell, or Mush Draper, as soon as the chance presents itself. A polite thank you will come back, no doubt, together with a small present of money.

Paulus Weamsley is a loyal Cromwell man, and his place at Austin Friars is promised, as soon as his usefulness at court comes to an end. In the meantime, he can use his knowledge to further his own ambitions, and decides to catch Lady Helge alone as soon as he may. Though far from being a beauty, the woman is obviously open to the amorous advances of gentlemen.

"Play my cards right, he mutters, "and I shall be astride that brood mare before the week be out."

*

"I can explain!" the Duke of Suffolk declares, the moment he is thrust into Thomas Cromwell's presence.

"You can?" Cromwell asks, icily. The room falls silent, with an air of imminent menace, and Suffolk's lips are dry with fear.

"Yes… well, that is to say… no," the duke stammers out, at last. "It was just a silly caper. You know how it is."

"No, I do not, My Lord Suffolk," Cromwell replies. "Pray explain it to me. Explain how the king was allowed to gallop across country, late at night, with nobody but you and that idiot Rich for company. After that, you might tell me why you did not warn me, or at least report on the affair afterwards."

"The king was in no danger, Master Cromwell," Suffolk explains. "None of us were. We were in disguise."

"Disguise?" Cromwell cannot believe his ears. "How so?"

"We wore masks," Suffolk says, somewhat lamely.

"Oh, that explains everything," Thomas Cromwell roars. "You wore masks. My God, Charles… but you are such a blasted idiot. Dress the king up as a Christmas angel and he would stand out. Lady Anne described him… and you to me… mask or no mask. What, in God's good name, possessed you, man?"

"Hal insisted," Suffolk admits. "You know how he is when he gets one of these ridiculous ideas in his head. He tells me to round up the fellows, and away he goes. The only chance of staying his hand is to get you to talk sense into him… and you were not there, sir. I caught hold of a page, and sent him for Rafe Sadler. Did not young Stanhope do my bidding?"

"Roger Stanhope is a second cousin of the Duke of Wiltshire's mother, Lady Margaret Butler," Cromwell replies. "He is a Thomas Boleyn supporter, and most likely he ran straight to him instead."

"I say, that is unfortunate," Suffolk says. "I cannot understand why Hal even allows Boleyn to keep his title. First Earl of Wiltshire indeed!"

"So, no warning was received," Thomas Cromwell continues, wearily. "The three of you leap onto your horses, and set off like…"

"There were more of us than that," says Suffolk. "Why, Tom Wyatt was there, along with that toad Richard Rich, and so too was old Dan Wildwood, Roger Wharton, and Sir John Russell. There might have been more, perhaps as many as ten of us, but I cannot really say."

"Very well, you are forgiven for not warning me," Cromwell says, "but I have yet to hear how events unfolded. What happened when you arrived… and leave nothing out, My Lord."

Charles Brandon is still drawing breath, so thinks he might just survive this unexpected disaster in one piece. He composes himself, decides that the truth is now the best course of action to take, and begins his report.

"We rode there… and arrived about

the ninth hour," he starts, "and milled about a while."

"Milled about?" Thomas Cromwell wishes to bang the duke's head on the oak panelled wall, but refrains for the moment.

"Yes, you know. Milling. We trotted our horses about the courtyard, shouted a few boisterous remarks, and barged one another, until that silly bugger Wildwood fell off into a heap of horse shit." Suffolk smiles at the recollection, and wonders if the man still smells of the stables. "Then Hal dismounts, and says we must search out the foreign ladies, like wild eyed bandits, and make them all afraid of us."

"What a clever prank," Tom Cromwell mutters, and grinds his teeth. "So, you stormed the high tower, and lay siege to the maidens within… no doubt. Judas strike you all!"

"Hal went first, but the steps soon tired him, and he was forced to pause for breath," Suffolk explains. "After a moment, he was able to carry on. We came to the lady's door, which was guarded by two soldiers, and we fell on them, and drove them away with kicks and shoves."

"Bravo." Cromwell can see it all in his mind's eye, and it makes him wince. "I wonder why the soldiers did not draw their weapons, and slay a few of you?"

"Yes, that is so. They were big,

burly chaps, with poleaxes and breastplates. I dare say they were simply overcome by our martial appearance."

"Or recognised a gang of inebriated nobles, and left them to their silliness," Thomas Cromwell guesses. "Perhaps the king's fox mask was not enough of a disguise."

"Oh, I was the fox," Suffolk says. "We strutted around the room... save for Tom Wyatt, who kept himself apart... and the king demanded favours from the ladies. It was only then that we realised how ... plain... the Cleves women were. Big, solid looking mares, with huge bosoms, and plaited hair, piled high on their heads, or wrapped in coils over their ears. Ugh!"

"Then what?"

"Hal made some disparaging remark, and fled the chamber, with the rest of us hard at his heels." The Duke of Suffolk pauses and thinks hard to see if he has missed anything out. "Damn me, Cromwell, but they were not a pretty bunch of wenches. Big, fulsome girls, with large noses, and feet ... oh, such enormous feet they had. I can only hope that the Flanders Mare was not in the stable when we called, and that she will emerge, like a butterfly from the dung heap."

"Do not be such an utter *pintle*, Charles," Cromwell says, with cold disdain.

"It now becomes clear to me that you are simply an idiot… rather than a traitor, and I must forgive you for your utter stupidity. Now get out of my sight. I shall see you next at dinner."

The Duke of Suffolk bows, and hurries away, thankful to still have his eyes… and his life. He will try to keep his wits about him from now on, for he senses a sudden, though subtle change in the political climate. Upon his return from the jaunt with Henry, he had recounted the adventure to the Duke of Norfolk, over a friendly bezique game of *piquet*. The old fellow had played the queen of spades with the seven of diamonds, and then positively roared with laughter.

"So the old stallion has seen his brood mare, has he?" Norfolk told Suffolk as he scooped up his winnings. "Good, for that will make it all the easier for me."

"Damn and bugger it," Suffolk says to himself. "Perhaps I should have told Cromwell about *that* too!"

*

"You let him off too lightly, Master Tom," Mush Draper says, once the duke has scurried away, and Thomas Cromwell wags an index finger at him.

"Not so, Mush. You really must learn to *listen* to what is said, and from it deduce that which is *not* said."

"What have I missed?" Mush asks. "I must be at my best for when I travel to Sardinia."

"Ah, you still wish to slaughter every member of the hateful Brotherhood then?" Cromwell asks. "I hoped that time, or the example of Edmund Tunnock, might change your mind. Poor Tunnock has spent ten hard years tracking down the enemies of a long dead cardinal. Revenge is not always sweet, my boy. Let others take on the Brotherhood."

"It is now a vendetta," Mush replies. "They killed two of Isabella's family, and tried to kill Miriam, amongst others. Now, sir, what did I miss?"

"Those who were there," Thomas Cromwell tells his favourite lieutenant. "Suffolk is a courtly fool, and forgot. Tom Wyatt is a poetic fool, and did not think it important. Sir John Russell is, however, a horse of a different colour. We pay him, do we not?"

"A hundred a year, and expenses," Mush replies.

"His only task is to keep an eye on Henry, and report back to us, at once," Cromwell says. "It has been almost four days now, and he has yet to send word. Why is that, Mush?"

"Perhaps he thought it too trivial."

"He should report everything,"

Cromwell says. "He tells us how many times Sir Thomas Heneage wipes the king's bottom for him each day, and what he ate for breakfast. Why not inform us that His Majesty rode across the county, without any soldiers to protect him, and then raided a lady's bed chamber?"

"I do not know."

"Then find out." Cromwell realises his voice has become harsh, and he softens it a touch. "Russell has either failed us, or done someone else's bidding."

"Shall I arrest him?"

"God's teeth, Mush. Use your brain, lad. I only want to know if he is becoming too friendly with our enemies. Have him watched, and check his reports scrupulously. Look for that which he omits, rather than tells us."

"Yes, Master Cromwell."

"And do not sulk so, my boy," Tom Cromwell says, in a fatherly way. "You have not called me Master Cromwell for years. I know you think me infallible, but I am not, and there are still those who would ruin me, just for the sake of it."

"Norfolk is the only one left," Mush replies. "What can he do to us now? The king still suspects he acted treasonably during the northern rebellion, and Henry holds a grudge over the bad advice he gave him about Cardinal Wolsey."

"Henry cares nothing for Wolsey," Cromwell says. "That is why Tunnock and I had to exact payment from his enemies. Who do we have watching Norfolk just now?"

"James Lower. He is the Duke of Norfolk's falconer these days, and sends us word of the damned fellow's movements."

"Send for him," Thomas Cromwell says. "I can smell mischief in the air, once more, and from Norfolk's direction. Let us speak with James lower, and see what he can tell us."

Mush Draper bows low, and slips out of the chamber.

3 The Witch

The atmosphere within the great dining hall at Hampton Court reminds Tom Wyatt of the recent funeral of Queen Jane Seymour, and he longs to slide away and find a friendly card game to join. Someone coughs, and the noise echoes about the vast chamber like a pistol shot. The king turns, and glares at the culprit.

It is to be an evening of glaring, and sour looks, the poet thinks, and wonders at how obvious is the dislike between the king and his new bride. The moment their eyes met, the fate of the evening was set firmly on the road to disaster. Even now, with the first two courses done, Henry has failed to say a single word to Anne of Cleves, and Wyatt decides to speak.

"How do you find England?" he asks the woman, Helge, who has been seated across from him at the second table.

"On a boat," the girl replies, solemnly. "Up and down, *ja*?"

"Quite. You like England?"

"No."

"I see." The poet struggles to make headway. "Your mistress has many fine jewels… precious stones adorn that which is more precious still… her smile might fade the stars."

"Ah, you are the court jester!" Helge says, and rips apart the joint of lamb she has appropriated from the huge serving salver. "You are to make us laugh, *ja*?"

"I am Sir Thomas Wyatt, roving ambassador to the king, and court poet, madam," Wyatt replies. "Do you not have poets in Cleves?"

"Kleffs," Helge says. "It is said this way. Kleffs… not Cleaves, like an axe. My lady is Anna, and our home is the Duchy of Kleffs."

"I see," Wyatt says, and subsides back onto his stool.

"My poet seems content with your lady, madam," Henry says, with some effort. He cannot hear the conversation, but expects Wyatt is charming the solid looking lump of Germanic womanhood towards bed. "See … they converse in a most proper manner."

"Yes, but he wastes his time, Your Majesty," Anne says without thinking. "Helge does not like weak looking men. Back home, we judge our lovers by their … what is the word… lust?"

"Ah, you mean their lusty good humour, and love of the hunt," Henry tells her.

"No… by how they use a woman … in bed," Anne says. "My Helge prefers other, more satisfying pastimes."

"She sews then?"

"No… if there is not the man… she prefers…" Anne stops in mid sentence, and wonders if the king might not understand sexual love between two women. She is still recovering from the shock of finding the fat old man of whom she has complained to Cromwell is, in fact, her new husband. "Never mind."

"And you, madam?" Henry asks. "How do you like your men?" This, Anne of Cleves feels, is a trick question, and she replies as advised by her mother who, quite rightly, says all men are still unruly little children.

"I have no knowledge of them, sire," she says with a broad smile. "No man has ever touched me."

"I can believe that," Norfolk mutters to the king's right, and he receives an icy stare from Henry.

"Then we must remedy that at once," Henry says, and is rather pleased at his own spontaneous reply.

"How so, Your Majesty?" Anne says. The king stammers and blusters his way through an inarticulate answer, which gives the impression that he is little more than an idiot. The evening is teetering on the brink of disaster, when Wat Turner's lads carry in a great silver platter. For a moment, the great hall falls silent, then a low mutter starts as they march right up to the new queen.

"Oh, *ja!*" Anne of Cleves squeals in delight, and claps her hands. "Roast sucking pig. My favourite!"

At the next table, Helge slides a hand up the thigh of Lady Jane Rochford, and whispers in her ear. Lady Jane wonders if she has misheard, or that the message is meant to be passed on to some gentleman further down the table. At last, she begs some clarification from the big German girl.

"I'm sorry, my dear… you want to put your tongue where?"

For answer, Helge moves her hand, and Lady Jane finally understands. She grips the girl's wrist, and pushes her hand away from that part reserved for her next lover.

"Spoken for," she mutters. "Though I am sure your tongue will find another nest this night."

*

"Did you see the king's face when he saw his new queen?" Miriam asks, later that night. "He likes her not."

"I warned Cromwell," Will Draper says, as he unfastens his doublet. "He has gone too far this time."

"Warned him of what?" Miriam asks.

"He asked Holbein to improve on Anne's looks," her husband explains. "Henry was expecting a finer featured girl… and one who was a little slimmer. I fear the reality has irked him, and he must contemplate a life with a woman he cannot love."

"She is not unpleasant looking," Miriam protests.

"No, but she is not as represented." Will sighs. "Fortunately, Henry does not know what Cromwell did, and thinks him as surprised as he. Let us pray it remains so."

"By tomorrow morning, Henry will be quite reconciled to it," Miriam says.

"I hope so, for Anne of Cleves is well thought of by the emperor, and England needs his friendship. Damn, what is it now?"

There is an urgent knocking at the bedroom door, and a servant comes in with a message. John Beckshaw is outside, in the courtyard, and begs his presence at once.

"Examiner business…at this hour?" Miriam frowns.

"Go to bed, my dear," Will Draper tells his wife, "and I shall see what this is all about."

He dresses, fastens on his sword and goes out into the chill January night. John Beckshaw, and four Examiners are huddled together by a fountain, in earnest conversation. They fall silent as their commander approaches, and Beckshaw salutes smartly.

"My apologies, sir," he says, "but the matter is urgent. I have been ordered to make an arrest ... by Sir Richard Rich."

"The Attorney General has his own officers," Will says. "Why does he seek to use my men?"

"He is here alone," Beckshaw replies, "and needs to make the arrest at once. It seems that a woman is accused of witchcraft and he wants…"

"Witchcraft?" Will almost laughs out loud. He has no time for witches and spells, yet knows some still place great store by their existence. "He wants some old crone arrested before midnight, so as to foil her sorcery, and thinks that is a goodly use of our time. The damnable dunderhead. Where is he?"

"Here, sir." Sir Richard Rich has come upon them almost silently. "The king knows of the matter, and wishes me to make the arrest at once. It seems the evidence is strong, and the woman is thought to be a great danger to the community."

"A danger to herself, more like." Will Draper calls for his horse to be saddled. Moll, his faithful old Welsh Cob will get little rest this night. "I shall come along.

Where is this crone now?"

"Mistress Farriby's house is but a short ride," John Beckshaw tells him, and Will is taken by surprise.

"Elizabeth Farriby from Topham Hall?" he asks. The young woman is a friend of Miriam's, and has recently come into possession of a manor house and three hundred acres of land just beyond the king's parkland. "I know her… through Miriam. The girl is no witch, Master Attorney General. What are the charges?"

"That she did conspire with the devil, sour a neighbour's milk, use witchery to kill chickens, and curse three people to death."

"Are you mad, Rich?" Will asks. "If we burned a woman every time the milk went sour, or a yokel fell from a barn roof, there would be no-one left in the bloody shire."

"The king disagrees," Richard Rich replies, and produces a warrant, signed and sealed. "He fears witchcraft, and will have it stamped out once and for all time."

"Elizabeth Farriby is not a witch," Will Draper insists. "She is the only daughter of one of my wife's seamstresses, and made an orphan after the last bout of sweating sickness."

"How comes she to own a manor house?" Rich asks. "I doubt seamstress work pays that well. Or did she earn her sudden advancement in some more lascivious way?"

"Have a care, Rich," Will says, as he mounts Moll. "The girl has been fortunate, and inherited from a distant relative. She is well educated, well mannered, and an unlikely witch. Who brings these silly charges? Some jealous neighbour … or a spurned young man with little sense?"

"This is my investigation, Draper," Sir Richard Rich replies.

"I seek only to clarify matters."

"You seek only to protect your own," Rich snaps. "This is not a personal matter, sir… but a case of suspected witchcraft. It is my intention to arrest this woman, and investigate the claims against her. If she is innocent, she will be released, and if she is guilty, she will be punished as the law demands. A good burning serves to keep the rabble in its place."

"How many women have been arrested for sorcery in England since you became Attorney General?" Will asks.

"A dozen or so," Rich says, defensively. Old women are easy meat, of course, and each burning makes him look good in the king's superstitious eyes. "Within my immediate jurisdiction."

"And how many did you find to be innocent?" Will asks of the man.

"None," Rich says with a sly smile. "It points to my ability to sniff out a witch, sir."

"It points to your inability to distinguish truth from lies," Will says. "It is not enough to find a victim, then gird them about with lies, so as to make them seem guilty. What about proof?"

"I follow the law, sir!" Rich protests.

"I doubt you know the difference between justice and the law, Rich," Will replies. "Go carefully, or I will show you my kind of justice."

"You wish to threaten me?"

"With all my heart," Will snaps. "I find I am good at both the making, and the carrying out of threats!"

*

"Madam, your king is without." Henry is standing outside the closed drapes of Anne's bed, and awaits her permission to join her. Clustered at the door behind him are several gentlemen of the court, and three of the Cleves ladies, who are there to bear witness that the union is properly consummated.

Once Henry is seen into bed, they will withdraw, making the usual ribald remarks due to this occasion. The following day, these same witnesses will confirm that the task was completed with vigour, and the formal exchange of vows will take place. It is only then that Thomas Howard, Duke of Norfolk, will take the king aside and ask him, in truth, what he thinks of his new bride.

"Pray enter, husband," Anne answers, and Henry parts the curtains. He is relieved to see that his new queen is swathed in a heavy flannel nightgown, which covers from neck to ankle, and leaves his lust un-aroused. "I am ready for you."

"As I am for you… madam. Out! Out I say!" Henry realises that Norfolk, Wyatt, Heneage, and the others are still loitering, and he sends them about their business. "I have no further need of you gentlemen."

"No, sire… nor of our advice," the poet calls, and they all laugh. The fiction of the king's monumental sexual appetite, and skill with the ladies is bolstered, and they troop off, slapping one another on the back. As they make their way down the corridor, Helge, who is at the rear, finds herself taken by the elbow, and urged aside. It is the young servant, Paulus. He whispers into her ear, and she smiles and nods. The boy is pretty enough, she thinks, and it will pass an hour.

In the queen's chamber Henry finds himself at a loss as to how he might proceed. Anne sees this, and pulls open the front of her nightgown. Her breasts, once exposed, are large, and not unattractive, but the king has developed a marked dislike for her which he cannot quite explain. He signals for her to cover herself again, and sits back against the pile of cushions provided.

"You are tired, my husband?" Anne says, hopefully.

"It has been a long day," he replies, as he senses a possible escape rout.

"Then you must rest, sire," Anne says with mounting relief at the prospect of a reprieve. The thought of this old man's hands on her are enough to sicken her to death. "I would not have you do yourself an injury on my account. The king must preserve his health, and save his vigour for the nation."

"Just so, my dearest madam," Henry tells her. "You have it in a nutshell. I shall sleep… and then, come the morrow, we must see what we must see." In that moment, the king knows that he cannot perform his marital duty, and that he has not one scrap of desire for his new queen. He has walked into a trap, and wonders how he could have been so ill advised. It is only in the early hours of the morning that he thinks about the portrait, and curses Hans Holbein for his devilish talent.

"He fooled us all," Henry thinks.

"He tricked me, and poor Tom Cromwell, into seeing that which is not there. He has used his magical skills to mask the truth from our eyes. We have been taken advantage of... but why?"

*

The manor house sits in silence at the edge of a neat little village, and it is a little after the midnight hour when a troop of horsemen canter into the courtyard, and dismount. Under orders from Will Draper, John Beckshaw and his men are as quiet as they can be, and refrain from the usual formidable way of securing a prisoner. It seems that stealth is preferred in this case, and that his commander wants to avoid distressing their target.

Sir Richard Rich is for forcing down the door, and dragging the hapless victim from her bed, but Will Draper is a dangerous man to argue with, so he keeps silent. Beckshaw knocks, gently at first, then a little louder, and a servant arrives, carrying a thick tallow candle, to demand their business at so ungodly an hour.

"Is that you, Michael?" Will says, and the old man opens the door wide.

"Why, Sir Will... what brings you here at this late hour?" he says. "Pray, do step in out of the chill air."

"I wish to see your mistress," Will tells him, softly. "I fear there have been some serious charges laid against her."

"Charges?" The old man looks out then, and sees the King's Examiner's men. "Armed men, coming to a decent woman's door at midnight? What tomfoolery is this, sir?"

"Bring her forth!" Sir Richard Rich demands, then cowers back as Will turns on him, angrily.

"Have a care, sir," he snaps at the Attorney General. "It is a long, dark ride back… and these men are mine. Were you to have an accident on the road…" His meaning is clear. Not so long ago, Rich had tried to implicate Miriam Draper and some of her ladies in a spurious witchcraft case, and Will has promised to kill him if he moves against his family again.

"This is a case brought to me, Draper," he hisses. "I do not gain by its prosecution. The charges are made by some honest citizen, and the king already knows about it. Fail to arrest this witch now, and it is your own neck, not mine, that will be at risk."

"Fetch Elizabeth," Will tells the old man. "Have her dress warmly, and see that a horse is saddled for her."

"No, sir… I cannot."

"You dare defy a king's man?" Rich yells, and makes as if to strike the unfortunate servant. Will catches his raised fist, and pushes him firmly away.

"Why not?" he asks Michael.

"She is not here, master," the old man explains to the king's man. "She is visiting an old seamstress friend of her mother's, who has fallen gravely ill."

"Then where is she now?" Will asks.

"Why, at the palace, sir."

"The palace?"

"Yes, sir. Hampton Court," Michael says. "She travelled there yesterday. Mistress Brown is a seamstress there, and recently took a fall from which she struggles to recover."

"God's teeth, man," Sir Will Draper snaps at Sir Richard Rich. "Did you not think to find out Mistress Farriby's whereabouts before bringing us on this wild goose chase?"

"I could not know… I mean, the accuser never mentioned that she was not at home." Rich is made to look silly, and John Beckshaw and his men have had a night ride for nothing. One or two of them growl complaints, and the mood is ugly.

"Then we must return to Hampton Court at once, and hope the lady is not already on the return journey," Will says. "This simply shows how our two offices fail to work together, Rich, and I will tell the king so, when next we meet."

Richard Rich holds his tongue. Draper might have the upper hand now, but things are about to change. He recalls the look on the king's face when he first saw the Cleves women, and he knows that Henry cannot be content without someone to blame for his savage disappointment. With any luck, he will quarrel with Thomas Cromwell over the new marriage, and anyone connected with Austin Friars shall be tainted by the outcome. Happier days might yet be coming.

They mount their horses, and set off on the return ride, which is accomplished in silence by a band of men made morose by a wasted journey. It is still dark when they arrive back at Hampton Court Palace, only to find out that Elizabeth Farriby is lodged in the servants quarters occupied by Mistress Abigail Brown, the king's seamstress.

"Place a guard at their door, but do not disturb them from their slumber," Will tells John Beckshaw. "The lady can be formally arrested as well tomorrow as now. Then get yourself back to your own dear Pru. I am for my own bed, and will see you at breakfast. I shall consider the evidence against this innocent girl then."

"You should… ugh!" Sir Richard Rich finds himself being held off the floor by his coat front, with Will Draper's face close to his. One look into those darkened eyes, and Rich's ingrained pomposity evaporates away. For a brief moment, he sees death looking out at him, and his nerve goes completely.

"I should thrash you, Rich… for being a fool, and a scoundrel. Now get away from me, before I resort to using even worse violence on you." He drops the man, and thrusts him backwards, so that he almost falls over his own feet. The Attorney General of England feels tears of shame pricking his eyes, and flees for his own chambers. Tomorrow, he tells himself, things will be very different from this.

4   The Accused

"The banquet was simply superb, Master Turner," Miriam Draper says, as she surveys the great heaps of soiled pewter plates, dirty forks, and soiled tableware being heaped up in the great washing vats, filled with hot water.

"Thank you, madam," Wat Turner replies, with a crudely executed bow, and a wide smile. "The praise is high, because of the quarter it comes from. The delicacies you supplied were eaten, right down to the last morsel. As for the venison… so tender, and so tasty… I can scarce say."

"Ah, yes, the venison. I import the live animals from Normandy," Miriam explains. "They are a quieter breed, and easier to herd."

"How long do you hang the carcasses for, madam?" the master cook asked.

"My master butcher insists on at least twenty one days, if you want the best flavour," says Miriam. "The king's venison tends to be more muscular, because of their wild nature, and should be hung much longer."

"A month, at least," Wat Turner confirms. "The sinews take that long to start becoming gamier. What did you think about my stuffed bird?"

"Genius, my dear Master Wat… absolute genius," Miriam confesses. " I could use a fellow like you in my…"

"No, madam!" Wat holds up a hand. "Do not say it. I am too much a part of Hampton Court. I live here, shall cook here, and then die here. My old master, Cardinal Wolsey, alas, wanted the same end. Forgive my blunt refusal, but I am a blunt man, and must speak in a blunt way… bluntly."

"I had not yet made the offer," Miriam says. "So, there is no harm done. Let us forget my crass attempt at stealing you from the king. I know even the two hundred a year I was thinking of would not tempt you."

"Two hundred… pounds?" Wat Turner is stunned at such an abundant offer, which is somewhat better than the twenty four pounds he now gets. "Each year?"

"Well, a flat rate of four pounds a week," Miriam Draper confirms. "Which is… let me see now… oh, I am so bad at my numbers."

"Two hundred and eight pounds a year," Wat says.

"With free bed and board, of course."

"Madam, you seek to turn my head." The old cook has never seen so much money, let alone possessed it.

"Not at all," Miriam says. "I understand that you do not wish to leave Hampton Court, but if the king accepts my proposals, that would not be necessary. He is thinking of making the Draper Company his royal caterers…. For everything. Banquets, state dinners, informal luncheons… the lot."

"Then you would have no need of me, or my lads," Wat mutters, as he tries to work out what is afoot. "Henry will not pay wages whee he does not have to."

"If you worked for the Draper Company, you would be my senior *chef de cuisine* ... as the French would say... and able to select your own staff. You would supervise the king's personal diet, and run the kitchens… exactly as you wish. The only difference would be that you hold yourself ready to look after my own list of nobles, when they throw a banquet. That means you would be responsible for feeding half the dukes and barons in England."

"There are not enough hours in the day," Wat says.

"You would merely supervise," Miriam reminds him. "I do not expect you to peel every carrot, or skin every hare."

"The king…"

"The king has other things on his mind," Miriam says. "At breakfast, he had not one word to say about his marriage night, and he could hardly bring himself to look at poor Anne. I fear for the future of that marriage, and the safety of the poor girl."

"Perhaps, but it is done now. Right after breaking their fast, they retired to the royal chapel at Greenwich, where Archbishop Cranmer tied the knot," Wat says. "God bless them both, and make their union into a fruitful one. Now, where am I to be based?"

*

"Your prisoner is taken, Master Attorney General," Will Draper says to Sir Richard Rich. "As you instructed. I spoke with the king before he left for Greenwich, and he advised me to take some heed of you in this matter. I took the liberty of informing him that you were in two minds about the case, and wished me to investigate it with you."

"Out of the question," Rich snaps. He is surrounded now by his own men, and feels more confident in his stance.

"The king thought not. I have his orders… in writing, and with his small seal upon it. He expects a full and frank report from me, once the matter is satisfactorily settled."

"You have deliberately misled His Majesty," says Rich. He is becoming red of face, and a small, nervous twitch has developed in his left eye. "What expertise have you in witch finding?"

"Enough to know Elizabeth Farriby is innocent," Will tells the Attorney General. "A blind man might see that!"

"She is to be conveyed, in an open tumbrel, to the scene of her guilty acts, and put to the question extraordinary," Rich pronounces. "So shall it be ordered."

"She is returning, as we speak, to her home… and in my private carriage, sir." Will Draper can feel the waves of hatred coming off the man, and almost grins in his face. "Once there, we will convene a board of investigation, and listen to all of the evidence, and speak with any witnesses that you may know of."

"Damn it, the girl sours milk… and has killed chickens with her conjurations!" Rich is almost raging.

"An axe would be easier," Will says, "and the milk in my porridge was slightly curdled this morning… but I do not intend burning Master Wat Turner for it."

"Wat … who?"

"The king's cook," Will says. "He assures me that chickens die of many causes, and that curdled milk is a result of it being badly stored, and left overlong in the bright sun."

"Chickens do not go mad, then die, unless witchcraft is involved," Rich persists.

"We shall see," Will Draper says.

"If a crime has been committed, I will discover it… and then apprehend the culprit. We leave in a half hour."

Richard Rich glares after the man he has come to hate so much, then orders his horse. As an afterthought, he tells his sergeant at arms to bring a bodyguard of a dozen men, and for them all to be armed with muskets. If this Farriby girl is popular, there might be a disturbance.

"If there is a crowd, and if it seems to be hostile," he tells his man, "then you have my permission to discharge your weapons over their heads. If, by any chance, that fool Will Draper gets in the way of a shot… I would be generous to the man who did it."

"How generous, sir?" Sergeant Toby Wilton asks.

"Ten pounds?"

"That might get a man hurt, sir," Wilton advises, "but twenty would ensure a good clean kill. You must make your thoughts plain though, for should my aim waver, and a man die … ever so accidentally… what of the punishment?"

"For an accident?" Richard Rich considers. He can always hang the fellow out of hand, and justify it to Henry as a way of placating the King's Examiners. "A verbal reprimand, and an order to get in more target practice. What say you, Sergeant

Wilton?"

"Let us pray the chance offers itself."

"Good man. You shall go far in my service."

"I aim to please," Toby Wilton replies, and they both laugh at the unintended jest.

*

Elizabeth Farriby is at a loss as to how her sudden good luck has vanished in the blink of an eye. She has just entered her twenty first year, and finds herself the subject of the gravest accusation that can be laid at a woman's door, short of infanticide. She is taken prisoner, no matter how gently, and is to be tried as a witch. The outcome, as any fool knows, will be a slow, painful death.

"Calm yourself, Mistress Elizabeth," Will Draper counsels the girl. "I can only help you if I know all of the facts."

"Facts, sir?" Elizabeth is quite distraught. "I know only that yesterday I was the happy inheritor of a fortune, and today, I am to be burnt at the stake as a witch."

"If Richard Rich has his way, you will suffer that fate," Will says, "but I am here to thwart him. Why would he want you accused of so wicked a crime?"

"I do not know the man at all, sir,"

Elizabeth Farriby says to the Examiner. "I swear he is a stranger to me."

"He claims never to have met you either."

"Then there is no malice, Sir Will," the girl reasons. "Can it be that he is honest in his intentions… and really does believe me to be in league with the devil?"

"Rich *is* the devil, my girl." Will Draper ponders. "Might you have wronged him in some way?"

"Never, to my certain knowledge," Elizabeth affirms, hand placed over her heart.

"Forgive me, but has he ever tried to…" Will gestures vaguely with his hands, to suggest some grappling movement, and the girl shakes her head. She understands the insinuation, but can refute it easily.

"I have never been with any man, sir, as you well know," she says. "Now I have wealth, I might make a fine marriage, and would not ruin my chances with such lewd behaviour. I tell you, the man is utterly unknown to me."

"Then who has accused you?" Will asks.

"They say I was denounced by a woman from the village," Elizabeth says, "but I do not believe it. I have grown up about here, and was born in one of the houses by the river. I know almost everyone here, and we live in peace and harmony. I even own some of the houses now, and intend lowering the rents. Does that make me into a witch?"

"Someone does not feel harmonious towards you, Elizabeth," Will says.

"Of course, but I cannot begin to guess," the girl replied, and in so open and honest a manner that Will was thoroughly reassured of her innocence.

"Then I must find out who it is, and question them."

"Pray do, sir, for I am in a sorry state. If not for your kind intervention, I would be in chains now."

On a pile of burning faggots, more like, Will thinks to himself as he leaves her chamber. Old Michael is loitering on the stairs, and beckons for him to come over.

"What is it, old man?" Will asks. "Can you shed light on this darkness for me, and so save your mistress?"

"Your weasel faced fellow, Rich, is offering a reward for anyone who can testify *against* Mistress Elizabeth. He means to make quite sure of her guilt, sir."

"How much?"

"A pound for information laid," the old man says, with disgust in his voice.

"Let it be known that I will pay twice that, to any household that remains silent," Will says. He calculates that it will cost him about a hundred pounds in bribes, but that is but a day's profit from just one of his wife's many business ventures. "If anyone can tell me about this so called witness, I shall gift them five pounds… and no questions asked."

"Well then, I am a lucky man," Old Michael says with a gap toothed grin. "For you want to speak with Mistress Nell Gifford. She lives in the house down the lane, and is supposed to be a dear friend of the mistress."

"What does she know?" Will asks, but the old man can only shrug his shoulders. His fund of information is now exhausted. The King's Examiner takes a purse of silver from his belt, and gives it to the old man.

"Here, and do not spend it all on drink, Michael."

"It is for the church, sir," Michael replies, rather stiffly. "This money will pay for a window, or a new bible. We are God fearing people around here, sir. Suffer not a witch, the bible says, and we would not. If Elizabeth Farriby is a witch, we would have burnt her ourselves… at once."

"Thank you, friend," Will says. "I must see this Nell Gifford, and hear her tale."

"Call on Jeb Buckley first," Michael whispers. "Ask him about his chickens, and the manner of their death. His farm is the one you can see from yon window."

*

"Well, Henry, that is that!" The Duke of Norfolk affects a hearty tone, and slaps the king on his shoulder. "You look tired out by your wedding night, and no mistake. Did your Flanders Mare gallop well for you then?"

"I beg your pardon, sir?" Henry stares at Norfolk in utter disbelief. "I cannot believe what you have just said. You liken the queen to… to a horse?"

"Oh, not in a detrimental way," Norfolk says. "You must recall how we jested about the race for your hand, and how Tom Wyatt did liken it to three fine thoroughbreds at the gallop?"

"Oh, yes… that." Henry remembers the light hearted jesting, back when he felt sure he would have the pick of the field, and it makes his blood run cold. "The three horse race."

"The French filly was found to be too willing, and the Luxembourg mount lacking in looks. I meant only that, having chosen your fine Flanders Mare, you did give her a royal ride of it!"

"Damn and blast it, Tom," Henry says, and draws Norfolk closer to him. He only resorts to using the old duke's first name when he is about to confess, or is in a corner and needs help. "This mare is not to my liking. Not at all, sir. When put to the fence… I fear that I stumbled."

"What… you could not…complete the course?" The Duke of Norfolk hides a smile of triumph. It is even better than he could have hoped for.

"I was left at the starting line," Henry confesses to his noble advisor. "Never have I failed to satisfy a woman so abjectly. Am I not known as the famous Tudor Bull?"

"Sire, your many bastards attest to your virility," Norfolk tells the king. "If there was a failure… it is not yours. Could you have been the subject of some spell… too much wine… or was the food too rich?"

"I know not, Tom, but my pintle was as flaccid as a dead pheasant," the king says. "The woman did show herself to me, in all her ampleness, but nothing stirred. The wretched creature is not the one I was expecting."

"Well, I must confess that the portrait was not that exact a rendition," Norfolk muses. "These things happen, of course. The artist can become carried away with his subject."

"You mean that Holbein cheated me?"

"Unlikely, sire." Norfolk rubs his

heavily stubbled chin, as if contemplating all the facts. "Why would he … how might he prosper from it … *unless* he was bribed to make one girl look much better than the others?"

"Then my enemies have done this to me," Henry says.

"How so, sire?" Norfolk shakes his head. "I grant the girl is not the painting, but in all other respects, she fits the bill well. She is a sturdy wench, with wide hips, and might sire a dozen strong sons for you… were you able to rise to the occasion. She is also a favourite of Emperor Charles, and that makes the Holy Roman Empire into out strongest ally. The match is a good one, bar your physical repulsion of the girl."

"Oh, you swive her for me then!" Henry growls. "The political match is a good one… any fool can see that… but my own feelings have been trampled on."

"Come now, sire," Norfolk says. "How can you blame poor Cromwell for this? He is no friend of mine, but he loves England, and has done his best for the sake of the realm."

"Thomas Cromwell had as little idea of the girl's looks than I had," Henry replies. "Why must you always seek to dun him so, Norfolk?"

"No, sire, I seek to defend him,"

Norfolk replies, smoothly.

"You do?"

"Why, yes. The only way Thomas Cromwell might be to blame is if he *deliberately* tricked you into this wedding."

"He would not… would he?" Henry is confused, but he is also angry at finding himself tied to a woman he does not want to have carnal knowledge of. "Cromwell loves me. You spoke, some days ago, of Cromwell being a traitor, and I demanded proof. Now you seem to support him. What are you up to?"

"Nothing, sire. I have simply realised that the poor fellow is not evil. He seeks only to make England strong. He is, if anything, as great a patriot as you or I. Only not so well bred, of course," Norfolk replies. "Cromwell loves you… yes… though, that love can lead a man into overstepping his authority. I do not believe Cromwell conspired against you deliberately, and I am sure it can be proven."

Norfolk knows the king thinks highly of Cromwell, and that any overt attack will end in ignominy and failure. It is time to approach from another angle, and try to get Henry on side.

"How so?" the king asks. The idea that Norfolk might prove Cromwell's true worth is such a novelty that he wants to hear more.

"If Master Crom… my pardon, the Duke of Essex, has acted against your best wishes, he must have had accomplices. That means people will talk out of turn. Let me investigate him, but with a view to finding him blameless."

"How so?"

"Let me ask about, and see if anyone has a bad word about him," Norfolk says.

"You spoke of having a witness against him once," Henry says. The conversation, but a few days before had ended with Norfolk demanding to have his man heard. "Where is he now?"

"I have him safe, sire," Norfolk says. "Let me look into Cromwell's character… then present both cases to you. It is my belief that the worst thing I find will be that he has been careless in the choice of your bride."

"Damn it, Norfolk, I chose her myself," Henry moans.

"Did you, sire?" Norfolk says, then smiles. "And how did Cromwell take that? He likes his own way, like most powerful men."

"He was keener on the Burgundian girl," Henry says. "We discussed it, and I decided against her. I suppose Tom was a little disappointed, but he took it like a good subject, and agreed that I knew best."

"Then he argued against Anne of Cleves?"

"Well… not exactly argued," Henry confesses. "He just seemed reluctant to accept her, but his reasoning was not sound, and Sir Rafe Sadler sided with me."

"Ah, Sir Rafe Sadler. There is a bright star in the firmament, sire."

"What does that mean?"

"Nothing, but that his rise has been quick."

"I discovered the fellow, and realised his worth," Henry says with real pride in his voice.

"Where, Hal?" the Duke of Norfolk asks, ingenuously of his perplexed king.

"Where?"

"Under a stone… or working below stairs?" Norfolk asks.

"No, he was a training as a law clerk … at Austin Friars."

"And what of his friend, Mush Draper?" Norfolk probes. "Is he not an Austin Friars fellow?"

"Well… yes, that is so. They produce some fine minds, Norfolk. Whereas your fellows are all hunting, fishing, and swiving dunderheads."

"You shame me, sire. Who can I select to help me look at Lord Cromwell's motives then?"

"Damn it, man. Must I think of absolutely everything?" Henry asks. "Call on Sir Will Draper, and make some use of his Royal Examiners."

"Will Draper, sire?" Norfolk rubs his chin. "Remind me… where did that fellow come from?"

"Irish, I think," Henry replies. "No… not so. He fought the Irish for me, and came to me from… Cromwell."

"Then I shall look into the matter alone, sire," the Duke of Norfolk says. "For I seem to be quite hemmed in by those fellows." The poison is dripped in to Henry's ear, and Norfolk will let it fester. The king will start to think of how many of his best men are ex Cromwell people, and it will make him wary.

"Do as you wish," the king growls. "I weary of this constant in fighting. But mark my words, Norfolk… I am not happy with this marriage, and would see myself out of it!"

Norfolk bows, and leaves the chamber. He is a step closer to humiliating Thomas Cromwell, and having him drummed out of office. Such an act would see him firmly back as the king's main advisor, but leave him with a thorny problem. No matter what the outcome of his investigation, the marriage is sound, and should be excellent for England. How then, after but a few days, can the king discard another wife, and not start a war with the Spanish, the Germans, and half of Italy?

"God's bollocks," Norfolk mutters, "but this politicking is damned thirsty work!"

*

"Did your fat husband do his duty last night?" Helge whispers, as soon as the queen returns to Hampton Court. Anne has been close mouthed until now, but cannot hold back the tears much longer.

"He hates me," she confesses to her closest friend. "The king has not even kissed me, Helge. He went pale, and shook like a virginal boy when I showed him myself. What am I to do?"

"First night nerves," Helge says. "Too much wine often makes a man limp. He will be better next time."

"No, he wishes to be rid of me. I can tell." Anne knows the story of how easily Katherine of Aragon, and then Anne Boleyn were discarded, and fears for her life. "What am I to do, Helge?"

"Nothing for the moment. Do not give him any reason to put you aside," Helge says. "Make him ask you for a divorce, then make your demands."

"He will have me arrested," Anne cries, and Helge simply giggles at her.

"How can he? Your father's cousin is the Holy Roman Emperor, and Charles is fond of you, is he not?"

"That is true." Anne realises that her position is not quite so hopeless, and that she might yet escape with her life, and her dignity in tact. "Charles would turn against my husband."

"Henry knows this. The Lord Cromwell knows this, and so does all of England," Helge says. "When the time comes, we must bargain hard. This England is a wonderful country, with many fine houses, and handsome people. Let the king give you a palace, and a pension, if he wants rid of you. In return, promise to keep his secret."

"Secret?" Anne asks.

"Why, yes… that he is not a man in bed," Helge replies with a knowing smirk. "There are young servants in his palace who can perform better than he … believe me. He will not want his shame broadcast across the entire continent!"

5 The Witness

If Sir Will Draper thinks he is to have things all his own way in this investigation, he is sadly mistaken. As he leaves the manor house, a coach arrives, and disgorges Miriam, Pru Beckshaw, and Marion Giles. They are here to ensure their friend is treated with kindness, and scrupulous honour.

"My dear, there was no need for…" Will starts, but he is cut short. Miriam is thriving on the sense of indignation she feels in her breast.

"Elizabeth is no witch," Miriam declares. "We are here to see she is found innocent, husband. I have written a note to Master Thomas, and begged for his full support."

"That will not be necessary," Will replies, a little put out by his wife's high handed approach. "You forget your place, madam. I am the King's Examiner in Chief, and you are… not."

"Bosh," Miriam says, and smiles sweetly. "Pru has *seen* Mistress Farriby's innocence, and Marion has medical expertise. She can sniff this curdled milk, or some such thing."

Will sees that there is no arguing with his wife, and bows to her companions.

It is then that a happy thought occurs to him, and he sees how they might be useful to him, and kept from under his feet whilst he investigates.

"Very well, madam," he says. "You must make funds available at once. Say two or three hundred pounds. Richard Rich, is a conniving swine, and offers cash inducements to find those who might bear false witness."

"Then I will offer more to those who remain honest," Miriam replies. "I have a hundred in the coach, and can have more within the day."

"Excellent. Then I must ask Pru to tread warily. For should Rich suspect her of having some sort of unusual gift, he would add her to the investigation, despite me. Two witches burn better than one, I fear. If you *see* anything, Pru, come to me privately. Trust no one else."

"And what can I do for you, sir?" Marion Giles is a newcomer to their circle of friends, and is the daughter of a noted apothecary. Had she been born a man, her position as a physician to the king would be assured. Instead, she makes beauty creams and potions for bored noble ladies. She is just turned thirty, yet has that elegance, and alabaster-like skin that makes a woman truly beautiful to discerning men.

"I am about to visit a farmer, whose

chickens all died suddenly," he says.

"You suspect poison?" Marion asks.

"I have an open mind," Will replies. "Come with me, Mistress Marion and give me the benefit of your advice."

"We shall both go with you," Miriam says, sweetly. It is not that she mistrusts her husband, but Marion is single, and of a most comely appearance. Even a saint might falter if left alone with such a creature. Will smiles to himself, as he sees a glimpse of jealousy in his wife's eye, and is pleased that she still cherishes him so well.

*

It is but a short stroll to the small holding of Jeb Buckley, who has a couple of milking cows, some goats, and a flock of chickens. He supplies the manor house, and the attached village with eggs, fresh milk, poultry and meat from his four acres of well managed land.

He sees the military looking gentleman approaching, with three attractive ladies in his wake, and wipes his hands on his leather work apron. It is only when they are within a dozen yards that he thinks to look at the man's face. He grins, and throws Will a smart salute.

"Captain Draper, sir… is it really you?" Jeb says as he sees Will's approach. "Where did you steal such fine clothes?" Will stops in his tracks, and wonders at the man's effrontery.

"You know me, fellow?" he asks. "Speak up!"

"Ho! And a fine accent to go with these fine clothes," the farmer replies. "Last time I saw you was in a ditch outside Dublin. We were covered in shi… mud… and fighting off a gang of ragged arsed Irishers. It's me , sir… Corporal Jeb Buckley."

The years roll away, and Will sees that despite a thickening of the waist, and a thinning of his hair, the man still has a soldiers bearing.

"I recall a foot soldier of that name," Will says. "I almost had him flogged for stealing a horse."

"An honest enough mistake, sir," Buckley says with a wink. "Now I think of it, my promotion came after you left to go bounty hunting in Wales. What a young scoundrel you were back then."

"Nothing changes," Miriam says. "Your Captain is now the Chief King's Examiner, and a knight of the realm, Master Buckley. I am Lady Miriam, his wife."

"Bugger me, madam," the older man says, "but I always knew the lad would get on. What do you want with me… Your Lordship?"

"I am investigating Elizabeth Farriby," Will says, and Jeb laughs out loud.

"What ever for?" he asks. "The girl is as honest as can be."

"Witchcraft."

"Jesus!" The old man steps back. "How can that be?"

"Your chickens died," Will says, and realises how lame it sounds. "The Attorney General claims it is through sorcery. He also says your milk was soured."

"It went sour, right enough," Jeb says, "but the cow has had an udder infection. That often makes the milk turn sooner. It was not witchcraft... though Elizabeth was visiting me when it happened. Perhaps that is how the story came to get about?"

"And the chickens?"

"That was two days ago," Jeb Buckley explains. "The damnedest thing... pardon my soldier's language, ladies... but they started dashing to and fro, and leaping in the air. Then they dropped down dead. I lost about half the flock... twelve good layers, and a fine cock... in a few moments. Oh... damn."

"What is it?" Will asks.

"It happened just after Mistress Gifford passed by, and she was out walking with Elizabeth. I called to them, and Elizabeth passed the time of day with me."

"And Mistress Gifford?"

"I hardly know her to nod to, sir," Jeb confesses. "She is a fine looking girl, but has only lived in the village for a couple of months past. They went on their way, and I fed my birds. Next thing is… they are going mad, and dropping down dead. I suppose, if you put the two things together it might sound a little odd."

"Did you see Elizabeth go near your chickens?" Marion Giles asks, and Jeb Buckley frowns, deep in thought.

"No, miss… but she looked at them, and said as how they looked hungry," he says. "Then poor old Mistress Jane Townley up and died yesterday morning. Her neighbours heard her screaming, as if being attacked. They rushed around to her cottage, but it was too late. She was dead."

"Murdered?" will asks.

"Lord, no." Jeb shakes his head. "Some sort of a fit. She was all curled up, and twisted limbed, and we had to get her in the ground quickly."

"Why so?" Marion asks of him.

"Begging your pardon, My Lady… but her corpse began to stink like …"

"Rotting fish?" Marion says, and they all look at her.

"What do you perceive, Mistress Marion?" Will asks.

"I am not sure yet," Marion replies. She is a woman of the sciences, and does not like to guess without all the evidence. "Where are the chickens?"

"Why, plucked and hung in my shed, madam," Jeb tells the apothecary's daughter. "Waste not want not, I say."

"Take me to them." Jeb looks to Will, who nods his approval.

"Behind the cottage," he mumbles, and leads the way. The chickens are plucked and cleaned out. They hang from a row of hooks, over a barrel which contains their innards. Marion bends over the barrel, and sniffs. Then she examines the dead birds.

"Where is their feed?" she asks. Jeb points to a sack which leans in one corner.

"I dip my bucket into it, and then scatter it on the ground. Chickens like to scratch around for their food." Marion nods her understanding, picks up a handful of feed, and smells it.

"Have you any more?"

"No, madam."

"And this is the sack you took feed from the other day?"

"It is. I half filled my bucket, and went outside to the run," Jeb says. "That is when Elizabeth Farriby spoke to me. I put the bucket down on the ground, and passed the time. She and her friend left, and I fed the birds."

"I see." Marion glances up at the birds. "Twelve?"

"Madam?"

"There are only twelve chickens, Corporal Buckley," Will says with sudden realisation. "Where is your cock bird?"

"Oh, I see," Jeb's face suddenly falls into disarray. "Dear God, sir… but they are too tough for my pot… so I gave it, out of charity, to Mistress Townley!"

*

"Colonel Draper seems to think we have all day," Richard Rich tells his servant. "Have a bench and chairs set up in the hall of the manor, and bring the accused down from her room."

"The King's Examiners guard her door, sir," the man reminds his master. "I fear they might knock me on the head if I get too presumptuous."

"Take my sergeant at arms, and four armed men," Rich insists. "Order the Examiner's men to stand aside… in the king's name, and bring her down. Then fetch our witness."

"Yes, sir. Anything else?"

"Order the villagers to collect enough faggots for a good pyre," Rich tells him. "Just in case the girl is found guilty. I want her tied to a stake, and burned before this evening."

"They will refuse," the man says. He has kept his eyes and ears open, and he understands how things stand in the village. "They reckon that this girl is innocent."

"Then have two men march them into the nearest woods, at musket point, and force them. Threaten them in the king's name if you must."

The man bows, and leaves about his business. The small court is set up, and all those concerned assembled, before noon, and Sir Richard Rich assumes the dual roles of both prosecutor, and judge. Elizabeth Farriby is brought down, under guard, and forced to stand in a makeshift dock.

"Very well, let us begin," Rich says. "Elizabeth Farriby, you are charged with witchcraft. It is alleged that you did try to ruin your neighbour by souring his milk, and causing the death of his chickens. It is further claimed that you murdered one Jane Townley, a spinster of the parish."

"Why would I?" Elizabeth cries, and the Attorney General smirks at her in contempt.

"I am here to establish the facts, girl. Not wonder at your deluded reasoning," he says. "How do you plead?"

"I have never …"

"Not guilty then," Rich says, and gestures for his secretary to make a note of the fact. "That you were present when the milk turned, and again when the chickens died is clear, and damning proof of your guilt. As for this poor old woman you killed by sorcery… we may never know what slight offence she offered to you. However, you must have your trial. Bring in the witness… Nell Gifford."

The chamber door opens, and a young, well dressed woman with a string of pearls about her throat, steps into the room. She curtseys to Richard Rich, and throws him a timid little smile.

"Have no fear, my girl," Rich says. "Speak the truth, and all will be well. It is the opinion of this court that Elizabeth Farriby is in league with Satan, and has practiced the black arts. Have you ever seen her work her charms?"

"Never, sir!" Nell Gifford says in a soft, lilting way.

"Then what do you wish to tell this court, my dear?" Richard Rich is not a romantic, but this Gifford girl appeals to him in that way, and he finds himself wanting to encourage and protect her. "I am not an ogre, you know."

"No, you are not big enough, Rich." Will Draper and his small entourage are pushing past the guards at the door, and grouping themselves behind the accused. "How dare you start proceedings without me?"

"Your warrant from the king entitles you only to investigate," Rich replies, haughtily. "My writ gives me full powers in the prosecution. You may remain, but I must ask you to hold your tongue."

"I shall hold yours," Will Draper replies, and touches the knife at his belt. "Mistress Farriby has a right, under English law, to ask for a defender to speak for her. I am prepared to fill that roll, should she wish."

"I do so wish," Elizabeth Farriby says from the dock. "I am innocent, sir. Even my friend, Nell, has said she has seen nothing of witchcraft when in my company."

"Then why is she here?" Will asks Richard Rich.

"That is what I am trying to establish," Rich snaps. "Now, unless you wish to be arrested for contempt of the king's court, let us get on with the trial."

"As you wish," Will says, and takes a seat close to the accused and her friends. "Pray continue with your ordinary questions, and let us consider the *questioning extraordinary* if we are not satisfied with *this* woman's testimony."

"Enough, sir!"" Rich is enamoured of Nell Gifford, who smiles at him so sweetly. "You cannot submit a witness to torture."

"No, sir… but you can question a *perjurer* so." Will Draper has scored a hit, and the Attorney General's face turns a strange colour. "If Mistress Gifford lies, under oath, she has committed a felony, and can be put to the question extraordinary. It is amazing what a pair of hot pincers can do to extract the truth."

"Please, gentlemen, I am here to relate my story," the young woman says. "Elizabeth is my landlord, and my friend, these past months. We have much in common, and I hold her dear to me. I have nothing to gain by blackening her name, but felt obliged to report the matter, after the recent strange death in the village."

"Then speak, my dear," Rich says. "We seek only the truth, and the plain truth will set free the innocent, and condemn the guilty."

"I thought nothing of it when Jeb Buckley's milk soured, other than that both I and Elizabeth were walking by his farm at the time. Afterwards, I recalled the odd look on my friend's face. She was staring into the byre, where the cows were kept, and seemed to have a far away look about her."

"Tosh," Miriam says, and Rich gives her an angry glare, which she returns ten fold. "An odd stare indeed!"

"Lady Miriam must not understand how the evil eye works," Rich says. "Witches often use a magical look to perform their mischief. Go on, my girl."

"Then all of the chickens went …

quite mad," Nell Gifford says. "It was odd that they died just after she… Elizabeth… spoke with Jeb Buckley."

"Perhaps they did not like the conversation," Will mutters.

"After that, I started to wonder if black magic was involved in both instances. There was a case back in Devon, when I was a child, where an old woman caused a flock of sheep to panic, and charge off a high tor."

"Terrible," Rich says. "Did you suspect your friend?"

"No, not then," Nell Gifford tells them. "It was only when poor old Jane Townley died that I began to worry. You see, Jane was a tenant of the manor, and paid only a widow's mite in rent. I know Elizabeth was trying to ease the old woman out of the cottage, and it occurred to me that she might have … done something."

"Used magic, you mean?" Rich asks, and the girl shrugs and looks down.

"That is a lie!" Elizabeth can keep silent no longer. "I wanted Jane to move into an alms house in the next village. She was almost seventy, and half blind. It would have helped her… not me, Nell Gifford. How can you think otherwise?"

"Silence, or I will have a scold fitted." The scold would seal her lips, and mark her down as a disruptive prisoner.

Elizabeth sighs and sits back. Richard Rich nods in satisfaction. "Then what happened, Mistress Gifford. You may speak freely here."

"I thought to visit Elizabeth at the manor, and tell her of my fears. Even then, I could not think ill of my friend."

"And?"

"As I approached, I could hear Elizabeth speaking with someone… a man with a deep, unnatural voice. She was laughing, and the man cried for her to hang on. I ran inside, and heard a crash, as if something had fallen from the roof. In the middle of the room, lying amidst the floor rushes, was a besom."

"A switch of hazel branches, bound to a wooden stave?" Rich glared around the room, as if making a telling point.

"Yes."

"The common conveyance of a witch," Rich says, with a note of triumph in his voice. "And what of the man?"

"There was no-one else in the room… save for Elizabeth's black cat."

"Then it is clear to this court that you interrupted a witch, whilst conversing with her 'familiar'… the cat… who was exhorting her to fly about the chamber on her besom."

"Good grief!" Will Draper stands up, and strides into the centre of the room.

"This woman accuses Elizabeth Farriby of looking strangely at a cow, smiling at some chickens, and dropping her broom, whilst sweeping up. As for the talking cat… well, we have all come across one of those after a heavy night's drinking, Sir Richard. This is nothing but the ramblings of a highly strung young lady, who needs to think before she speaks."

"The evidence is clear," Rich replies. "There are clear signs of witchcraft. The milk… the chickens, and the death of Jane Townley. There is no rational explanation, other than the presence of a witch. As everything seems to indicate Elizabeth Farriby's involvement, I am inclined to find her guilty."

"This is madness!" Miriam cries, and Will shushes her into silence.

"However, I am aware that she does not fit the usual criteria of being a witch, and think we must investigate more, before I pronounce sentence."

"Thank God," Miriam mutters to her friends.

"So, the accused will be taken to the Tower of London, and put to the *question extraordinary*. Let us see if the hot irons, and the rack will loosen her tongue, and bring forth the truth. The sentence of death by burning is suspended, until after the official torture is concluded. Court is dismissed."

"I protest," Will says. "There is evidence to show Elizabeth Farriby is innocent."

"You have a witness?" Rich asks, a tone of disappointment in his voice. The king fears witchcraft, and if he can appear to be stamping it out, he will stand in good stead with His Majesty.

"No, not as such," Will says. "Certain circumstances point to a different interpretation of events."

"No witness, you say? Then this court is adjourned until Friday next. The accused will be put in heavy chains, and must be transported to London forthwith, and put to the question in two days time. If you have anything else to report… I suggest you are quick about it, Sir Will. Now, Mistress Gifford, your ordeal is finally at an end. Will you join me for luncheon, my dear?"

"Why, thank you, sir," the girl says. "It has been a most frightful few days, and I am distraught at finding out my friend is a proponent of witchcraft. I wonder if she is just confused by her sudden wealth. Must she die?"

"I fear so," Rich says, and offers his arm to the girl. "The king is most strict about the stamping out of witchcraft. Since my appointment, he has refused every appeal, and always confirms my sentence. The king and I are close friends, you see."

"Poor Elizabeth."

"Quite," Rich says. "Do you like venison, my dear?"

"Oh, yes!" Nell Gifford links the Attorney General's arm, and looks longingly into his watery eyes. "Might we also have oysters? I am told they have a most enervating effect."

"You shall have a dozen… no two dozen," Rich says happily, as they stroll outside. "You are a brave girl. Have you a beau?"

"Not I, sir. I am without fortune… apart from a small allowance from an old aunt in Exeter. It seems I must find a man who wants me for my other charms."

"Excellent, my dear, quite excellent," Richard Rich whispers in her ear. "How nice it is to meet a girl of such rare innocence… and such abundant charms."

"Sir… you flatter me," Nell says, and grips his arm ever tighter.

6 A Question Extraordinary

"How is my guest faring, Master Donne?" The Duke of Norfolk enjoys his little jests, and talks of the prisoner as if he were an honoured visitor. "Have his nerves settled down yet?"

"Hardly, My Lord," Rupert Donne, the Duke of Norfolk's best agent, and own private torturer says. "Captain Tencher led him to believe he was about to be skinned alive, and the thought of it almost unhinged the poor creature's mind."

"The bloody stupid oaf." The duke does not clarify which one he means to curse, and Donne can only smile, and nod in agreement. "Can one really do that?"

"Skinned alive, sir?" Rupert Donne considers it for a long moment. "It is possible, of course, though I really do not see the point. So much skin, and for so little effect."

"I know of a fellow who had his dead enemy's skin peeled from his body, and used to bind his family bible," Norfolk says.

"How amusing," the torturer replies. "Should Your Lordship ever hate someone enough, I would be happy to give it a try."

"I shall keep that in mind, Master

Donne," Norfolk says to him. "It might be the closet some of my enemies ever get to Almighty God…eh? Has the Plank fellow recovered his wits yet?"

"Since being delivered into my hands, I have seen to his comfort, and promised him his life, and a large bag of gold, if he can compose himself, and give a full account of that which he has recently overheard. He seems to believe me, and has calmed himself enough to stop gibbering with fear."

"Stout fellow," the Duke of Norfolk says. "Promise him his heart's desire, Master Donne. You can always kill him afterwards, I suppose."

"As you wish, My Lord," Donne says. "Shall I have him brought in, so that you might question him?"

"Why not?" Norfolk decides. This Judas Plank swears he has damning evidence against Cromwell, and it might be enough to sway the king, and bring down Austin Friars. The duke knows he is playing a dangerous game, of course, but can tolerate Thomas Cromwell and his men no longer. "Bring a couple of flagons of cheap wine, so that his tongue is not tied."

"I fear that the problem will be in stopping him talking, sir," Rupert Donne explains. "He is pathetically keen on surviving, and might make things up, just to please you."

"That is no good to me." Norfolk bites his thumb nail, and spits. "I must have proof that what he says is close to being true."

"Then let me question him," Donne says. "In that way, he might well temper what he claims, recall the actual words uttered, and stay within the bounds of reality."

"As you wish, Master Donne," the Duke of Norfolk tells his cleverest torturer. "Do exactly as you think most fitting … but get me my evidence."

*

The landing at the Tower of London is slippery with moss, and the small boat's commander finds it hard to keep his footing. He turns the bow rope twice about the iron post provided, and uses his long boat hook to swing in the aft part of his craft. The obligatory guard jumps ashore then, and offers his arm to the prisoner.

Elizabeth Farriby steadies herself, and steps ashore. The Assistant Warden of the Tower, Master Robin Crabtree, approaches, and bows to the girl. He is an impressionable young man, in his middle twenties, and finds himself admiring the lack of artifice , and the natural beauty of the girl.

"My Lady," he says, with his heart

pounding in his chest, "I am Robin Crabtree, Assistant Warden of the Tower of London, and I am here to escort you to your quarters. I hope they are suitable for your current needs."

"Then I am not to go to a damp prison cell?" Elizabeth says, in an eerie repeat of the words once used by the late Anne Boleyn upon a similar occasion.

"No, Mistress Elizabeth," Robin tells her. "I am a loyal friend of Sir Will Draper, and he begs me to attend to your comfort, even whilst the false charges against you are investigated. You are to occupy the chamber once used by Queen Anne."

"That is a most sobering thought, sir," Elizabeth Farriby says. "Considering how the poor woman met her end."

"Dismiss the thought from your mind," Robin Crabtree tells her. "I can see that a foul travesty of justice brings you here, and I pledge my protection. Will Draper shall do right by you, and you will be returned to your husband, safely."

"I am not married, sir."

"That astounds me," Robin says, offering her his arm. "How can such a magnificent treasure remain unclaimed?"

"Would that Sir Richard Rich thought of me in so pretty a way, Master Crabtree," Elizabeth replies. "Then I might now be a free woman."

"Please … can you not call me Robin, sweet lady?" Robin Crabtree replies. "As for that toad faced little bastard, Rich… may he die, and rot in everlasting Hell!"

*

"Sit down, Master Plank," Rupert Donne tells the prisoner, as soon as he is led into the chamber. "Might I name to you, His Lordship, the Duke of Norfolk? Sir… this is Judas Plank, who I can recommend to you as a most honest fellow. He comes to us with important information, and with no desire for reward."

"Then he is, indeed an honest chap," Norfolk recites. "If he has information to my liking, I will force him to accept my generous bounty."

"Than you, sir." Judas Plank cannot raise his eyes from the ground, for fear of being seen for what he is… a coward… a liar, and a traitor to those who trusted him.

"How came you to be near Arundel, Master Plank?" Rupert Donne asks. "You are amongst friends now, and you are safe from the duke's enemies."

"I was passing through… coming back from Austin Friars."

"What was your business there?" Donne enquires.

"I am a journeyman haulier, sir,"

Plank replies. "I had just delivered a cargo to the house, at the behest of a foreign gentleman, called Holbein. A German, I think."

"What was this cargo?"

"Paintings," Plank says. "Portraits of three noble women, for the king. Holbein took them to Thomas Cromwell's house first, for him to admire."

"And you unloaded this cargo?" Donne asks.

"I did. Then the foreigner paid me, and bid me get off on my way," Plank says. "I thought to visit the kitchen, and beg a drink of beer, to keep me *whilst* on my way… so did not leave Austin Friars at once."

"Can you prove any of this?" the torturer asks.

"I can, sir," Plank tells him. "I have signed bills of lading, and I can describe the pictures in detail. Who else could do that, unless in close order to them?"

"Signed by whom?"

"One by Holbein, and a second receipt by Cromwell." Plank scratches at a boil which has appeared by the side of his nose. "Then they went into a chamber filled with books, and spoke to one another. I saw Thomas Cromwell, with my own eyes."

"How did you know him?" Donne asks. "Have you seen him before?"

"No, sir, I have not… but Holbein

referred to him as 'Cromwell'… and then, a little later… as 'Master Thomas'."

"Why would they speak to each other with you present?" the duke puts in, and Judas Plank almost leaps out of his skin.

"Beggin' your pardon, My Lord… but they could not see me, for I was in the entrance hall, concealed… quite by accident, you must understand… amongst a stand of outside cloaks, and other such heavy garments. Once they started talking, I was feared to slip away, lest they saw me and thought me to be spying upon them."

"So you were forced to stay, and spy?" Donne says. "This clearly attests to the man's honesty, My Lord… and his proof of being there is irrefutable. Master Plank's memories of the event are clear, and my scribe will take down his every word. What was said, Judas… and by whom?"

"They did slander the king, sir, and say…"

"No, we must have the very words," Donne tells him. "From your memory to the written page. So authentic a document will carry great weight with any court… or the king."

*

"Wine, mistress?" Robin Crabtree offers. The chamber is well appointed, and furnished to royal standards. "The late queen used to like this one, I am told."

"Please, call me Elizabeth," the girl says. "Might I call you Robin, good sir?"

"I pray you will," the Assistant Warden replies, effusively. "For I would be as good a friend to you as Sir Will and Lady Miriam. They are fond of you… yes?"

"Miriam took me under her wing when my dear mother died," the girl explains. "They supported me, and then found me work… until my good fortune."

"Your good fortune?" Robin asks.

"Yes, quite out of the blue beyond, I received a letter from the Court of Chancery. It seems that a gentleman in Cornwall passed away, and named me as his beneficiary. I am left a manor house, called Topham Hall, another house down in Exeter, some hundreds of acres across two counties, livestock, and a fortune of over a thousand pounds."

"Was he a relative?" Robin asks as he hands over a crystal cut glass of amber wine.

"No, I knew him not." Elizabeth sips at the nectar. "Sir Joshua Benson seems to have no link to me at all."

"The name is unfamiliar, and I know most families of good standing at court." Robin muses. "Was he an old man?"

"In his middle sixties, I do believe… and a proper country gentleman… but that is all I can say," Elizabeth tells him. "Miriam Draper spoke with Sir Rafe Sadler at the law courts, and he is handling the business for me. It seems he must write to a lawyer in Exeter, and verify the full facts. In the meantime, I have possession of Topham Hall, and money to live on. Things seemed to be going well for me, when this absurd accusation came up."

Made by a friend, I am told," Robin Crabtree says. "Why would this Gifford woman use you so badly?"

"I know not," Elizabeth shrugs her slender shoulders, and Robin's heart flutters. "She came to the village two months ago, and asked to rent a cottage of mine. I agreed a fair rate, and we soon became close friends. Nell was amusing, and we would walk and chatter away the days. She was almost like a sister to me."

"Then why accuse you?" Robin asks. "Does she stand to inherit from you, or benefit from your death?"

"On the contrary. Not only does she not stand to make anything… she might well lose her cottage." The young girl shakes her head in confusion. "I can only think that she believes what she says. Nell Gifford must really think me to be a witch."

"Capable of sorcery and murder?"

Robin laughs at the obvious stupidity of such a claim. "It is she who is mad, more like. I think her mind is addled, and that is why she has this mad fancy."

"Then pretty girls cannot be witches?" Elizabeth asks, and the man blushes.

"None as pretty as you, Elizabeth."

"Sir, we have just met."

"My pardon. I shall say nothing more."

"Pray, do not stop on my account, Robin," she says, and smiles at the handsome young man. "If Sir Will trusts you, then I would be a fool not to. If you say I am pretty… then I must believe you!"

*

"It was Holbein who spoke first," Judas Plank says to his small audience. "He bid me put the portraits in the library. That was when Cromwell said he thought my name was unusual. I explained to him that there were many Planks where I came from."

"But not so many a Judas?" Donne says, and Plank frowns as he realises how he had been twitted.

"Cromwell says 'It is for the best that we view them, before letting the king have a look' and the foreigner agreed with him."

"Then you went to the kitchen?"

"Yes. For a moment. I came back,

and it was then I found myself hidden from sight. 'I commend your artistry', Cromwell is saying to Holbein. 'Is this the Luxembourg princess then?' and Holbein says 'It is, sir' back to him." Judas Plank takes a long pull at the wine he has been offered, and wipes a filthy hand across his mouth.

"Did Cromwell make a comment about the woman?" Rupert Donne asks.

"Yes," Plank replies. "He asked if she really had such an obvious squint. '*Most noticeably*' says Master Holbein. Then he says she has a good body on her, and Thomas Cromwell just laughs and says 'the king still likes to admire the mantelpiece, even when he is giving the fire a good poke' straight out."

"He said that?" Norfolk asks, and he chuckles, for it sounds just like something that Cromwell would say amongst those he could trust.

"Yes, and he then said 'the king will not accept such an evil eye', and they both laughed. Then they turned to the Burgundy woman's portrait, and Holbein told of how well bred she was, coming from the French royal line. Cromwell says the king will be impressed, '*for he is such a snob*' and I almost choked with trying not to be outraged. Our own dear king, used so badly, sirs."

"Quite," Norfolk says. "Go on."

"I hear Holbein say 'Her beauty is

marred by a twitch of the right eye, which makes her entire face look lopsided. One must hope it is not catching'. Then Cromwell claps his hands, as if in pleasure."

"You are sure of this?" Norfolk asked. "It was Cromwell who laughed, and clapped his hands?"

"My Lord Norfolk, Thomas Cromwell could scarcely hide his pleasure, and then he declares that the Cleves woman is the prettiest. Holbein tells him that she is a clever wench, but not too clever for the king. It is then that Thomas Cromwell says: 'Henry does not like to come second to anyone. The lady is rather old at twenty four. I wonder no other man has come knocking at her bed chamber door. Is she still a virgin?' Just like that, sir."

*

"How will they use me?" Elizabeth asks her young gaoler.

"It will not come to that," Robin replies, with more certainty than he feels. "Will Draper is on your side."

"And the Attorney General of England is not," she says. "I wonder who has the king's ear today? They say Henry lives in fear of sorcery, and that he shakes with horror at the very sight of a black cat."

"Hush, girl. Do not speak about the king in such a way," Robin tells her. "Even these walls have ears, and I cannot protect you from yourself."

"What will they do to me?" Elizabeth asks.

"They will demand a confession."

"I am innocent."

"Then they will put you to the question," Robin says. "The Tower torturer must confirm what you say. If you are innocent, he will find out. Of course… most change their minds to avoid the terrible pain."

"So, if I plead guilty, I will avoid the torture?"

"Probably. Sir Richard Rich wants someone to burn, and does not hold a personal grudge. Confess, and he will allow you an easier death."

"Then what must I do, Robin?"

"If Will Draper does not save you, I will," the young man says. "I will find a way to get you away from here."

"Truly?" Elizabeth asks, but she cannot see how it could be done. "They would arrest you also."

"We can flee to the coast, and take ship for France," Robin tells her, but he knows it is a dream. In five hundred years, only one man has ever escaped from the Tower of London, and kept his freedom. "They will never follow us there."

"Yes," Elizabeth says, softly. "That

is what we will do."

*

"He asked if she was a virgin?" The Duke of Norfolk cannot believe his luck. His niece Anne Boleyn died because of her loose morals, and here is Thomas Cromwell idly wondering if the Cleves woman is of the same ilk. "What did the foreigner reply to this outrageous question?"

"He did not seem to know." Judas Plank wrings his hands, and hopes he is furnishing the right answers to the great Norfolk and his man. "The painter claimed she was surrounded by useless old men, and mincing sodomites. Thomas Cromwell said the king would often jest about such men… in a lame way."

"Lame indeed?" Rupert Donne glances across to make sure this is all being taken down by the secretary. "He said Henry was a *lame* king?"

"Yes, sir. 'Then the girl will seem pretty enough, and has yet to be swived?' Cromwell asks."

"How did Holbein answer this?" Donne asks.

"Let me think… ah, yes… 'Of the three, I found Anne to be the most honest', the painter says back to him." Plank replies. He sticks as close to the actual words as he can recall, and hopes for the best. "Then Cromwell says: 'It is Anne of Cleves who must become our new queen. She is suitable in so many ways. With her beside Henry, the Church of England will become stronger, and the Germanic States will become allies. The emperor will not object to the union, and the new alliances will form a noose about the neck of France'. Then Cromwell went on about bat shit for a while."

"Bat shit?" Norfolk grimaces. "Do not write that part down, you imbecile!" The scribe pauses, and waits for Judas Plank to continue.

"Then the painter says: 'Your future seems to be assured, Master Thomas. I salute you,' and Thomas Cromwell says he shall pay Holbein very well for his cleverness."

"This is still not enough," Norfolk growls and Judas Plank sees he must tell it all. He clears his throat, and leans towards the scribe, as if begging him to copy down each word faithfully.

"Holbein asked 'when will you show the king his new bride to be?' Cromwell said: 'Soon. Though I must seem impartial. Henry hates to think he is being *maniper ... maniperlated*. He shall choose his new bride *without* my help."

"The cunning swine," Norfolk says.

"Holbein asked if Thomas Cromwell was sure Anne would be picked, and he said: 'Just between you and I, Hans, I wrote to her father last week, and advised him to start the girl on her way. She will be in England in a week's time.' The painter seemed worried at this news, and said: 'Let us hope Henry is happy with the lady you have chosen for him.''

"This is more like it." Norfolk smiles at these damning words, and begins to pace up and down the chamber. "Go on, man."

"Cromwell sounded drunk, and said: 'Let me tell you this. The king *did not deserve* his last queen. She was far too lovely a creature ever to be his. I think God took her to save the girl from his *crude* attentions.' At that moment, this other fellow turns up, and demands that they shut up, for fear of being overheard."

"Then that is all?"

"Apart from the new man... Thomas Cromwell called him Rafe... who wanted to know what he was writing up, and Cromwell tells him it is the king's marriage contract... *to Anne of Cleves*."

"Then the whole damned marriage was a farce," the Duke of Norfolk says. "Contrived to put Anne of Cleves on the throne of England, whether the king likes it or not."

"And our Master Plank has given you the clear proof that you need," Donne says.

"Indeed, he has," the Duke of Norfolk says. He crosses to the scribe, and snatches the paper from his desk. He reads, with his lips moving, and confirms that all is exactly as it should be. At length, he hands back the damning document, and the clerk quickly dusts it with sawdust, and blows it dry.

"Make two further copies," Donne commands the man. "One for the duke, another for myself, and the third to be locked in My Lord's strongroom."

"Yes, master," the man said, and bowed himself out of the room. Judas Plank sat quite still, with his eyes fixed at a place on the reed covered floor. The duke stood in front of him, then put a hand under his chin, and raised his head so that their eyes met.

"If Cromwell falls, I will laden you down with gold, Master Plank, and give you enough land to keep you until the end of days."

"He shall fall, My Lord," Plank told him. "For, as God is my witness… I have spoken only the truth. Cromwell is a traitor, and I will tell it to any man." Norfolk nodded his head, and glanced over to where Donne was awaiting his instructions.

"Keep him safe, Master Donne. For soon, he will repeat his story to the king!"

7 The Examiner Calls

The sprawling cluster of law offices about Lincoln's Inn reminds Will Draper of the Venetian ghetto, with every single room coveted and filled to capacity, not by rich Jewish merchant families, but with highly skilled lawyers, busily vying for trade. A young lad recognises him at once, and runs forward from the shelter of one of the close packed buildings.

"Hold Moll for you, Colonel Will?" the lad asks, as he pats the old mare's forehead. "I can rub her down for a penny."

"Still hanging around these villains, young Teddy?" he asks the lad, and hands over his reins. Moll will be rubbed down, watered, and generally cosseted by the youngster, and readied for the return journey. " Here is a shilling. Find her some decent forage, and keep the change. It will keep you honest."

"Too late for that, sir," Teddy Brown says. "I am surrounded by men of law!"

"Well said," Will replied, with a grin. "Is Sir Rafe Sadler about?"

"Master Rafey, you want?" the lad says. "Inside the second door, and a good climb to the most upper floor, sir. He is working on the king's new land reform bill.

The clerk, Rawlings, will show you up. I dare say you could find him yourself, but the old fellow would be out of a job."

Will Draper follows the elderly clerk up some rickety stairs, and past several open doors. In one office, he sees Barnaby Fowler, and gives him a cheery wave, in passing. On the third floor, young trainee lawyers are busy copying legal papers out for their masters and, in one corner, a child is busy penning quills, and cutting slots in their points for the scribes. They clamber up one more steep flight of stairs, and he finds Rafe Sadler, bending over several open law books. His friend looks up, and frowns.

"Bad news, Will?" For the King's Examiner to come calling does not bode well "Who are you after… not one of mine, I hope?"

"Rest easy, Rafe," Will says. "I come only to pick your considerable brains, in the hope of helping poor Elizabeth Farriby."

"Elizabeth?" Rafe has not heard of the arrest, and wonders what the poor child could be involved with. "Is she in trouble?"

"Arrested, by Richard Rich, and accused of witchcraft," Will explains. "I believe you are handling her legal work for her?"

"I am." Rafe puts down his quill,

and pours out two glasses of a tawny coloured port wine. He offers Will one, and sips at the other. "Though there is nothing criminal in any of it. A simple matter of straightforward inheritance, or so I thought."

"Oh?" Will sits down on one of the rickety stools that are dotted throughout the building. "Is there a problem?"

"That is for me to find out, I suppose," Rafe says. "Mistress Farriby is set to inherit a considerable estate from Sir Josh Benson, who was once a successful merchant, both here, and in the west country. He died without issue… or so I first thought. It seems that some twenty odd years ago, our Sir Josh was something of a *dandycock* with the ladies. After a torrid *affair de la coeur* with one of the king's seamstresses, he left her with child. That was back in the year 1519."

"Elizabeth Farriby?"

"The very same," Rafe says. "This remained a closely kept secret, until his death. Benson's lawyer, Master Edwin Carmody, of Exeter, was left with instructions to contact young Elizabeth, and inform her of her good fortune."

"But surely, bastards cannot inherit their father's estates," Will says. "Cannot some closer relative intervene?"

"If directly willed to the said bastard, things become rather murky," Rafe Sadler explains. "The illegitimate child cannot take precedence over a legal wife, or child born in wedlock. Or even a brother, sister or close nephew or a niece. It is my job to establish that no other claim can be made, prior to Elizabeth's own."

"Of course. What did you find out?" Will asks. "Pray tell me that Nell Gifford's name has come to your notice."

"Nell Gifford?" Rafe frowns. "The name means nothing to me, my friend. How is she involved in this affair?"

"I do not know yet." Will empties his glass. "Pray continue with what you found out."

"Sir Josh Benson never married. Elizabeth Farriby is his only issue. However, he had both a younger brother, and a sister. The brother, Montagu, died a year before Sir Josh. He was a widower, with two sons. Daniel and Walter."

"Then they must come first, surely?" Will asks. He does not quite see where all this will lead, but it might explain why someone wishes Elizabeth Farriby arrested for witchcraft. "Two nephews must out bid one bastard daughter."

"Walter died in 1533, from the sweating sickness," Rafe confirms, "and Daniel… the older brother… in 1536, after a hunting accident. It seems he put his hunter at a ditch, and took a bad tumble."

"Then surely the sister has a fair claim," Will says.

"Amelia Benson married late, was widowed, and had two children. Both died young. Amelia moved to live with her brother, Josh, and passed away … after a lingering illness when she was forty one years old."

"A most unhappy family history, Rafe," Will Draper concludes. "Then we are left with poor Elizabeth."

"Her mother was named, in Sir Josh's last will and testament, as the single beneficiary. On her pre-deceasing Sir Josh Benson, the illegitimate daughter comes into the entire estate. In total, she is worth about ten thousand pounds, and will have an income of over two thousand a year."

"What if she is found guilty, and executed?" Will asks. "She has no living relatives."

"In that event, the property would pass to the crown," Rafe says, and smiles. "I cannot think Henry would condemn a girl to death, just to lay hands on an estate worth less than he spends on a jewel for his new wife. Nor can Richard Rich benefit, other than gaining a sordid reputation for finding witches."

"Then Elizabeth Farriby is not being accused to cheat her out of her estate?"

Will asks.

"Not that I can see," Rafe Sadler replies. "It seems to me that Mistress Farriby is the victim of circumstances. Might she be accused honestly?"

"Of witchcraft?" Will almost snarls the words. "How can you, a rational man of the law …"

"You misunderstand me, Will," Rafe says. "I have no time for witches and warlocks, or black cats and demons, abroad at midnight. I do not believe in magic … white or black, and I cannot think how any sane man would give it credence. I mean, merely, that some honest person, of limited intellect, might misinterpret what they see. A cat leaps out of the dark, and it becomes an evil imp, or a horse sickens and it is because of the evil eye."

"There is some truth in what you say, my friend," says Will Draper. "This Nell Gifford seems such a girl. She sees the evil eye in a casual glance, then ties an old woman's death into her friend, by virtue of her being the old dear's landlady."

"Then half of my clients are witches," Rafe tells him. "For England runs on rents and leases. Has this girl any real evidence?"

"None. She claims to have heard Elizabeth conversing with the devil, and just missed seeing her flying around the room on a besom!"

"Good God, the girl is unhinged." Rafe rummages on his desk, and comes out with a slim volume. "Here, this is a treatise on lunacy. Was it a full moon? Doctor Arthurius writes that a full moon can unhinge young women, or any of a *hysterical* lean, and make them behave in a mad way."

"What is this 'hysterical'," Will asks.

"It pertains to a woman's privy parts, and how they can make that woman seem frenzied, or overwrought. Doctors say it is hysteria induced by bad airs within the womb."

"Good God! Modern medicine is beyond my grasp," says the Examiner.

"Even so … they might have a point where witchcraft is spoken of, and a lady having her … monthly curse… might become hysterically inclined."

"Nell Gifford seems sane enough," Will replies. "That is the problem. The girl speaks well. She is educated to a reasonable standard, and puts her case in a clear way. Yet all the while, she laments ever accusing Elizabeth, and claims to be her best friend."

"And is she?"

"It would seem so," Will confesses. "She is of the same social standing as Elizabeth, and the accused says they are close, and have been since she came to the village."

"From where?"

"Does that matter?" Will asks, and Rafe Sadler shrugs.

"I doubt it, but it seems odd that this Nell Gifford should turn up, just as Elizabeth inherits… and that she becomes friendly with her, even though she is the girl's landlady. Does she have any family hereabouts?"

"No, she is an orphan," Will confirms. "That is why the two grew to be friends, I think. Nell seems, to my mind, a most unlikely accuser. She condemns in one sentence, and tries to absolve in the next. Richard Rich thinks she is a good witness, because he only hears the evil, and has already condemned Elizabeth in his eyes."

"Then she is taken?"

"Of course. Fortunately, he has her lodged in the Tower, and I have many friends there. Robin Crabtree is keeping an eye on her, and seeing she is well cared for, and the Torturer in Chief, Abraham Wake, is in my pay. He will do nothing to the girl without warning me."

"Perhaps, but he must do his duty if pressed," Rafe says. "If not, then Rich will replace him. How long have you before they start questioning Elizabeth?"

"Two days."

"Then you must either have this girl, Nell Gifford, change her mind … or discredit her. Investigate her past, and find out something unsavoury." Rafe Sadler rubs his sparse beard, and considers. "Might not some of Master Tom's more dubious associates be able to find something to soil her with?"

"She is a twenty year old orphan," Will says, "and as sweet a thing as any man might meet. If I had not known Elizabeth Farriby, I might well have believed her myself."

"Then you must prepare for the worst," Rafe advises his friend. "If you cannot prove her innocence, you must spirit her away somehow. Therein lies the problem. Help her escape, and Richard Rich will have good reason to arrest you. The king fears witchcraft, as does a child, and he will side with his Attorney General, if only out of fear. Even Thomas Cromwell would be hard pressed to help you then."

"Damn, but it is a mess," Will says. "I have John Beckshaw and a dozen men questioning the entire village, in the hope of establishing how the old woman died. If that can be shown to be natural, the charges diminish. Then we must only disprove the charge of killing the chickens with her evil eye."

"Can Doctor Theophrasus help

you?" Rafe suggests. "He is the king's best physician."

"He is in Milan at the moment," Will says. "It seems that the Duke of Milan has gout, and has heard of his amazing powers."

"Yet we do not call him a sorcerer," Rafe says. "Only Nell Gifford thinks Elizabeth Farriby is a witch. Were I to be defending Mistress Elizabeth, I would call every man and woman in the village as witness, and ask them one question: *Is this girl a witch*, and I would demand a one word answer. In the face of a hundred denials, even the king might waver."

"Yes, there is great wisdom in what you say, old friend," Will Draper concludes. He stands, slips his hands back into his riding gloves, and takes his leave. "Good day to you, Rafe. I shall think on your advice, and try to find my way through this maze of circumstance."

"Farewell, Will," Rafe replies. "Nothing happens without a reason. Find it, and all will become clear to you."

*

"Sir… you are far too forward, I think." Nell Gifford speaks sharply, and pushes Richard Rich's hand away from her tightly laced bodice top. "Do you think me the sort of *woman* who frequents low taverns? I thought you better than that. I am an orphan in this world, and must live on a hundred a year. I have no-one to guide me in the ways of courtship, and cannot tell if a man is honest or not."

"Oh, I am honest, my dear," Rich says. "It is just that I am overcome by your comeliness, and would touch your snowy skin."

"Now you talk like a poet," Nell Gifford says. She stands, and allows her skirts to fall back over her exposed ankles. She knows Rich has been admiring them as they ate, and is not surprised now he has tried to take a liberty with her. "Oh, such snowy skin, you say, even as you try to unlace my bodice. Do you think I value my virginity so little, sir?"

"You are a virgin?" Richard Rich gulps, and clasps his hands in his lap to stop them shaking. "Then you must have a guardian, my sweet girl. I am Attorney General, and if you put yourself under my wing, I will guard you with my life."

"Sir… are you offering marriage?"

"Not *per se*," Rich says. "For I am, most unfortunately, already married. It is a sham, of course, but I cannot put the damned woman aside."

"Then what do you offer me?" Nell asks. The skinny little fellow is not her idea of the perfect man, but she is interested in what he has in mind. "You are married, sir… and I am not."

"I could find you a cottage," Rich proposes. "I might see my way clear to paying the rent. In return, you might look upon me in a more kindly light. I could visit… often … and protect you."

"You would make me into a whore?"

"Not at all," Rich explains. "You would be the mistress of the Attorney General of England. You would rank amongst the greatest in the land."

"I would need clothes, jewels, and money." Nell wonders how rich he is, but does not forget that mistresses can be discarded easier than wives.

"Of course," Rich says. "What say you, my girl?"

"You make a tempting offer… but there is a problem."

"Tell me, and I shall remove it at once."

"Why, my reputation, of course," Nell Gifford replies with a blush of the cheeks. "I have accused my friend of witchcraft. What if she is found to be innocent, and returns to this place?"

"I do not follow," Rich says.

"She will not look upon me kindly, sir," Nell complains. "Why, she might even dun me in the street, and turn everyone against me… just for being honest about what I heard and saw."

"The girl is as guilty as sin," Rich says, "and will burn at the stake for it. I know she is a friend, but the law is strict on this matter. It is a pity you did not actually see anything else. I mean to say, what if you had seen the cat changing shape? These devils can do that you know."

"How odd!" Nell looks astounded. "Why, that is exactly what I saw, now I come to think of it. The cat was rolling about on the floor, as if just resuming its mortal shape."

"Excellent. And you will swear to this?"

"I will." Nell answers.

"Then I regret that Elizabeth Farriby is your friend, for as sure as anything, she must burn."

"Oh, dear." Nell Gifford's eyes cloud with tears. "How could she have deceived me so? Let me think about your kind offer, Sir Richard... and I shall give you my answer *after* the trial."

*

Marion Giles has the demeanour of a beautiful ice queen, and her insistent demands are driving the village's young vicar to distraction. He is used to preaching to farmers and milkmaids, not arguing with a stunningly attractive gentlewoman. He is at a distinct disadvantage, both physically, and intellectually.

"What you ask is impossible," he says.

"How so?" Marion replies. "Is it against the law?"

"Well … not as such," the Reverend George Farrall admits."

"It is, or it is not," Marion retorts. "Why argue with me over such a simple thing. There are no relatives to consult, are there?"

"No. It is just … not right."

"Perhaps, to your narrow mind, it is wrong," Marion says, "but I am a trained apothecary, and I do not hold with your simple Christian beliefs. Now, will you do it, or shall I find myself some sturdy young men, and do it myself?"

"Madam, you task me," Farrall says.

"I am a mistress, sir," Marion says, " and I will task God if need be. Pray, do not try to stop me."

"I see that I cannot," the vicar replies. "Mistress Giles, you have my permission… though God knows why. Master Sexton, fetch two spades, and help me dig up poor Mistress Townley!"

*

The cheap wooden cask comes out of the black earth with ease. Jane Townley has only been at rest for a couple of days, and the soil was not yet compacted, or frozen. The two men raise the box, and place it on the open grave side. As they do, the vicar mutters a prayer for the dead.

"Lid off, please," Marion says. The vicar hesitates, but sees the look of determination in Marion Giles' diamond blue eyes. He uses the edge of a spade to prise open the wooden lid, and crosses himself as the contents are revealed.

The old woman is contorted within the confines of the flimsy wooden casket, and her face is twisted into a look of primeval fear. It is as if she has seen Satan, the vicar thinks, and mutters a quick prayer.

"I must examine the body," Marion tells the man. "Will you try to stop me, father?"

"I am not a father," George Farrall says. "That is for papists and the like. Do what you must, ma… mistress, and I shall see to the reburial, before the entire village descends on us with scythes and pitchforks at the ready."

Marion smiles at the thought, and bends down to look at the mortal remains of Jane Townley. It is as she suspected, and the signs are there to see. That the woman has met an unnatural death is obvious, but the reason eludes her. Perhaps Will Draper can throw light into so dark a corner.

"Very well, fa… oh, what do I call

you?"

"George will suffice, Mistress Giles."

"Then George it shall be," Marion says to him. It is only now that she realises the fellow is staring at her in something close to rapture. "I have seen enough. Pray put the poor wretch back into the ground."

"Can you refute this madness now?" George asks.

"You do not believe the girl is a witch then?" Marion asks.

"No, I do not," the vicar replies. "I have no time for spells, evil eyes and magic potions. My faith preaches that we should forgive, and understand our fellow man. Have you read Tyndale, Mistress Giles?"

"You must call me Marion, as it seems we are allies," she says, and links his arm. "Escort me back to my friends, and tell me all about why you are a priest."

"We do not like that word," George Farrall tells her. "It has links with the bad old faith. What kind of a religion bars most of its followers from reading the holy bible? The English bible is there for all to read, and it gives the true, unsullied, word of God. There be no mention of the desolation of purgatory… for one."

"Then I might go straight to Heaven … or Hell?"

"The former, surely," the vicar says,

with a gentle bow to her. "I cannot see any evil in you. I think you are Heaven sent to us, my lady."

"Marion." She looks down into the eyes of this strange little man, and sees something other than the usual lust. "I think you are a very good man, George Farrall. Does your dear wife follow your protestant beliefs?" The question is asked, and Marion finds herself holding her breath for an answer.

"I cannot afford to take a wife, madam… not on my meagre stipend," George Farrall says.

"Pity," Marion says, with a smile that suggests the opposite, and she links him even more tightly.

*

"You jest, surely?" Miriam is at supper with Marion and Pru, and cannot believe her ears. "You mean the funny little fellow with the thin lips?"

"He is not short," Marion says. "Rather, it is I who am tall, and his lips are just as they should be. He is most honest, and has a caring nature. Why, from what I hear, he beggars himself to keep his parishioners from starvation."

"That is not a reason to love him," Miriam says. The very idea that her friend is willing to give herself away to a village priest is beyond understanding. "You cannot marry him."

"No, I cannot," Marion replies, "for he has not asked me."

"Then let that be an end to this foolishness," Miriam tells her. "Tomorrow, we return to London, and this unfortunate episode can be forgotten."

"Do you love him?" Pru asks.

"That has nothing to do with…"

"Yes, I do." Marion cuts across Miriam. "I am thirty two years old, and have never felt this way about any man before. George but looks at me, and I know I want to be with him… for the rest of my life."

"Then tell him," Pru says. "Refuse this man, and the world will end in storm and tempest."

"Oh, damn it," Miriam groans. Pru sees things, and only a fool would disregard her prophesy.

"Then I shall," Marion says, and jumps up from the table. "I must go to him, now!" She leaves the chamber, and throws a cloak about her. She runs out into the night, and finds George Farrall standing in the front garden with a forlorn look in his eyes.

"Marion," he starts, as soon as she appears, but then he falters. Marion Giles smiles, and takes him by both hands.

"I know, George," she says, happily.

"I know."

They kiss, awkwardly. George tries to explain how poor he is, and Marion hushes him by telling him of her own small fortune.

"You must preach each Sunday, and be a kept man during the week," she says. "Do not attempt to argue with me."

"How can I?" George says. He is a foot shorter than her, and a poor catch in most women's eyes, but his inner kindness, and love of his parishioners seems to have won over this woman of rare beauty in a moment. "We must find another preacher… so that we may wed. Do I have to speak with your father, or have you a master or mistress to convince?"

"I am my own woman, George Farrall," Marion tells him sternly, "and that is enough."

"Oh, yes my dear one."

Inside, Miriam and Pru spy from the window. It is Pru who speaks first, because she knows it must be said.

"I made it up."

"You made it up?" Marion asks.

"Yes. All that storm and tempest stuff," Pru says. "I just thought it might help her decide. It is transparently obvious that she loves the poor man. God help him."

"Amen," Marion says, and they

both giggle.

*

Even when lodged in the very best chambers available, the Tower of London is still the most daunting place in England. Built to dominate the city, first by William the Conqueror, and then strengthened by a succession of Edwards and Henrys, the citadel seems designed to make brave men cower. The prospect of ending her days in one of the less well furnished towers makes Elizabeth almost weep in anguish. It is only her own strength, and the kindness of Robin that keeps her from utter surrender.

It is easy to see why innocent men would confess under the ministrations of the Tower's staff, and how great wrongs could be done, in the name of justice.

"They say Richard Crookback murdered his own nephews in this place," she murmurs. Robin takes her hand in his, and smiles his support at her.

"Old tales." The Assistant Keeper tries to think of a cheerier thing to tell her. "Mortimer once escaped from here, you know. He climbed down the privy, and into the moat. They say that the Bishop of Hereford, or some such place, was waiting in a rowing boat."

"Then he lived?"

"He fled to France," Robin replies. "Then he returned, and drove the king from the throne."

"Which one?"

"The one in Greenwich, I think."

"No, which king?"

"Oh… I can't remember. He was a …rather odd fellow. Very fond of one of his ministers, I hear."

"Ah, that kind of love," Elizabeth says. "Did it last?"

"They chopped off his head," Robin says, but he is getting confused over his facts, and cannot recall exactly who killed who anymore. "You must not linger over such morbid things."

"Then stop telling them to me," Elizabeth replies, gently. "Just sit with me, and hold my hand. I cannot face the dark alone."

"You never have to," Robin tells her, gallantly. "I will be beside you, all the way, and when it is darkest… we will hold hands and step on together."

"I am scared, Robin," Elizabeth confesses. "Let us pray Colonel Draper can bring some sense to all of this. After all, were I a witch, would I not just fly over the high walls on my besom, and escape?"

"They would claim some reason why you do not," Robin says. "Granted, Master Cromwell is a most legal fellow, and obeys the laws of England, but there are others who do not. They will twist whatever you do, or say, to make you look guilty."

"Then I must pray," she says. "For the strength of the Lord God conquers all."

"Amen," Robin says. He has seen many honest men go to the inquisitors, and he has heard their prayers, even as they screamed out their guilt, just to halt the agony. Somehow, in this terrible place, God seems to have grown quite deaf to the needs of his suffering humanity.

8 Proof

Marion Giles has studied at her father's knee since her mother died when she was just four years old, and knows as much, if not more, about the herbs, elements and compounds, as any apothecary in England. By the time she was fourteen, she could diagnose an illness, and prepare a remedy better than her father.

"They will ask for a spell, or a charm to ward off the sickness," her father would tell her. "Do not be tempted, even out of kindness. Always make clear to your patient that it is the medicine that helps, and that anything else is witchcraft. Never claim to understand the black arts, my girl, or it will destroy you!"

The words drove deep into her mind, and she was resolved to spurn anything but proven medicinal fact in her daily work. Now, of course, she spends her days concocting sweet smelling unguents for idle rich women to rub on their skins, or making up powders to ease headaches, or stifle runny noses.

No matter how many times she hands over one of her apothecary's remedies, someone will always ask the same ridiculous questions: Should I take it at full moon? Must I recant Satan as I swallow it down? Is there a magical amulet to go with it? The list of stupid ideas is endless, and she meets each enquiry with a cold smile, and the same answer.

"Do whatever you wish to do," she says, "but it will not effect my medicine."

"Deep in thought, Mistress Marion?" She is startled by the sudden interruption, and almost drops the glass she has just raised to her lips. "I hope it is about this witchcraft foolishness."

"A foolishness that might get an innocent girl burnt at the stake, Colonel Draper." She sips at the cold milk, and lowers the glass to the table. "Will you join me for breakfast?"

"I have eaten," Will replies. "I called at the manor, and Elizabeth's servants fed me. They tell me strange things have been going on, whilst I was in London. Can you explain?"

"Strange things?" Marion has to puzzle for a moment. "Oh, you mean digging up the grave? That, surely, is something you would have done, given time."

"Yes, but I am an officer of the king," Will replies. "I have the authority, whereas, you do not."

"The vicar gave his consent."

"Oh?" Will wonders if any man can deny this woman. "And why would he do that?"

"The fellow is in love with me, of course."

"Really? So, he simply said ' I love you, Marion… let me get a spade'?"

"Almost word for word," Marion tells Will, and she smiles at how simple love can be. "I thought it prudent not to let the body lie too long without examination. The worms work fast, and I needed to see her before there was too much change."

"A gruesome task for a lady," Will mutters.

"That is what poor George said."

"George?"

"George Farrall, my sweet vicar," Marion explains. "We are to be wed in a day or two. Though that matters not to this investigation, of course. It was the chickens, you see. That is what first started me thinking."

"You must explain, madam." Will sits, and drops his cap onto the table. He is still dusty from the road, and poor Moll is almost done after a hard ride.

"I went to speak with Jeb, the man who tends to them."

"Yes, I was with you," Will reminds her. "You made some play of how one of the birds was gone, and then you looked at the chicken feed. I recall you became tight lipped then, and I know better than to push you, Marion. What was it that you discovered?"

"That the chicken feed was…"

"Poisoned?" Will smiles and nods. "I had already guessed that was the case."

"No, I examined the feed, and it was, without a doubt, *not* poisoned. The entire bag was untainted. Jeb opened it, that fateful morning, and drew from it. Then he fed his birds."

"And they died."

"Just so."

"From what?" Will asks.

"The chicken feed, of course," Marion replies. Really, she thinks, men can be so narrow minded… even the cleverer ones, such as the colonel.

"That does not make sense." Will sounds scornful, but even as he speaks, he understands what this remarkable woman is saying to him. "Damn me for an idiot, Marion. I forget that England contains more than one clever woman. You rival my dear Miriam, if no one else can. I should have seen it at once. The feed was not poisoned… until it was in the bucket!"

"Exactly so," Marion says, enjoying her moment. "It is the only possible answer. Jeb half filled the bucket, and would have fed the chickens there and then, save for an unexpected intervention."

"Elizabeth came strolling by, with her so called friend, Nell Gifford." Will

Draper slaps his gloved hands together.

"That is so. Jeb and Elizabeth… even Nell… agree to that, do they not?" says Marion.

"Yes, I had it written down, and dated," Will tells her. It is something he has started doing of late. The mind is a strange place, and things can be easily mislaid in it, so the King's Examiner has his men write reports, as soon as time allows, and then, if possible, have them witnessed by those concerned. It is a laborious process, made all the more difficult because so few outside the clergy, or the nobility have the skill. To be literate means instant promotion to officer status for ill's recruits.

"A wise move," Marion says. "In this way, a guilty party cannot change their words without suspicion falling on them. So it is that all three attest to the casual meeting. Jeb, being a man, put aside his duty to speak with two remarkably pretty young girls."

"Leaving the bucket of feed unattended," Will says. "It is hardly something that you would think needed guarding. Elizabeth says they spoke of a few things, then she and Nell prepared to go on their way. Jeb then picked up the bucket, and threw the feed to his chickens. Moments later, they started to jerk about, and die."

"Then we have proof," Marion says

to him. "But of what? We now know the feed *must* have been poisoned … unless you believe in the evil eye?"

"I do not. Such distorted thinking belongs in the dark ages. Someone poisoned that feed in the bucket," Will replies. "That is why the sack is untainted. The only ones there were Jeb, Elizabeth, and Nell. It was one of those three."

"Yes, but we cannot claim it to be any one of them in particular. All three had the chance to pour poison into the feed."

"Pour, you say?" Will puzzles at the certainty of what she says. "Why not a powder, or some other way?"

"No, it must have been a liquid," Marion tells him. "A powder, or pellets of some kind would not have diffused so quickly, and the chickens would have been affected in stages. Instead, they all died, within a few seconds. I have been giving some thought as to what this concoction could be."

"And do you know yet?" Will asks. He is sure that this could be a vital piece of evidence, and that the nature of the poison might well point to whom it was who administered it.

"It is a clever potion," Marion says. "Not one a poor country poultry keeper would understand."

"Then we are back to Elizabeth and

Nell once more," Will says. "Neither girl has any reason to do such a thing. They both claim to be close friends."

"Someone poisoned the feed," Marion says. "I could not tell which poison had killed the birds, because Jeb had them plucked and cleaned. That is why I needed to see the body."

"What did the old lady reveal to you?" Will asked.

"Her face was contorted into a rictus smile, there was a scarlet rash down her arms, and across the neck, and her body was twisted, as if in utter agony," Marion Giles tells him. "There are many poisons to be found in the hedgerows, or marshes around here, such as Monk's Head, or Hemlock… but this one was a little different. The symptoms I saw, clearly displayed on Jane Townley's corpse, point to Bella Donna … or Deadly Nightshade, as some call it."

"How hard is it to come by?" Will Draper asks.

"It grows tall in woodlands, and hedgerows, but the soil about here is not really suitable for its propagation. The leaves and berries are most poisonous, when reduced to a draft. In very small doses, it can ease nagging toothaches, or allow the sleepless to sleep, but in larger amounts, it is quite deadly. The chickens lasted only moments, so the dose they digested must have been highly concentrated. Then Jeb sent the cock bird to Jane Townley's house, as a charitable act."

"You think it killed her?" Will asks.

"It depends how strong the dose she took was," Marion explains. "I have seen animals eat from a poisoned carcass and then die. Though it is a rare thing to come across. There is, of course, another possibility."

"Yes, I know. Whosoever it was who poisoned the chickens, did it to make Elizabeth look bad. Why not go further, and dispose of a woman whom she wanted out of her cottage?"

"If Jane Townley ate the gifted bird, it might be enough to kill her," Marion says, "but the immediate rash, the convulsions, and the swiftness of death points to a much more concentrated dose. It could be that the killer administered the Bella Donna in a drink of some kind. I think we should search the poor woman's house, in case something remains. Let us pray the culprit has not thought the same thing, and acted to remove the evidence."

"I shall get my men onto it at once, Marion," Will Draper says. "You have been a great help to me in this matter. How can I ever repay you?"

"Come to my wedding, and dance."

"You drive a hard bargain," Will Draper tells her, with a wry smile. "I am no dancer, my dear friend. What of this vicar you wish to marry… can he dance a fine jig?"

"I really do not know, Marion says. "No doubt I shall find out at the wedding feast."

"You must let Miriam and I arrange it for you," Will says to her. "You can use Draper House. We have plenty of room, even with the three children capering about the place. You might like to use our great hall for the wedding feast."

"Why, thank you, Will," Marion says. "We are most grateful for the offer." In truth, the arrangements have already been taken over by Miriam Draper, who intends for her friend to have a fine wedding, and a huge banquet to follow. "My husband to be, and I, thank you."

"Think nothing of it," Will says. "I shall have the search done at once. If nothing else, it will establish if the old woman ate the cock bird…"

"Or was murdered," Marion finishes.

"Then you think as I do?" says Will. "You know who the culprit is?"

"Of course. It is obvious to anyone who knows the facts, but there is no reason for it. Nell and Elizabeth were friends. Nell has nothing to gain by accusing Elizabeth of witchcraft, so why try to condemn her to so cruel a death?"

"That is for me to find out," Will says. "Nell Gifford came here a few months ago. She has no relatives here, and only Elizabeth Farriby as a friend. Everyone says they were close. They shared walks, ate together, and amused themselves the way minor gentry should. There was never a cross word, and the two girls were not even love rivals."

"There is something else," Marion says. "If Nell meant Elizabeth great harm… why accuse her of witchcraft? Would it not have been simpler to drop some Deadly Nightshade into her wine cup one night, and make it look as though she has had a terrible seizure of some kind?"

"Perhaps she feared suspicion falling on her?" Will conjectures. "She is all alone with her friend, who suddenly dies. It would look odd, at least."

"Not if she was not there," Marion explains. "Make the dose smaller, and leave as soon as she drinks it down. Nell would be back at her own house before Elizabeth started to convulse. It would be put down to a sad accident of nature. Nell would only come under suspicion, even from you, if she stood to gain financially in some way. Does she?"

"Not at all," Will Draper confesses. "Nell Gifford would gain nothing from Elizabeth's death. In fact, whoever inherited Elizabeth Farriby's estate might well throw her out of her rented cottage afterwards. Nell rents from month to month, and has no long lease to protect her. Scant reward there for a murder, is there?"

"No, but there must be a reason," Marion says.

"Oh, there is always a reason," Will Draper tells her. "That is for me to investigate, and uncover, I suppose."

"Then good luck to you, Will," Marion Giles says, "for there are those who have their own darker motives to see Elizabeth Farriby condemned. Why, a successful prosecution would much advance our Attorney General in the mind of the king.

"Oh, yes. Sir Richard Rich is a damnable scoundrel," Will agrees. "Let us hope he allows us the time to uncover the truth of this matter. I do not want an innocent girl to go to the stake."

*

Sir Richard Rich knows better than to try speaking with the king whilst he is walking in the gardens with one of the household ladies. This one, Lady Meg, is a widow, and seems to have caught Henry's eye. She is a healthy looking young woman, with the glow of life in her cheeks, and the king finds her overt charms put him in a good humour. He loiters, and hopes for an early summons.

"Sire, I fear the servants have let one of your household dogs out, unattended," she says to the king. Henry frowns, and looks about for the errant animal. Then he spies Richard Rich lingering near the rose arbour, and guffaws with laughter. It is a cruel sound, and it makes Rich start with fear.

"Oh, my sweet Lady Meg, but you are almost as sharp as Tom Wyatt," he says. "Richard Rich… my pet dog, indeed! How very droll of you. Look at the poor sort of a thing, waiting to be patted or kicked, like … yes, just like one of my dogs. He should take care, especially around the palace, for little dogs do not fare very well here."

"Oh, you mean poor little Porkoy?" Lady Meg says. "I remember that poor little thing. He was ever sniffing around … and getting under *that lady's* feet, My Lord."

"Come now, my dear," Henry rests a proprietary hand on the woman's nicely rounded backside. "You may mention the *putain's* name without me going into a rage. I know all there is to know about that one, and her infamous brother. Boleyn well deserved the cruellest death possible."

"Then you know how he kicked the poor beast out of the window?" Meg asks.

"What?" Henry is quite taken aback. "No, I did not… for I was told the thing jumped to its death."

"No, sire, Tom Wyatt told me he was kicked out of a high window, by George Boleyn. The man had no hesitation, I hear, and did it through his jealousy."

"Then he is better off dead," Henry says. "What says Tom Wyatt about that?"

"Oh, I happen to know that Master Wyatt agrees with you wholeheartedly, sire," Lady Meg says. "He is a staunch defender of Your Majesty, and of your honour. Whereas others, like yonder puppy dog, look only to themselves, I fear."

"Yes, he is a selfish bastard," Henry mutters.

"Yet he sits at the high table, with his betters," Lady Meg says to the king, "instead of at their feet… cringing."

"You dislike him, ma'am?"

"I loath him," she replies. "The king is too benevolent with those who do not serve him well. At best, he is little more than a petty clerk. See how he hangs about, hoping to whisper in your ear, my dearest Majesty?"

"I suppose I must see what he wants."

"He wants to hurry on with this witchcraft nonsense," Lady Meg says. "He seeks to condemn some poor girl, just to show up Sir Will Draper."

"What, he still irks my Examiner General?" Henry says, with surprise in his voice. "These people should realise how I love my dearest friends. Did you know I once jousted with Will Draper?"

"I was there, sire. I thought he would best you, but you stood firm, and won the day. Such heroism!"

"Yes, it was rather, wasn't it?" Henry says, with a beatific smile on his face. "One moment, my dear. You, Rich, come here, sir… at once!"

"Your Highness wishes to…"

"*Your* king is sick of being baited so, Sir Richard." Henry gestures to the rolls of paper under the man's arm. "I am at my leisure, and yet you dare intrude? Well, what is it now?"

"Sire, I have further proof against the witch, Elizabeth Farriby. It shows her clear guilt."

"Does it, by God," Henry says. He can feel Meg watching him just over his shoulder, and knows that she expects some regal gesture from him, as the famous victor of the long ago joust. "And what does my Examiner General say to it?"

"Sire, I have not yet had the time to…"

"Then find it, Rich!" Henry roars now. "Find the time. Present all your evidence to Will Draper, and await his report. Only then ... mark me well, sir... only then may you proceed. I cannot have the King's Examiners Office undermined by the Attorney General's men... willy nilly. It is not seemly, and I have spoken to you of this before. Is that clearly understood?"

"As you command, sire!" Rich is almost falling over his feet to escape, and almost forgets to bow.

"Splendid," Lady Meg murmurs, and links the king's huge forearm. "Such manly grace is seldom met with, my dearest Majesty."

*

"How did it go?" Tom Wyatt throws back the heavy woollen blanket, and moves over to make room in his bed for so welcome a visitor.

"Well enough," Lady Meg tells him, as she lets the dress fall about her slender ankles. "Henry yelled at Rich, until he was quite blue in the face, and told him to defer to Will Draper. The king fears witchcraft, as does a small child, but he hates having his wishes thwarted even more."

"I see, and how did you avoid his bed tonight?" the poet asks, and runs his hands over her nakedness. He has primed Lady Meg to be of some help with the king, and is happy his ploy to aid Will has worked out so well.

"I flattered him until even a fool would know I was doing so, yet he just believed everything I said. Then, when His Majesty mentioned that I might wish to see his new portrait, which hangs in his private chamber, I readily agreed. On the way, I made as if I felt a little faint. He asked if I was unwell, and I said that it was but the curse come upon me early, and he almost died of fright. He made his excuses, politely, and let me go on my way. Perhaps he should look to his new queen for his pleasures, rather than try to swive a poor young widow such as I?"

"I do not think they see eye to eye," Tom Wyatt says, as he pulls her to him. "Some say he has not even tried the wares yet!"

"I doubt Anne of Cleves will lose much sleep over that," Meg replies, with a smile. "I think the king wants only the reputation of a great lover… without any of the hard work!"

The poet smiles at the thought of the king being unable to rise to the occasion, then thinks of a clever play on words, and so extemporises:

"*The queen, an object of royal lust,*
evades poor Henry's timorous thrust,
and keeps her virtue for another day,
from her ageing stag at bay."

Lady Meg giggles at the very rudeness of the couplet, and runs her tongue down over Wyatt's chest.

"My poetic lover," she whispers. "How poor Queen Anne would welcome a poet, sooner than a king, into her bed!"

*

"Mush, are you awake?"

"I am now," Mush says, and rolls out of bed. He has a dagger in his hand, but slips it under the pillow when he recognises the huge outline of Richard Cromwell, picked out by the moonlight.

"We must talk," Richard says.

"It is late," Mush says.

"No, it is early," Cromwell's nephew replies. "The fourth hour, I think. I need your advice."

"I thought you to be in Norfolk," Mush says.

"So I was," Richard replies. He produces his tinder box, and sparks it into life. Soon two candles illuminate the proceedings. "I was near Norwich, visiting Edmund Ambrose."

"Old Edmund still lives then?" Mush asks. The man, acting as a striking double for Thomas Cromwell, almost lost his life in an attempted assassination. "I thought Doctor Theophrasus said he was all but dead?"

"All but. My uncle feels indebted to Master Ambrose, and keeps he and his family in considerable comfort. It is true that Edmund is taken up with some terrible growth in his body, but yet he lingers on. I took this month's money for his poor wife, and we see to his children's education."

"Master Cromwell always looks after his own," Mush agrees, "though I do not see why I needed to know all this at such an ungodly hour, my friend."

"I tell you that, only in passing," Richard Cromwell says. Since his poisoning, he has lost some weight, and is not as strong as he once was, but he is still a most formidable man. "I did my duty, as my uncle told me, and stopped over at the Swan's Neck, on the London highroad."

"Ah, where Big Jenny plies her trade," Mush smirks. "I trust she is still a good swive. I dare say she is the only lass in England who can match you in both size, and gusto."

"Very funny," the younger Cromwell replies. "Will you hear me out, or not?"

"My apologies… do go on," Mush says.

"Yes, Jenny is lodged there, and yes, we did pass some time together. It was during this passing of time that she spoke of a man who calls himself Donne."

"What?" Mush is wide awake now. "You mean Rupert Donne… Norfolk's pet torturer?

"The same."

"What did she tell you?"

"That he seems to be very well heeled these days," Richard says. "She says he is a regular customer. Sometimes turning up three or four times in a month."

"For swiving her?" Mush asks.

"Not quite," Richard replies, and there is a broad smirk on his face. "It seems that he likes to be tied down, as naked as Adam on her bed, and beaten with sticks or whips."

"Are you jesting with me?" Mush asks.

"Not at all," his friend says. "It is how he becomes aroused, and able to perform his duty. Jenny says she often makes his cheeks glow red… and I do not mean his face."

"The man has a perverted nature," Mush says, "but what of it? It will make a humorous story around the Austin Friars breakfast table. Nothing more."

"Whilst she beats him, he rants on about how clever he is, and the wicked things he has done. The idea is, I suppose, that he is confessing… but to a lusty whore, rather than a priest. He was wailing about skinning a fellow to make a book, would you believe, and then … in mid stroke… he said he was going to ruin a great man. Jenny laughed, and said what great man would he dare try to best?"

"And he said…" Mush starts to nod his head. "Cromwell?"

"Yes, he is going to destroy my uncle," Richard concludes.

"Is she sure he meant it?" Mush asks.

"Yes, she is sure. Big Jenny has been on our payroll for these past four years. She is a favourite of the local gentry in Norfolk and Suffolk, and they become loose tongued in her company. She pretends to be a half witted jade, and they are careless of what they say. Then I visit her, once a month, and we exchange silver for information. It is seldom more than some minor crime, committed by some feeble witted son of a baron, but this is different."

"Yes, it is. Rupert Donne is the Duke of Norfolk's man," Mush says. "He organises the duke's spies for him, and acts as chief interrogator, and torturer. If he is going to attack Master Tom, it is at the behest of his master. We must know more."

"There is no more for me to pass on," Richard Cromwell tells his friend. "Jenny used all her charms on him, even slapped him like a naughty child, but he must have caught himself, and would reveal no more."

"That will not do," Mush says. "Donne is one of the most dangerous men in England, and if he is set upon our master, the very walls around Austin Friars may crumble."

"Uncle Thomas is in soundly with the king, and we need fear no man." Richard argues. "Norfolk is a spent force. What can he do, but offer violence to us? In such a case, he would be outside the law, and Henry would have him brought to trial."

"Then Donne must know something," says Mush.

"There is nothing to know," Richard replies, with a confident tone in his voice. "We run the law courts, and handle everything that comes in from abroad. The king cannot speak to any foreign diplomat without us knowing what is said."

"There should be no threat from the emperor, at least," Mush says. "He is pleased with the new marriage."

"More so than the king," Richard Cromwell tells him. "Anne of Cleves' lady in waiting, Helge, has a loose tongue. She sleeps with any man … or woman… who wants her, and talks openly about her mistresses dislike of the king."

"Damnation," Mush furrows his brow. "Can that be it, my friend? What if the king is angered about this marriage?"

"How can that affect Uncle Thomas?" the younger Cromwell asks. "He was careful to offer some mild opposition to the match. He spoke up for the Burgundian girl, knowing how Henry would choose. In this way, the king saw him to be open and honest. He even thanked him, and said he admired a man who spoke his mind."

"Then Henry believes himself to be at fault for the marriage?" Mush smiles at the cleverness of his patron. "Even if he seeks to throw her aside, Master Thomas can sigh, and remind him how he favoured the Burgundian."

"Just so. If this Rupert Donne hopes to bring us down, then it is some other thing he has in mind." Richard spreads his hands wide, as if to say there, that is the extent of my thinking. "That is why I come to you, my friend. Can you think what it might be?"

"I cannot," Mush says, honestly. "The New World adventure is still thriving, Henry has his best ship safely back in English waters, and Cromwell runs the country perfectly well. He helped bring about the king's divorce from Queen Katherine without mishap, freed him of the Boleyn's, and placed him next to the Seymour's. Granted, the marriage ended in tragedy, but the king has a son by it. A healthy and legitimate boy to ascend the throne."

"Perhaps it is about money?" Richard asks.

"Have you ever once known Master Cromwell take a bribe?" Mush retorts. "There was never any need. Every deal he ever did made Henry richer. He could open his accounts now, and a team of auditors might go through them, and find nothing out of place. It is not about money."

"Then what?" Richard says. "I am at my wits end, wondering what this fellow has on us."

"Then we must solve the riddle," Mush says. "Where is this man now?"

"He travels about Norfolk and Kent, doing his dirty business," Richard replies. "I do not know where he is just now."

"When will he next visit Big Jenny?"

"She says he will be back in two weeks time," Richard says. It seems he cannot go longer without her particular talents."

"Then in two weeks, you and I will visit Jenny, and lay in wait for Rupert Donne," Mush explains. "She shall have him bare all, then tie him, securely to the bed. Once the beating starts, we will step in, and introduce ourselves. With him tethered to the bed, and at the mercy of our strong right arms, he will talk, and we shall have proof of his actions."

"The fellow actually enjoys Big Jenny's beatings," Richard Cromwell says. "He would get pleasure from it."

"Not the way we shall do it," Mush tells him, and they huddle down to discuss the finer points of the adventure to come. It is their chance to confound one of the Duke of Norfolk's plots, without recourse to Will Draper, or his King's Examiners for aid.

Thomas Cromwell seems to lean towards the stiff necked investigators assembled by Will Draper more these days, and seldom lets his own young men have their heads. It is time those very young men showed him their true worth.

9 Findings

"Might I have the pleasure to name Captain John Beckshaw to you, sir?" Will Draper says, then turns to his junior officer. "John, this good gentleman is Parson George Farrall."

"Reverend rather than Parson, my dear sir, if you don't mind," Farrall replies. "Though I am just as easy with 'George', if it please you."

"Then I am to be John to you, dear sir," Beckshaw says to the little clergyman. "I hear you have stolen the jewel in the crown of Draper House, George…. save for Lady Miriam… and my good wife. Mistress Marion is a rare beauty, and will make a rather fine wife for you."

"Yes, it appears I am to be wed," George replies, still bemused at the swiftness of his betrothal. He is a willing enough victim, for all that, and thanks God for moving in so mysterious a way. "You and your wife will attend the wedding, and the feast afterwards, I hope?"

"Only if we resolve this terrible business," Will puts in. "I must leave you both now, but I commend you to each other. Search the old lady's house, and cast about for anything that either proves, or disproves Mistress Farriby's case."

John Beckshaw salutes smartly, as Will climbs into the saddle of his old Welsh Cob. Moll is an old girl now, and the King's Examiner in Chief wonders if she would be better off turned out into one of his wife's many pastures. Moll would appreciate the rest, he thinks, and he could do with a new stallion… to suit his elevated position.

"Shall we?" George says, and he pushes open the low door to the cottage, once rented by Jane Townley. He steps inside, and signals for Beckshaw to stoop. "You are a head taller than I, so take care. The rafters are low too, and would give you a nasty bump."

"Damned awkward.. Begging your pardon, vicar… but it is. I am almost touching the … hello… what have we here?" The captain of the Examiners runs his fingers along a dusty crossbeam, and comes up with a tightly tied black bag.

"The poor woman's savings?" George queries. John Beckshaw crosses to the kitchen table, loosens the ties, and tips out the contents for them to peruse.

"Dear God!" John Beckshaw steps back in horror, and cracks his head on the low beam behind him. "Damn me!" he curses, and rubs at the sudden pain in his crown.

"It is a tongue," the vicar says, softly. ""And this is an ear. The tongue is not human, I think… but the ear is most certainly from a man."

"What can this mean?" John asks.

"Let us continue our search," George says, "and draw our conclusions later. The two men move about the small cottage, and poke into every crevice they can find. Over the course of the next hour they amass a considerable pile of strange items. John Beckshaw finally calls a halt, and they go out into the daylight for a breath of air that does not reek of the devil.

"Have you ever seen such a collection of horrors, sir?" George Farrall asks. "There are at least two animal tongues, a human ear, what looks like some human finger bones, and a mixture of powders and potions I have never seen before."

"We must have our Mistress Marion inspect all of these things," John Beckshaw says. "Her knowledge is far better than mine, when it comes to witchcraft."

"Witchcraft?" George crosses himself, and spits onto the ground, without thinking. "You really think that this is what we have uncovered, John?"

"I do," the Examiner colonel replies. "Let us hope your betrothed can shed some light on things for us. It seems that, if a witch ever lived in this village, it was not poor Elizabeth Farriby, but her old tenant, Jane Townley."

*

"How is Elizabeth bearing up?" Marion asks. "It must be terrible, confined within the walls of the Tower of London."

"She is being well looked after," Miriam Draper replies. "It seems that one of my husband's young men works for the Warden of the Tower, and has taken the girl under his wing. They are quite smitten with one another, I believe."

"Then love truly is in the air," Marion says. "I have spoken with George, and he agrees that we must put off our wedding until this awful business is concluded. I cannot set a date, when Colonel Draper may have need of me at any moment."

"What news is there since last we spoke?" Miriam asks her friend.

"Captain Beckshaw sent for me, this morning," Marion Giles tells her. "He wished me to look about the old woman's cottage. He had found some things used in black magic. She had all the wares of a witch hidden about the place, and must have been practicing her arts for many years. I wonder if Elizabeth suspected her of it?"

"Possibly. There was some talk of her wanting to turn the woman out of the cottage, and see her settled in an alms house," Miriam says. "Perhaps she meant to put a stop to the foolish old woman's practices, without actually denouncing her?"

"Then that gives Jane Townley a motive to ruin Elizabeth, rather than Nell Gifford." Marion Giles shakes her head in frustration. "Things become cloudier, rather than clearer. If Jane Townley was a witch…"

"Not a real one, of course," says Miriam. "I do not believe you can conjure up the devil with potions and incantations. Such nonsense is for ill educated country folk to believe in."

"And the king, I fear," Marion Giles says, softly. "Henry thinks he can be cursed unto death, and that black cats talk to Satan when the moon is full. He believes milk can be soured, that evil eyes exist, and that old women can leap onto their besoms, and fly to the moon and back. The man is little more than a superstitious…"

"Hush now, my dear," Miriam counsels. "It is not our place to speak thus of the king. Whether black magic works, or not, Jane Townley believed in it… as does Henry."

"True, and she would have a knowledge of the old ways with plants and the like," Marion confirms. "What if it was she who brewed the deadly Bella Donna concoction?"

"Then why not give it to Elizabeth?" Miriam Draper asks. "I would think it the easiest way to stop her from turning her out of her home. A few drops in her wine, and that would be that."

"Besides, she was nowhere near the chicken feed," Marion Giles concludes.

"Perhaps she had her 'familiar' poison the grain?" Miriam says. "Though why then kill herself afterwards?"

"Kill herself?" Marion frowns. "You think of things that have not yet crossed my mind, Miriam. I wonder, can it be that Jane Townley died, because of the chickens?"

"How so?"

"Oh, I do not know," Marion confesses. "This entire affair is a puzzle. Let us hope your husband can throw the light of reason onto the darkness of ignorance. Where is he today?"

"Riding to Hampton Court Palace," Miriam confirms. "He seeks an audience with the king."

"Will he get it?"

"Who can tell, these days?" Miriam says. "Henry's moods seem to swing from hour to hour, these days. If the rumours about his new marriage are true, I can see the road ahead may become a little rough."

"For Colonel Will?"

"I do not think so," Miriam says.

"Master Cromwell should be safe enough too. It seems that he counselled against the marriage, when others advised the king in favour of it. No, Henry made his own bed, and must lie in it, I suppose."

"Though not with Anne of Cleves," Marion mutters, and they both giggle like young girls. They leave it unsaid, but they both believe the queen is happy not to have to sleep with such a husband.

"Thee are those who will warm his sheets for him quickly enough," Miriam concludes. "My husband tells me of several new ladies at court who keep the gentlemen occupied. I trust he does not speak from experience."

"Oh, Miriam!" Marion Giles laughs. "Your dearest Will would sooner die than fiddle another tune."

*

Gossip is the life blood of any royal court, and the quality of such gossip is measured by whom it involves. Some juicy piece of news about Norfolk, or Suffolk might do the rounds for days, but anything concerning the king will cause weeks, or even months of speculation.

"They whisper about me, Will." Henry is standing in his favourite pose. Legs apart, and balled fists planted on his broad hips. "They whisper about my private life, and I see it in their eyes."

"Sire?" Will Draper has just entered the throne room, and has no idea what the king means. "Men always whisper about those who are greater than they are… or whom they fear."

"Fear?" Henry smiles, and nods his fleshy head. "Yes… they do fear me. Even so, I will not have my private life gossiped about by lesser folk."

"I have heard no such gossip about you, sire," Will Draper says. "Though men know where I stand with you. Perhaps they hide their feelings behind false smiles, lest I box their ears for their impudence, and kick their arses out of the palace."

"Yes, what matters it a jot how I conduct myself with the queen?" Henry says. Ah, that is it, Will Draper thinks. The king does not like his new wife, and he vainly assumes the world is interested in every detail.

"Does she so displease you, Your Majesty?" he asks, then places his hand on the king's shoulder. "Forgive me for asking so pointed a question, but your welfare is my duty, sire. And duty is the most important thing in this world to me."

"Well said, Will," Henry replies. "Would all my subjects were so honest as you. I speak man to man when I say this, my dearest friend: she does displease me greatly, and I find myself quite unable to warm to her. The woman is not … *as pleasant* as she should be. I simply cannot believe her to be a virgin."

"Sire, that is something you should be expert at detecting," Will says, flattering the king's childish ego. "Your conquests are legion… if the tales be true."

"Oh, they are … of course," Henry replies, turning a little red faced. "It is just that she is a little slack breasted, for her age, and seems … too worldly for my liking."

"Have you spoken to your ministers about your marital misgivings, sire?" Will Draper asks. As always, he sees the old advice is for the best. Ask Tom Cromwell, is the answer; for he never fails with goodly advice. He has been telling the king this for the best part of the last decade, and sees no reason to alter his recommendation at this late date.

"I have spoken to the fellow, and Cromwell says he can see no way out," Henry replies. "It seems a somewhat harsh thing for him to say, do you not think, Will?"

"I cannot believe he meant it like you think, sire," Will tells the king. "He is a man of the law, and speaks only of legal matters. I should think his personal wish is to help you all he can."

"All he can?" Henry sounds almost

on the brink of exploding, but contains himself. Norfolk has warned him that Cromwell has great friends, and that Will Draper is one of them. "If you should have to choose between Cromwell and I…"

"Your Majesty!" Will's exclamation makes Henry recoil a half step in surprise. "Thomas Cromwell loves you, and would never do anything to hurt the crown. That is why I love the fellow. It is not conceivable that he should do anything against you. As for me making a choice … there is none to make. How can any man go against his king, and remain a true man?"

"Well said again, my friend," Henry tells him. "You shame me for doubting you. No matter what, I shall always remain your truest friend, Will Draper."

"Then thank God you overcame me that time," says Will, and flatters for all he is worth. "Else there might have been another sitting on your throne now."

"Would you have hurt me then?" Henry asks, a little upset at the prospect.

"I am a soldier, sire. Not a born gentleman." Will taps the hilt of the sword only he and Suffolk is allowed to wear in Henry's royal presence. "Once the blood is up … who knows. You stood up to me fair and square, and if you had been wanting, I might well have forgotten myself, and laid you down… as poor Suffolk once did."

"By God, yes. To have two such friends makes me fill with pride, Will. Charles Brandon thought he had killed his king with that one lucky blow. I was distracted by a lady in the crowd, as I recall."

"They have that about them, sire," Will says, happy to be over a dangerous moment. "You either love them, or hate them. I do well recall how you did love Queen Jane. Perhaps it is love of her that makes you shy of this new queen?"

"Yes, by God, but that must be it," Henry says. "The woman is not fit to replace my lovely Jane Seymour. I must see how best to put her aside."

"Then I beg you, sire," Will says. "Send for Thomas Cromwell, and tell him your mind. When first you spoke, he thought only of the legalities of the marriage. Let him now think of the more intimate aspects."

"You are right," Henry says. "It is only what I was thinking to myself. Cromwell is my man, and will serve me well in this, as in all other matters. I would not believe ill of him, unless the proof was unavoidable."

"It sounds as if you have been given poor advice, sire," Will guesses. "Let us hope that inferior men do not mislead you."

"Just so," Henry replies. "Time and again the likes of Sir Richard Rich and old

Uncle Norfolk offer me advice that does not sit well with me. They both argued against me elevating Cromwell to his Earldom of Essex. Save for Sir Rafe Sadler, yourself, Tom Cromwell, and Suffolk of course, I should heed no man."

"Then speak to Master Cromwell, sire," Will Draper concludes, and bows as if to leave.

"But stay a moment, Colonel Draper," Henry says, with a broad smile. "Did you not ask for this interview? What do you want of me? Ask, and it is granted."

"You are too kind, Your Majesty," Will says. In truth, he is eager to get away now, and ride to Austin Friars. Cromwell seems to have made a false move, and should be warned. "It was about this ridiculous witchcraft investigation."

"Ah, yes. I have already castigated that oaf Rich about it. He is withholding information from you, and I will not have it. It is my decision that nothing is to be done until your full report is ready for my study. The girl … for I am surprised at her youthfulness … is safe for now. Are not all witches old, Will?"

"I suppose they must learn when young," Will responds. "That is why young kings become old ones, and old soldiers become new gentlemen!"

"Ah ha!" Henry is fully restored

now. "You jest well, my friend. Come to dinner more often… and bring that pretty wife with you. The woman at my side just now is no match. I really must think up something witty along those lines … perhaps a clever epigram about old becoming young… what! Perhaps Tom Wyatt might suggest a word or two about … young soldiers who never grow old, but die gloriously in battle."

Sir Will Draper is out of the chamber, with his tongue firmly clenched in his teeth so as to bite back a caustic comment. No man ever dies gloriously in battle. Will has seen it too often, and knows that even as they fight, it is only to live, and when the end comes, it is with blood curdling cries of agony and fear.

Henry, King of England, the ex-mercenary concludes, is a bloody fool, and not the man to have at your side in a real fight. It is one thing to charge a rabble of French peasants, surrounded by five thousand trained cavalry, and quite another to stand beside a comrade and shield him from a bloody onslaught.

*

"An epigram?" Thomas Cromwell shakes his head, and stifles a laugh. "Did he really say that, Will?" He is in the chamber he uses as an office when at Hampton Court, and the Royal Examiner has done well to find him there. It has saved him a wasted ride into London, for which both he and Moll are most grateful.

"Yes, God help it, he is to make up an epigram," Will replies, as he pours himself out a goblet of the watered wine Cromwell has taken to drinking of late. "Would that I knew what one was."

"You must surely ask Tom Wyatt … as I am sure the king shall," Tom Cromwell tells him. "It is a form of clever poem with a witty ending. Rather like my life, I hope."

"Pray do not speak of endings just yet, Master Tom," Will Draper says. "Though I have just come from an uncomfortable meeting with His Majesty. His thoughts were very much upon his new queen, I fear."

"Oh, be damned to it!" Cromwell drains his own wine goblet, and refills it. "I do not know what is the matter with the fellow. Queen Anne is not, I grant you, an English rose. More like a Flanders Mare… as Wyatt calls her. But she is quite handsome looking, with a fulsome body, and a willingness to please. What more does he want? Why, he even chose her himself. I pushed forward the Burgundian trollop, without any success."

"Come now, sir," Will says, dropping his voice. "We that are amongst your closest friends know the truth of things.

Hans Holbein did his work well, and the king simply chose the way you really wanted. Why, you played him well, and with just cause, no doubt. I know Anne of Cleves brings us an alliance with the emperor, and puts the French king at a clear disadvantage, but our king likes her not, and that is the crux of it!"

"I know. He told me so, and I had to inform him that the marriage contracts had already been exchanged. He even stood in front of the blasted Arch Bishop, and made his vows. Under both English and Holy Roman law, that is that. It is why we had to find another reason to break the king's first marriage. That ridiculous fiction about whether or not she had lain with her first husband, Prince Arthur, was to contradict a point of law. It is how things work, you see. Henry is married, like it or not, in the eyes of the law."

"Then he wants to be un-married," Will Draper says. "He will come back to you, Master Thomas, and he will not take 'no' as your answer. If there is a law to make him married, then there must be one to make it otherwise."

"Can he not see what would happen if I let him put Anne of Cleves aside?" Thomas Cromwell says. "It would mean either a divorce, or an annulment. The divorce is out of the question… for there are not the grounds. She has not deceived the king in any way, and the marriage has been consummated."

"I doubt that, sir," says Will. "The king spoke of not liking the look of her."

"Perhaps not, but he made the mistake of remarking to Eustace Chapuys that he had '*been likened unto a stallion*' on his wedding night. The ambassador wrote to the emperor, and informed him of the king's complete satisfaction with the poor girl. He cannot now announce to the world that he failed to even clear the first fence. It would make him into a laughing stock, and bring his word of honour into disrepute."

"I only come to warn you," Will tells his old master. "The king wants rid of her, and he will have his way. What about an annulment… a mutual separation?"

"Ah, there you have it. Mutual. A funny little word, that can mean so much. Does Anne of Cleves agree with Henry's assertion that they are incompatible?"

"I doubt she would object," Will says, thinking of how any younger woman might view the obese and quarrelsome king.

"No?" Thomas Cromwell sighs at the younger man's firm assertion about something he knows nothing of. "If you were to put Miriam away, what would happen?"

"What has that to …"

"Everything. Would Miriam leave your marriage with only her dowry in her purse? Would she be content to watch you remarry, take her children from her, and keep her million pound fortune?"

"Good God!"

"Ah, you did not know she is worth a million pounds?" Tom Cromwell grins at his friend's look of surprise. "The wealth of England is almost three million a year, and she alone is worth enough to buy a small country. You might own Cyprus, or even Ireland, if she so wishes."

"Of course she would not want to lose the children, or the wealth… and I would never allow such a thing. I love her." Will is uncomfortable, knowing that the law makes his brilliant young wife into nothing more than his property. "I would not touch a penny of her money."

"Nor would you, my boy," Tom Cromwell says, "for she has it well hidden away from greedy eyes. Imagine what would happen if the king thought a mere girl was worth more than he has in his own treasury, and virtually owned the Flanders wool trade. Thank God you do love her, sir."

"She is my life," Will tells Cromwell. "You know it, sir."

"Of course, but the king does not

love Anne." Tom Cromwell taps a finger to the side of his nose. "You see? If she agrees to be put aside, she must give grounds for an annulment, even to our new English Church. She cannot claim her marriage to be unconsummated, because Henry has sworn he swived her silly on the wedding night, to at least thirty gentlemen... amongst whom was our own dear Eustace Chapuys. Is he then a liar?"

"Of course not," Will says. "He cannot retract so openly given an assertion."

"Because it would ruin his reputation, as a lover, and as a man of honour." Cromwell spreads his arms wide, as if inviting any bright suggestions that might solve the current impasse. "There is only one more thing to suggest."

"There is always a way," Will Draper mutters.

"Yes… if I care to suggest it," Cromwell says. "The queen can always become overwhelmed with religious fervour. It does happen to some highly strung mares, I believe. She can declare herself to be devoted to God, and unable to continue in her new marriage … despite it being a happy one. Everyone is then happy to let the marriage be annulled, and Henry can get on with finding himself yet another queen."

"Then, what is the problem?"

"Queen Anne is unhappy, no doubt… but she would be even more so, once locked away in a nunnery, with all her worldly goods stripped from her. Imagine that if you will. I doubt she will see it as much of a bargain when she is down on her knees four times a day, praying for the world's salvation."

"You paint a very sad picture," says Will. He does not understand why Thomas Cromwell seems so set on keeping the luckless marriage going. "What if the king insists?"

"He cannot, you must see?" Thomas Cromwell tells his friend. "To annul means both parties must agree. Anne of Cleves will never accept the convent life… even if it is a very comfortable one. She is in her twenties, and wants more. Do you think she came to England, just to be 'tried out' and cast aside? No, she wants to be queen, or failing that, live a life full of luxury."

"Cannot Henry just buy her off?" Will suggests. "A nice castle, set in a thousand acres of parkland, and some pretty jewels would do the trick with most women."

"Anne of Cleves is not '*most women*', Will," Cromwell concludes. "Even if she agrees on a parting of the ways, the only grounds are annulment, and that comes under church law. The great and the good are still finding their feet after the break from Rome, and they will want to be seen as scrupulous upholders of the new Church of England. If Anne agrees, they will have no choice but to have her placed in holy orders."

"My God, what a mess," Will says. "Then there is nothing you can do?"

"Let me be honest with you, my dear fellow," Thomas Cromwell tells his old friend. "I am more than content with this marriage arrangement, and see no reason to interfere. I have told the king that I can see no way out. Granted, I will wring my hands, and produce every written law I can to try and break the contract, but to no avail. Henry is wed to Anne of Cleves, and England is wed to the Holy Roman Empire."

"But why are you so obstinate?" Will Draper is yet to be convinced. "What gain is there in refusing the king?"

"Damn it, man!" Cromwell can keep his temper no longer, and leaps to his feet. "The king chose his wife. The king chose his allies. I advised him to marry the Burgundian girl, did I not? It is none of my doing, in the king's eyes. Let him complain to that idiot, the Duke of Norfolk, who urged him to invade the lady's chambers and so plight his troth. All I can do is advise him, and that advice is this: stay married, sire… and do not upset the Spanish emperor. Old Charles is a benign sort of a ruler, if you are not a heretic, or a New World native. He will support Henry, because he is a drinking friend of her father, and that means so much to us just now."

"But not so long ago, you advocated us raiding the Spanish treasure ships," Will says, somewhat bemused. "What has changed in so short a time, sir?"

"The French king, whose life you so gallantly saved, is about to pay us back by stealing our foreign possessions. His ministers are, very quietly, making a military levy. In six months time, François, King of France, will have forty thousand men under arms. Trained men, not peasants. He is hiring Genoese crossbow men by the thousand, and has even approached the Doge of Venice to hire a hundred of his strongest ships, and some of his remarkable Swiss pike men."

"The bastard!" The King's Examiner recalls how he was instrumental in halting an assassination attempt on the French king, and almost regrets it now. "How do you know so much?"

"The late Doge, Andrea Gritti was, as you know, an old friend of mine. I saved his life whilst we were both running away from the victorious French, some twenty odd years ago… but that is another story. Andrea swore to help me, and we became the great est of friends … at a distance. He died last year, but his successor, Pietro Lando is of a like mind. His first act was to write to me, and inform me of Gritti's death. Since then, we have kept in close touch, and he warned me of the French treachery."

"Then that is why you wanted this marriage?"

"Of course. With the emperor's twenty five thousand troops camped in the Netherlands, King François's own forces are at a distinct disadvantage. If he strikes at the *Calaisis* enclave, Charles will fall on his rear, and cause havoc. Now, the French army must sit on their backsides, and wait. In the meantime, I have Charles Brandon preparing an expeditionary force. Once he has his five thousand arquebusiers in Calais, things will settle down."

"Let us hope the king sees good sense then," Will Draper says. "Else we find ourselves embroiled in a bloody war."

"Would that not suit you?" Tom Cromwell asks.

"No more," Will replies. "Soldiering is for younger, single men. Miriam would not let me go, anyway."

"Good for her," Cromwell says.

"Let the king be, and he will come around. He will brood for a week, then some pretty young thing will slip into his bed, and he will forget all about his latest bride. I shall pension her, provided she leaves the court, and allows Henry his mistresses. After all, the king has a son to follow him, as well as two strong daughters. In a month or two from now, we will look back, and laugh at all this!"

"If God wills it," Will says.

"No... if I will it," Tom Cromwell replies, and they both laugh. "This little upset will not steer us from our course, my boy, and it will not hinder my future plans."

"Which are?"

"Give me time, my friend," Cromwell says. "Give me time!"

10   Exeter

The fifty six mile long trip to the busy port of Southampton is done in two days of hard riding, and a swift cog, part of Miriam Draper's own ever growing fleet, takes Will and his companion down the coast. They arrive in the Exe estuary, and take hired horses on to the bustling market town of Exeter.

"Four days!" Kel Kelton boasts as they enter the busy little town. "It would have taken us eight, or even nine, had we ridden overland."

"The king bids me take all the time I need for my investigation," Will Draper replies, "but Richard Rich is a slippery eel, and I dare not linger. Miriam's cog ran well before the wind."

"What now, sir?" Kel asks. He is not long married, and is in the happy situation of having two 'wives'. He is recently married to Thomas Cromwell's best cook, and lives, harmoniously with her, and Lucy, a young half Moorish girl who has just delivered a son into the world. The two girls are the best of friends, and take turns in seeing to their young man's wants. "Though I am in no rush to return home. My marital responsibilities weigh heavily on me, and I am glad enough of the break!"

"You are a rogue, Kel," Will Draper tells him, with a grin. "I can scarce cope with one wife. What does Cromwell think of it all?"

"He just shrugs, sir, and smiles," Kel replies. "I suppose he is thinking of his own younger days, in foreign parts. I dare say we have all been in them … *foreign* parts."

"Very funny," Will says. "You are here, as my helper, because I could not find Mush. It seems he is away, but poor Isabella has no idea where. I hope he is not chasing after Lady Mary Boleyn again."

"No sir, it is not that," Kel says, and almost bites off his own tongue. "That is to say… I doubt it, for that lady is married again, and living in far off Cheshire."

"You lie badly, Master Kelton," Will says. "Now, out with it, before I cut out your tongue. Where is he?"

"Norwich, with Master Richard."

"Norwich. What is he up to there?"

"I know not," Kel replies, truthfully. "It was by chance I heard he was visiting the place. Though it must be for some pleasure, and nought else."

"Why not?"

"Because Master Tom knows nothing of it," Kel says. "The gossip is that Richard has taken a fancy to Big Jenny, who runs a brothel just outside the town, and Mush is there to keep him company."

"Then that is why poor Isabella is unaware," Will says. It is unlike his brother in law to treat his lover in so poor a way, and he wonders if there is more to it. Isabella Lucretto has been Mush Draper's mistress ever since the successful Corfu expedition against the Ottoman Turks, and he brought her back with him. They seem to have a good relationship, and it is odd that Mush would put it at risk, all for the sake of some whore.

"Shall I find us a bed for the night?" Kel asks.

"Yes. Then ask about, and find me the whereabouts of the lawyer, Edwin Carmody. Exeter is not so large a town as to have many of that profession. When you have his whereabouts, come and find me. I shall be about the market square, talking to folks."

"Talking to whom?" Kel Kelton asks. "We do not know anyone here, do we?"

"I am the King's Examiner General," Will tells his young accomplice. "The warrants I carry mean I can speak with anyone I please. If this town has a mayor, his door must open to me, and I can demand information of any who live here."

"To what end, sir?"

"To my own ends," Will tells him.

"Now, be about your business, Kel, and I shall be about mine!"

*

"There is someone asking after you, Master Carmody." The lad, a stablehand at the Ship Inn has heard Kel Kelton making enquiries, and thinks to earn himself a penny or two from an interested party. "A right dangerous looking fellow, from London."

"Dangerous… oh, goodness." Edwin Carmody frowns, and fishes a penny out of his purse. "Then he is looking for the wrong man, young Dick. Did you tell him you know me?"

"No, not I," Dick answers. "I don't like foreigners much."

"Loyal fellow," the elderly lawyer says. "Now, run back, as fast as you can, and tell this man where my chambers can be found."

"He doesn't look like no lawyer to me," the lad moans, but does as he is bid. Kel Kelton listens to him carefully, and commit's the address to memory. The Ship Inn is the best house in town, and the rooms boast comfortable beds, and their own fireplaces. The food smells good, and the serving girls are eager to please this stranger, who seems to have a very full purse on his belt, as well as a wicked looking Italian made dagger.

The inn keeper is a friendly sort,

and is ready to offer any help Kel might need. For an extra penny a night, he will provide wax candles in their room, and for a shilling, he has two accommodating wenches to keep them warm. The young man accepts the candles, but knows Will Draper's thoughts on swiving outside wedlock, and declines the services of Bess and Nan.

After a swift mug of beer, and some bread and hard cheese, he sets out to find Will Draper. It takes him longer than expected, as the town is a maze of narrow streets, each of which seems designed to confuse the hapless visitor. The main square is busy, and on asking after his comrade, he is directed to a low tavern by the cathedral.

The place is crammed in between a stables and a tanners shop, and boasts the lowest ceiling Kel has ever seen. He has to stoop, and find his way through the gloom to a bar at the rear. Most of the customers are sailors, and they glare at the intruder. Kel smiles back, and drops his hand down onto the dagger at his waist.

"Ah, there you are, at last," Will Draper calls, and beckons him over to the empty barrel that serves as a table. He is sitting on a stool, flanked by two of the dirtiest rogues imaginable. They stink of fish, and are dressed in a rag tag array of old clothes, probably passed down from long dead relatives. "This is Palk, and this is Caleb."

"No, I'm Caleb," the fatter of the two men says. "As he be Palk, see?"

"Of course," Will says. "Master Palk has lived in Exeter all his life, and knows most things that go on. Unfortunately, he is not a great talker, and Caleb translates the noises."

"Noises?" Kel asks.

"Yes, Master Palk was a sailing man, some years ago, and he fell foul of a Spanish galleon. The Spaniards took offence at what they thought was attempted piracy, so cut out the tongues of the entire crew … save for the gentlemen officers, who they just hanged. Palk did a year in a slave galley, before escaping back to England. He has gone off the sailing life these days."

"No wonder," Kel says. "How does he talk then?"

"Noises, and with his fingers," Caleb says. "It ain't that easy, but we get by. Like I just told His Lordship here. What Palk don't know, never happened."

"And what does Palk know?" Kel asks his comrade.

"He knows Edwin Carmody."

"Save your money, Colonel Will," Kel says, brightly. "I had his whereabouts an hour since. He lives not a stone's throw from here. Behind the cathedral... as what the big church next door is called, and down Frog Street, until you come to a windmill. Your man lives at the big house on the left."

"Then we must visit him anon."

"We are expected later," Kel says. "He keeps his legal chambers above the main house, and says we are welcome at any hour we care to call."

"Then he knows of our coming?" Will does not like this, as it moves the advantage of surprise away from him.

"The lad at the Ship Inn ran and warned him," Kel admits. "I think he was after two rewards."

"What else did this lad have to say?"

"Nothing at all," Kel says. "I asked what sort of a fellow this lawyer was, but he would not be drawn."

"A young man who knows how to keep silent," Will says, and smiles. "There is an unusual thing. So, you know nothing more of Master Carmody?"

"I asked around. It seems he is not at all the kind of lawyer Rafe or Richard are. He knows no politics. Nor is he like Master Fowler, who stands in court, and argues his case. It seems he is the sort of lawyer who arranges legal matters for other folk. They want a lease drawing up, so they go to him. Or they might wish a will to be altered… all legal like."

"So I have been told by my friends here," Will says. "Master Palk has also intimated that he is not quite as honest as he should be."

"He is, begging your pardon, sir… a lawyer. Of course he is not quite honest," Kel replies.

"It seems he has been a lawyer in Exeter for almost thirty years," Will explains. "He came here, after some trouble in Barnstaple, and set up his practice. In his younger days, he was want to roister with the best of men."

"You cannot hang a man, even a lawyer, for that, Colonel Will," Kel answers. "What does this Palk know of him after those days? Is he a villain?"

"It seems not. Palk here, tells me that he is a generous fellow, who gives gifts to the poor, and helps to pay for the local hospital. In fact, he is almost a saint."

"Aye, that be it … a blessed saint," Caleb repeats. "My friend Palk says so."

"Unghh!" Palk puts in, and holds out his empty glass.

"You must buy your own liquor from here on, gentlemen," Will tells them. "I have business with my young servant. Take these coins, and do not spend them wisely. Good day to you both!"

"Must you keep referring to me as your servant?" Kel says as they leave the ramshackle tavern. "It makes me look like a…"

"Servant?" Will says, and laughs. "These people are simple souls, and would talk with a servant more readily than a fine gentleman."

"What, you… a fine gentleman?" Kel chuckles. "I have seen finer hanging on gallows, my friend."

"Perhaps, but for now, you must act as my servant, and refer to me as Sir Will, or Colonel Draper. I mean to impress this lawyer fellow, and for that, I must look the part. Hence, you are, for the nonce, Kel Kelton, my own personal servant."

"I trust this is going to pay well." Kel sees that his role is cast, and he can do little enough about it, for now.

"Examiner rates," Will says, and the young man's face falls in disgust. The ordinary Examiners make two shillings in a good week, whilst he can earn that in the blink of an eye back in London.

"Then I might have enough from it to feed my horse for a week … if only I had a horse."

"Act well for me in this matter, and I will buy you a fine horse," Will tells the younger fellow. "What say you to a sturdy

Welsh Cob, like my faithful old Moll, or would you rather have something with more pace?"

"Why, Sir Will, for a fine gelding, I would call you Milord, and gallop to Hades and back," Kel declares, somewhat taken aback. He is surprised at so handsome a gift, and expects even an average sort of a horse to cost him better than ten pounds. "Pray, do give me my instructions!"

*

Edwin Carmody sits in his chamber, and looks over the great pile of papers he has amassed concerning the estate of the late Sir Joshua Benson, gentleman of Exeter, and one time magistrate to the county of Devon. It is a formidable task, even to catalogue so vast an amount of documentation, and his clerk has barely started on the true valuation for the Court of Chancery.

"Well, Sir Will," he says to the tall gentleman who has just invaded his chambers, "here is what you seek. Though why Sir Rafe sent you, rather than writing to me, I do not know. Is this matter so urgent? I was led to believe that the initial settlement on...". He pauses, and runs a finger down the top document. "Mistress Elizabeth Farriby, has been made. Has she not taken possession of the estate known as Higher Topham, and the great house, rents, and land holding that goes with it?"

"She has, Master Carmody… these months past," Will Draper agrees. He looks about the room, and sees that the only chair is piled high with legal documents. He gestures to Kel, who is playing the runabout servant. "Boy … the chair." Kel nods, and tips the contents out onto the floor. The lawyer is too startled to protest, as this military looking gentleman sits down, quite uninvited.

"My pardon, sir," Carmody says. "I should have thought to look to my manners, but I rarely have guests. Might I have my servant bring some refreshments?"

"No need, my dear Master Carmody," Will says, with an airy wave of his hand. "As you do so correctly say, this Farriby woman has come into a part of the estate, but there are … complications. Sir Rafe Sadler is, as you know, a lawyer of great repute and minister to the king. If he commands, I must do his errands for him. It is most bothersome, being away from court at this time, but I have no choice."

"Bothersome, as you say," Carmody concurs. "It is a long ride from London, just to hurry along the doings of Sir Josh Benson's estate, no matter how vast it seems to be."

"Vast, you say?" Will studies his finger nails, as if he did not give a fig for the task laid upon him. "I was told it was merely a house and a few hovels. I thought the income was barely a thousand a year."

"Only on the part settled, sir," Carmody replies. "That part was unencumbered, and free to dispose of as stipulated. That is why I put Mistress Farriby in possession, at once. The rest of the estate is more complicated. You see, there are borders to define, rights to be investigated, and all debts and taxes to be paid."

"Oh, I see. How much are we talking about?"

"About forty thousand pounds," the lawyer tells him.

"What … you say this Elizabeth Farriby's inheritance is forty thousand pounds?" Will asks, startled at it being so much.

"I fear you misunderstand me, Sir Will," Edwin Carmody says. "The forty thousand is how much is owed to various creditors, and a portion set aside for Crown taxes. The entire estate, after these deductions, will come to somewhere in the region of three hundred thousand pounds."

"Holy Christ!" Kel murmurs, before he recalls he is to act the part of an obedient servant.

"Indeed," Will echoes. "Is there so much gold in Devon, Master Carmody?"

"Not in ready money, of course," the lawyer rushes to explain. "Half of that value is tied up in farm land. Most of the rest is in livestock, and property. Sir Josh, bless him, had a great love of horses. He owned a dozen stallions, just for hunting and racing, which are worth some three thousand pounds, and his flocks number around eight thousand. Then there is Topham Hall, already in Mistress Farriby's domain, and seven more great houses."

"All in Devon?" Will asks. He has never heard of one man owning so many grand houses, save Henry… and his own wife, of course.

"Goodness, no." Carmody almost blushes. "He bought a house for each of his mistresses to live in. He used to say that it helped him keep them separate, and in order."

"Then they are still living in them?"

"No, Sir Josh made provision for each one, and had them move out, upon his demise. The ladies caused no fuss, I assure you, sir." Carmody offers a document, as proof of his actions, but Will waves it away.

"Damn me, Carmody, I have fellows to do my reading," he says in a lazy drawl. "Father thought an education wasted on me, as I was set for the military life. Try reading an Irish rebel to death with a book, what? That's a good one. I must remember to tell it to the king, when next we dine."

"Sir, you move in heady company."

The lawyer is impressed by the stature, if not the competence, of his somewhat unwonted visitor.

"For all the good it does me," Will replies. "I am a fourth son, Master Carmody, and that means I am as poor as a church mouse. Why else do you think I run about for Rafe Sadler?"

"I see." Carmody frowns, then smiles, as if he has just had a sudden, happy thought. "As you are on business for the estate of Sir Joshua Benson, you are entitled to the usual expenses. Recompense for your time and trouble?"

"Am I?" Will looks blank for a moment, then grins. "Well, if you say so… who am I to argue the matter? Besides, that London trip was most arduous."

"Shall we say a hundred pounds?"

"Most arduous."

"A hundred pounds, each way then."

"If you think it to be correct, sir?" Will says.

"All above board, Colonel Draper," Carmody says. "The estate will reimburse you for your efforts. I assume Sir Rafe Sadler wishes me to hurry the business along?"

"He certainly does, Master Carmody."

"For any particular reason?"

"If so, he does not inform me of it," Will lies smoothly.

"Then your duty is done," the lawyer says. "A full statement of accounts shall be drawn up, and sent to his chambers within the month. Now, will you take wine with me, sir?"

"A splendid idea," Will says. "I suspect Mistress Elizabeth Farriby will be pleased at your efforts on her behalf."

"Of course," Carmody says, and looks a little perplexed. "Is that the entire reason for this visit, sir?"

"I do not follow, Master Lawyer," Will says, with a blank look on his face. "Is that not enough. This filly wishes her oats… so approached Rafe Sadler. I dare say he will get a fat fee, and a fair ride from the girl. I hear she is very pretty."

"Is she?" Edwin Carmody says. "I do not know her, other than through Sir Josh, who made certain allusions to a *lady* he once knew."

"What, only once?" Will laughs. "I hear that your Sir Josh was a considerable roistering devil, and did swive his way through every servant at court. I dare say there is more than one by blow bastard left in his wake."

"I think not, Colonel Draper." The lawyer stands, and seems on the point of closing the interview. Then he relents, and sits down again. "Forgive me, sir, but Josh Benson was a good friend to me, and was of great service when I first started to practice. I felt for him, as you would for a brother."

"I always hated mine," Will replies. "Then Mistress Farriby is a single acorn, fallen from the mighty oak. Damn me, but it is a shame I am married, or else she would make a fine match."

"Sir Josh's family was cursed," Carmody offers. "His own father died at Flodden Field, cut down by a Scot, even as the battle was won. Then his sister died of the sweating sickness. Prior to that, she had lost her two children and her husband."

"How careless of her." Will makes a good job of sounding almost totally empty headed.

"No, sir… lost as in 'dead'."

"Ah. What rotten luck."

"Then his younger brother, Montagu, died after he took a tumble from his horse. I think he put the beast at a ditch, and that was that. Broken neck, I am told."

"Damned bad luck," Will mutters. "This Montagu died without issue then?"

"Oh, I see what you mean," Carmody says, as if just thinking of it. "You mean to ask why they did not come into the estate. Well, let me remember. There were two sons. Ah, yes. Now I recall the bad business. The elder brother, Daniel, was waylaid whilst in Cornwall, and murdered for his purse. Two pounds and some shillings, I believe. They never caught the rogues, but some Welsh raiders were suspected. I was in Bristol at the time, and did not hear about it until much later."

"The fellow should have been better armed," Will says. "Or go about with a nasty piece of work like my man here. Kelton would slit your throat for a shilling, and eat your liver for another sixpence!"

"Quite so," Carmody says, and he goes ashen faced.

"What about the other son?" Will probes. "The unlucky fellow must have died young by the sound of it."

"Just so," the lawyer says. "And funnily enough, poor Walter Benson met the same fate as his father. That is to say, he died in a hunting accident. A crowd of young fellows were cavorting about the forest, letting fly at anything worth hunting, and Walter was hit by a crossbow bolt. He lived for a couple of days, before the wound festered, and he died. So very sad. Lovely boys, both of them. I suppose it was a mercy to the loving father that he died before they did."

"Yes, a real mercy," Will concludes. "Might I trouble you for an advance on my expenses, Master Carmody? With some gold in my purse, I might well be able to enjoy my stay in Devon."

"Will you tarry long, now you have done your duty?"

"A day or two, I think," Will says. "I am also tasked to find, and arrest, a fugitive from the king's justice. It is believed she fled to this, her home town."

"You seek a woman?" Carmody is now as white as a ghost.

"I do. The wench is wanted for perjury, and murder," Will says, nonchalantly. "You have lived here for many years, sir… and I think you might know her?"

"Oh, I keep myself very much to my self, these days," the lawyer replies, warily. "Might I ask her name?"

"You may, sir. The wench is called Nell something or other."

"Gifford, Milord," Kel puts in, as suggested. "I have asked in the low taverns, but she is unknown. I will look to the better inns tomorrow, and failing that, you might inquire at some of the great houses here abouts."

"Might I?" Will says, still playing the empty headed messenger.

"Yes, Milord, for she might be well known to the local gentry… as a servant, or a girl of low morals." Kel watches Edwin Carmody's face, and sees he has scored a hit with one of his remarks. "Once she is taken, we can have her put to the question extraordinary. I am most adept with a knife, and she will tell us everything after a few minutes with me. I've never seen a girl hanged before."

"And you shall not this time," Will says. "This Nell Gifford has done murder, using witchcraft, and for that she must roast!"

"Good God!" Carmody can scarcely stop himself from shaking. "This sounds like a bad business, and I wish you every success. Give me but a few moments sir, and I shall bring you your money… in full. I hope you will give my most friendly salutations to Sir Rafe Sadler?"

"I shall commend you to him, and to the king, as a most honest fellow, and a lawyer of great skill and probity."

*

"Probity?" Kel Kelton almost chokes with laughter as they stroll back past the magnificent cathedral. "You are supposed to be a dunderhead…and you use such a word… Milord?"

"Enough of your rascally humour," Will Draper replies. "Now all is known, what do you make of it?"

"Make of it?" Kel asks. "Why, that the fellow was surprised when you mentioned Nell Gifford. It was almost as if he knew her."

"Nothing else?" Will asks. Kel puzzles for a moment, then nods his head.

"Indeed there was something else," he says. "When I talked of searching her out, he flinched when I suggested you visit the local gentry's houses. As if she might be known in that vicinity."

"Very good," Will tells his companion. "You will make a fine Examiner, one day."

"At two shillings a week?" Kel smiles. "I dare say the wife would object."

"Which one?" Will Draper asks, and the young man has the decency to blush a bright red. "Join me as a lieutenant, at twenty pounds a year. In a year or two, you might make up to captain, at thirty a year."

"How tempting," Kel says. As Cromwell's special young man, he makes that much in a month these days, and hopes that things can only get better. He wants his own grand house, and for people to doff their caps to him in the street. One day, he might even become close to the court, and a favourite of a king, just like Will Draper. "Pray, let me think on it."

"There is no rush," Will says. "We have yet to solve this present investigation, though we are close to a satisfactory conclusion."

"We are?" Kel Kelton frowns, and

wonders what it is that he has missed. "How so, sir?"

"The old lawyer has told us almost everything," Will Draper replies, with a sly smile. "What think you of the Benson family luck?"

"Poor, to say the least," Kel says.

"Just so. Apart from Sir Joshua's young sister, they all seem to have met with violent ends. Granted, Sir Joshua's father died many years ago, whilst fighting the Scots, but it was an ill starred end for a man on the winning side. I wonder …"

"Yes?"

"Nothing. We may never know, but I would like to know if he raised and armed his own levee… and whom his captains were. A gentleman as rich as Sir Josh's father must have taken at least a company of horse, and several hundred foot soldiers up north."

"I shall ask around," Kel says. "I dare say the town is full of old soldiers, willing to gossip about a century ago."

"Just twenty six years since then," Will says. "You will find enough that remember. I am more interested in the officers than the ordinary soldiers."

"As you wish." Kel cannot understand this sudden interest in a long gone battle, or how it could throw any light on the current investigation. "You think Flodden was won by witchcraft?"

"There is no such thing," Will reminds his comrade. "It is all in the minds of simple folk, and foolish kings."

"Treason sir?" Kel remarks.

"Did I mention a particular one?"

"Now you play the lawyer," Kel says. "What else must I know? You seem to have discovered more than my mind has fastened onto."

"The second son, Montagu Benson, died after a riding accident," Will tells him. "I have seen a few such accidents that could have been murder. His own younger son, Walter is killed in a hunting accident, and the older brother, Daniel, is killed by an unknown robber… who stole his purse, containing two pounds and some shillings."

"An unlucky family, as you say," says Kel.

"I wonder how he knew?"

"Knew what?"

"That a man, travelling in Cornwall had that amount in his purse," Will says. "The pieces fall into place, Kel. Why, it is only Lady Amelia who died of natural causes."

"She had two children, after marrying late in life," Kel muses. "Perhaps they also died unhappily?"

"I shall look into that," Will tells his friend. "After all, you are going to be too busy on the morrow."

"My enquiries should only take a couple of hours," Kel replies. "What else is there for us to do?"

"You are going to ride over to Barnstaple, and make certain enquires for me. I must call on the Exeter gentry, and pay my respects," Will says. "They might know of Nell Gifford."

"Forgive me for saying this, Master Will," Kel says, "but your story was untrue. Nell Gifford is not here, but back in Surrey making eyes at Sir Richard Rich."

"I have not forgotten," says Will. "But Edwin Carmody's face paled at mention of her. I wager she is known about these parts, even if by another name."

"Another name?" Kel shakes his head. "Now I am confused."

"As is the lawyer. I have no proof, but I would swear he was surprised at how I spoke of Mistress Farriby. I made no mention of her trial, and spoke as if she were enjoying her life. It was not what he expected to hear. He actually expected me to say she was taken for a witch!"

11 The Journeyman's Tale

"Boy, run and find my nephew for me," Thomas Cromwell asks of one of the urchins who minds the front gate for his generous penny a day wages. "I have a task for him."

"Not here, master," the lad says, and wipes his nose on the sleeve of his black jerkin.

"I can see he is not here," Cromwell jests, "which is why I wish you to go *there* and bring him here. For if he is not here, then he must be there."

"Here or there, Master Tom," the boy replies, "your nephew is nowhere near."

"Then where is he?" Cromwell asks, becoming annoyed at the boy's unusually ambiguous answers.

"Norwich," the boy offers.

"Norwich?" Cromwell cannot recall asking his nephew to visit the town this particular week, and grows a little concerned.

"It is in Norfolk, sir."

"Yes, I know where it is, lad," Cromwell says, "but what is Master Richard doing there?"

"Can't say, master."

"Can't say, won't say?" Cromwell

asks.

"Can't say because I am not to, and won't say as it would offend you, master," the lad responds.

"Are you, by any chance, one of Barnaby Fowler's charity pupils?"

"I am, sir… when I can be spared," the boy admits.

"Then that accounts for your lawyer-like evasions," Thomas Cromwell tells him. "Why can you not say?"

"That would be the same as answering as to why I won't say, sir." The boy frowns. "Master Richard told me not to tell you, and Master Mush said not to offend you with it."

"What has Mush to do with all of this nonsense?" Cromwell is almost laughing, but a strange foreboding gnaws at his mind.

"He's with Master Richard in…"

"Norwich. Yes, I understand that. Doing what?"

"Visiting a lady, Master Tom."

"Ah." Cromwell finally thinks he understands. "You mean our agent there?"

"The whore, begging your pardon… an' I have said nothing of it to you, sir, or else Master Mush will gut me like a kippered herring."

"He will not."

"He says so, Master Tom, and I do

not wish to put his word to the test… me training to be a lawyer."

"I must speak with Barnaby Fowler," Cromwell mutters to himself. "Soon, if he does not desist, even my stable lad will be a man of the law."

"Not Jim, sir," the lad says, knowingly. "He is more your killing sort of a fellow. Master Kel teaches them how to throw a knife, and slit throats."

"Desist, boy," Cromwell says, and laughs. "You make my head swim. If Mush and Richard are in Norwich, I must beg your indulgence, and ask you to run to Draper House and…"

"The colonel is in Devon, sir."

"Damn and blast it!" Cromwell stamps his foot in the dust of the courtyard. "I am told nothing these days. Have I any young men to call on, lad?"

"Not clever ones, sir," the lad says. "They are all about your business. Master Mush has left six well armed fellows lounging about the kitchen, in case of trouble."

"I see. Then run next door, and beg Ambassador Chapuys to call on me for lunch. If I can get no work done, I might as well spend a few hours dining, and playing chess with an old friend."

"Yes sir."

"Then he is not in Norwich?"

Cromwell jests.

"What, old Chapuys?" The boy grins. "Bless you, Master Tom, but the old fellow has no time for tupping tarts these days. I wager he is almost as old as you!"

*

"What is it now, Norfolk?" Henry is slouched down on his throne, feeling sorry for himself. He has tried to speak plainly with the queen, but she is being most difficult, lapsing into German and waving her arms about. "I am busy."

"Yes, sire?" Norfolk glances about the near empty chamber, and sees only Suffolk playing cards with Sir John Russell, and a sleepy pair of guards by the door to the outer court. "Forgive my interruption, but it is important."

"Have the French invaded?"

"Not that I have heard, Hal," the duke replies

"Then what is so … ah, yes… Cromwell. You wish to whisper poison into my ear. The man will not see eye to eye with me over my new queen, but he is as honest as you are not."

"Thank you, sire," Norfolk says, and moves closer, so that Suffolk, a friend of Cromwell's, does not overhear them. "It is about my investigation. You recall I was trying to prove his honesty to you?"

"Is that what you were doing?" The

king wishes to chase Norfolk away, but with Cromwell regretfully confessing the marriage is sound, he has no one else to listen to his woes. "Very well, speak up, man."

"I looked at the crown finances."

"Without his permission?"

"I did not need it, sire," Norfolk says. "You gave me leave to look into matters, and Sir Richard Rich, who loves you well, was most obliging."

"I wager he was," Henry says. "One day, I shall hang that dirty little bastard … next to you, probably. What did you find?"

"Nothing, sire. I never thought that Thomas Cromwell was a thief. Your accounts are impeccable. Not a single penny piece out of place. Tom Cromwell has no need to steal from you, sire. He is worth forty thousand pounds a year, just from the Earldom of Essex you gave him."

"I suspect that you earn more from your own title and lands," Henry snipes. "Why, Norfolk alone must bring in fifty thousand."

"Oh, I am a rich man, right enough," Norfolk admits. "Despite owing most of it to the Jew bankers, I manage to live well, and pay my taxes to you, sire. Twelve thousand silver marks a year, and the running cost of a ten thousand strong militia." There, the king is reminded that

Norfolk pays his way, and controls a large private army, loyal to himself. "It is not about money at all, Hal. Thomas Cromwell … or should I say the Earl of Essex… is worth every penny he makes from us, as long as he is loyal to the crown. That is the only real kind of honesty required of him."

"Then you claim he is disloyal to me?" Henry smiles. He knows that Tom Cromwell, and all the Austin Friars party are devoted to him. Norfolk is, as always throwing mud, without a shred of evidence to support his ridiculous claims. "How so?"

"He trapped you into a loveless marriage."

"Utter rot!" Henry laughs out loud, and Suffolk glances over at them to see what the jest is. "Tom Cromwell was the only man who would speak to me honestly. When I favoured Anne of Cleves, he tried to dissuade me from the match by force of argument. Why, he wanted me to wed that flat chested Burgundian princess, did he not?"

"No, Your Majesty, he did not," the Duke of Norfolk replies, triumphantly. "The Earl of Blacksmiths has shown his true colours, and is seen to be nothing more than a scheming rascal."

"Proof, sir… or by God, I will…"

"Have my head?" Norfolk asks. If his head is forfeit if he is shown to lie, then what price must Cromwell pay for being shown to be a liar. "By saying this to me, you insinuate that to lie to the king is … what… sedition… treason?"

"Enough of this," Henry cries, his face growing dangerously red. "Either show your hand, or remove yourself from court… and not just for a few weeks, sir! Prove false to me now, and I will strip you of your title, and see you are a ruined man. Then, if Cromwell cares to argue his case, and shows you to be worse than false, I will let him take your life."

"Strong words, Your Majesty," Norfolk touches the magical amulet he always has about his neck, and hopes the fragment of Saint George's tooth within does its job for once. "Without further ado, I must demand you listen to my proof, at first hand. Let me present you with an honest journeyman fellow … a coach driver, who is sober, God fearing, and untainted by any sign of coercion."

"A coachman?" Henry asks. "You think some low fellow knows more about my marriage than I, Lord Norfolk?"

"Sire, listen to him, in private, and question him to your heart's content," Norfolk says, earnestly. "Then afterwards, you might deign to call me Tom, or my dear Howard again, and I may call you dearest Hal, whom I have always loved like a son."

"You hate your son, sir."

"He is not the man you are, Hal." Norfolk dares to reach out, and place his hand on the king's broad shoulder. "Come, Master Judas Plank awaits us. It is best other ears are excluded from this business. Though Charles is a friend to us both, he is close to Cromwell, and Sir John Russell is now an Austin Friars man."

"Russell is *my* man, and mine alone." Henry is uneasy at these casual insinuations about those around him, and he is beginning to feel uneasy about Norfolk. The man is so sure of himself, and seems confident he finally has the better of Cromwell.

"Ask yourself, sire," Norfolk says. "How comes Thomas Cromwell to know your business before the rest of the court? Who is it that takes your personal orders about the countryside, warning of your arrival? Who was it who guarded the door of Jane Seymour when she was confined with little Edward, and let Thomas Cromwell enter, along with your Jew doctor?"

"What, you actually know this?" Henry asks.

"I do." Norfolk smiles, secure in the knowledge that he has enough information to support his claims. "One of the ladies who attended your dear late wife is cousin to a lady of my most intimate acquaintance.

This lady heard the tale, first hand, and has told me, in confidence. It seems Cromwell wished to confirm the young prince had all ten toes before he came to congratulate you."

"Let us speak with your witness then," the king growls, "and later, you must find a new position for Russell. Perhaps as a captain in my Irish army?"

"As you command, sire," old Norfolk replies, now full of the joys of life. Russell will change sides, rather than have to fight in the bogs of Ireland, and Doctor Adolphus Theophrasus will lose face, if nothing else. "I shall attend to him, personally. As for the Jew doctor…"

"He is from Exeter," Henry says, firmly. The doctor is the best he has ever had, and he will not sacrifice him, just because he might be tainted with the blood of Christ Killers. "I know of no other man who can ease my gout so well, and his potions for relieving the cardiac passion are truly wonderful."

"Made up by Mistress Marion Giles," Norfolk sneers. "She is the tall blonde piece, Will Draper keeps at his great house. It seems he must have every pretty woman in London for his bed."

"Leave Will Draper be," Henry warns. "For even if, by some strange happening, Tom Cromwell *has* slighted me, the rest of his Austin Friars trained men have done me nothing but good."

The king stands, and urges the Duke of Norfolk out of the chamber. Charles Brandon, the Duke of Suffolk, and Sir John Russell see the movement, and stand, as if ready to follow, but Henry waves them back to their table.

"Take your ease, gentlemen," he calls. "Boring Uncle Norfolk wishes to go over some old navy accounts, and I would not ruin your game for so dreary a reason. Do not lose too much, Charles!"

The Duke of Suffolk smiles, and bows to the king. If he has learned anything over the last twenty odd years, it is to pretend he does not recognise when Henry lies. The king does not realise, but his voice changes, and his face blushes the colour of his once famous ginger hair. The duke makes a note to speak with Henry later, and try to find out what is afoot.

*

"Sir Kel Kelton, at your service, sir." Kel has few scruples when it comes to gaining an advantage over a foe, and thinks the spurious use of a title will add weight to his enquiries. Will Draper has despatched him the thirty eight miles to Barnstaple, to gather certain information, and he does not intend going back empty handed. "This is my warrant." He taps the rolled scroll tucked in his belt, which is positioned so as to display the small royal seal. In truth, it is an old order for some ship's provisions he has simply 'borrowed' from Tom Cromwell's study.

"My dear sir, let me have some refreshments brought, the alderman replies. "You say you come from Exeter?"

"From Hampton Court Palace at first, then by Exeter, Master Tidwell," Kel tells him. "Some wine, and a small repast will do admirably. The king wishes me to make certain discreet enquiries, and I am informed that you have served Barnstaple well for many years."

"I am a loyal servant of His Majesty," Alderman Tidwell enthuses. "You have but to ask it of me, sir, and I will aid you in any way I can."

"I wish to know all there is to know about a lawyer who has his practice in Exeter, but hails from your town. His name is…"

"Edwin Carmody," Tidwell says. "Master Carmody is … or rather was… the legal representative of Sir Joshua Benson. He often visits to see about Sir Joshua's holdings hereabouts. The old fellow has several hundred acres of good pasture, and makes a tidy sum from the wool trade. He also has … had… a manse down by the headland. It was once owned by the Bishop of Devon… the old Roman Catholic one… and he sold it to Sir Joshua when our blessed monarch reformed the church."

"Then you are not a Roman Catholic?"

"Not I, sir!" Tidwell is genuinely offended at the very thought of such a thing, though half the town's population still go to secret masses, and donate money to the papist cause. "I am a Tyndale man, God rest his poor martyred soul. When the papist Earl of Devon, William Courtenay, plotted against His Majesty, last year, this town closed its gates to him, and declared for Thomas Cromwell and the king."

"Might we return to this Edwin Carmody?" Kel says, firmly.

"Why, that is exactly what I mean to say, sir," Alderman Tidwell replies. "When Milord Devon was conspiring with some of the Pole family, it was Edwin Carmody who came here, and advised us as to the illegal nature of the earl's wicked actions. We begged him to write to the king for us, and urge him to leniency, as we were not for supporting that bastard Courtenay's shocking disloyalty."

"Most commendable."

"It was. We have much to thank Master Carmody for," Tidwell confirms. "He suggested that Sir Joshua endowed a school and paid for a hospice in the town.

The man is a saint, sir, and I cannot listen to a wrong word about him. How we rejoiced when the Earl of Devon was arrested, and then beheaded for his treason."

"A most happy outcome," Kel Kelton says, but he is not happy with this answer. His master, Will Draper, wishes to hear something bad about the fellow, so that his investigation is helped to its conclusion. "I trust Master Carmody was well rewarded?"

"His reward was in being able to help," Tidwell says. "Those were his very words, as he sat in the very chair you now occupy. The people applauded him in the streets, wherever he ventured, and his work in the alms houses was hailed as ground breaking."

"How so?" Kel says.

"Why, he had them all enlarged, and had Sir Joshua purchase the leasehold from the Devon estate," Tidwell explains. "Then he had his master sell it to the newly appointed Board of Governors for a pittance. The houses stand in prime land, and are now the envy of the whole town. The head of the governors, Master Lucas Younger, says there is not a finer man in all of the county."

"Is he married?" Kel asks. "Or does he visit the whore house, or perhaps keep a mistress?"

"Sir… you speak out of turn!" Tidwell is red faced and angry. "Master Carmody is not married, he has no mistress, and we do not have a whore house in Barnstaple."

"Then where do the young men go for fun?" Kel asks, and the alderman frowns at so impertinent a question coming from a man whom, he now thinks, looks far too young to be a knight of the realm. "Perhaps one or two of the lower taverns might have such wenches in them, but they are not prostitutes, sir. If they … entertain gentlemen… it is out of the goodness of their hearts."

"Of course," Kel says. Barnstaple is beginning to sound like the most boring town in all of England. "Though lawyers must, because of their profession, make enemies. Who has he wronged, or had imprisoned without cause?"

"No one that I know of," Tidwell says. "He is not that kind of a lawyer. He makes out wills, and draws up legal papers. There is no man alive who would cast dirt on so excellent a fellow. He is honest, truthful, and faithful. Why when he was with …"

"Yes, sir?" Kel asks, with a smile of triumph. "When he was with whom?"

"I speak of many years ago, you understand," Tidwell confesses, "and his behaviour in the matter was exceptional."

Time for the grand deception, Kel thinks to himself. He finishes his wine, and affects a tone that implies some great secret is to be imparted. To emphasise this, he huddles forward, and drops his voice.

"In confidence … I am here directly from the king," he says to the concerned alderman. "I have been instructed to investigate Master Carmody's past, but for the good, rather than the bad. His fine work for the king has been noted, and there is some talk of a knighthood… or even better, being offered to him."

"Goodness me!" Tidwell is impressed, for now he might well claim to be the friend of a knight of the realm, rather than a mere country lawyer.

"This exceptional behaviour you speak of?"

"It was many years ago, when he was a younger man."

"Nonetheless…." Kel replies. "Some deeply heart warming act might sway the king's ministers in his favour."

"Of course…. I see what you mean." Alderman Tidwell pours out more wine for them both, and gestures for Kel to help himself to the platter of choice cuts. "It must have been back in the summer of 1516 … no, I tell a lie, for that was the bad fever summer. More likely it was in the middle of '17, and we were all such a happy gang of roisterers back then …"

*

Judas Plank does not quite understand how his life could have changed so dramatically in these past weeks, and prays that his current good fortune continues. Master Donne, a most frightful fellow at first, has become his guardian angel, and guides him through his days with casual friendliness.

"It seems My Lord Norfolk likes you," Donne says. "You are in his good books, and he always rewards such men well. Look at me… a poor clerk one day, and a man of power and influence the next. I own lands, and command servants… as will you, Judas."

"But I have only repeated what I heard."

"Truthfully," Donne says. "Remain faithful to that truth, and do not alter a word. Repeat what you have said to the duke, and all will be well. I dare say that the Duke of Norfolk will be most generous… and as for the king…"

"The king?" Judas Plank almost passes out at the idea of speaking to Henry. "How can I?"

"Do it boldly," Donne advises. "Make it plain that you have no axe to grind… that Cromwell is neither a friend, nor an enemy. If asked, repeat your story, and remain always at the king's service."

Now he is here, sitting in a small oak lined chamber, with a table full of good wine and food at his elbow. The moment is nigh, and he expects Donne to enter at any moment. Instead, the door is thrown back, and it is gruff old Tom Howard, the Duke of Norfolk who fills the room, swiftly followed by the king.

Judas leaps to his feet, then falls to one knee. The king is impressed, because the coachman is dressed in clean new livery, and is clean shaven. He knows his manners, and actually smells of, of all things, oranges. The Duke of Norfolk knows how the king dislikes to come into contact with those commoners who are too common for his taste, and has had his Judas scrubbed from top to toe, then doused in his wife's own expensive citrus fruit pomade.

"Your Highness…. Might I present to you Master Judas Plank," Norfolk says. "Might I also commend him to you as a loyal servant of the king, and a man of soberness and propriety. I, myself, was so struck by his honest nature, that I refrained from using the question extraordinary on him. He speaks the absolute truth. Listen to his tale, and you will see for yourself."

"Very well…. Speak up man." The king takes Plank's chair, and attacks the food left out for the coachman. "Tell me all you know, at once."

"Sire," Plank starts, "I am a simple man. I know nothing. My ears heard words, and my poor head remembered them, but I know not what it is I heard. I am not a political man. Might I just repeat the words, and let you, in your infinite wisdom, know what they mean?"

"Ah, you are a wise fellow," Henry says. "Best not try to strain your mind wondering about things that do not concern the common herd. Speak out, and I shall judge." Judas Plank smiles, and bows again. Donne said the old fool was open to flattery, and he did not lie.

"It was like this, sire," he begins. "I was waylaid by a foreign gentleman, as was made known to me later as a painter of portraits , named Hans Holbein."

"Damnation… then Holbein *is* involved. I knew it to be so, in my heart," Henry says. "Go on…"

"He bid me carry some paintings to a certain house in London," Judas says. "It was my first visit to Austin Friars, but I had heard of the place, of course. He had me unload his paintings, and told me to go to the kitchen and refresh myself." This part is a lie, but such a minor one that it will slip past unnoticed. "I came to leave, but found myself hearing the words of the great folk in Cromwell's office. I took fright, lest I be seen, and thought a spy, and so I hid amongst the coats and cloaks hanging in the entrance hall. Then it was that I heard it all, and realised my life would be forfeit if I was ever taken by so base a crowd."

"Speak on," Henry says. It has the ring of truth, and that is more than enough for a man who lives with suspicion and distrust at every waking moment. Besides, he has been to Austin Friars, and knows the very cloak stand the man speaks of. If nothing else, he has been inside the place, Henry thinks.

"They spoke of the paintings, and of how Holbein had done them in the way Cromwell wanted. That is to say, one was made to be more attractive than the others."

"Did they say why?"

"To trick you, Your Majesty," Judas Plank says. "Master Cromwell spoke of how he would argue against you, for forms sake, then let you think you had made the final choice."

"If this is so…" Henry grinds his teeth. Then a thought comes to him that Norfolk might have told this Judas Plank what to say, and he resolves to play the thing through. "Repeat to me, word for word, that which was said. I shall listen to every word, and by the way they are said, know if it is likely to have come from my dear old friend Cromwell, or not. Do not deviate by a single word, you miserable fellow, or I shall see you pay for it with your life. Treason is a nasty business… whomsoever is involved."

"Sire, I will do as you order," Plank replies. "For I do not understand the words, and could not make up such infamy for myself."

"And no one else has made you speak thus?" for answer, Judas Plank pulls open his doublet, and exposes his bare chest. It is free of any marks of torture, and attests to the man's lack of coercion.

"I see how it might look, sire," he says, "but it is by chance I fell into the duke's hands. I was coming here to find some great lord who might listen to my tale, for though I am not sure what it all means, I know it was meant against you, and if nothing else … I am a loyal Englishman!"

Tom Howard almost cries out in joy at this sudden improvisation, for it reaches to Henry's very core. It speaks of loyalty to England and, more importantly, the king. Dear Christ, he thinks, I almost believe the cunning bastard myself.

"Then speak, sir… and be damned to the consequences," the king says, emotionally. He fears what he will hear, but cannot turn aside from it. Thus it is always the dilemma of the suspicious mind to think the worst, yet fear knowing it.

"Very well, sire … it went thus…"

12 Escape from the Tower

"I thought we were close friends." Eustace Chapuys stands before Thomas Cromwell, wringing his cap in his fists. His expensive, and much admired, ostrich feathers are crushed beyond redemption. The latest letters from the emperor's office have just arrived, and make for some uncomfortable reading.

"What have I done now, Eustace?" the Privy Councillor asks in genuine surprise. "I recall helping your emperor swindle the Fugger Banking Houses out of their share of gold from the Americas, and I seem to remember joining he and the king through his new marriage. Is it that which irks you?"

"The king, I hear, hates Anne of Cleves, though God knows why," the little Savoyard diplomat snaps. "I doubt the marriage will last out the year."

"Why not?" Thomas Cromwell says. "Many men never meet their wives, let alone sleep with them. Leave them to it, my friend, and they will come to some satisfactory accommodation."

"I doubt it, but that is not why I am so angry," Chapuys retorts. "When were you going to tell me about your expedition to the New World? When were you going to explain how you thought it wise to steal my master's lands."

"Ah, you mean the privately funded expedition," Cromwell says. "Nothing to do with me, Eustace. I believe Lady Miriam Draper and some rich investors seek to build an outpost, far to the north of the emperor's lands."

"So we believed," Chapuys says. "Your fleet was last seen sailing up towards the New Found lands."

"Where they will trade with the local natives, hunt for furs, and do a little logging." Cromwell has all the answers, and is sure he can divert Chapuys back onto the right path again. "I dare say they must be well into their first year by now."

"Just so. Admiral Santa Cruz, who is our man in the Floridas, has written to us with the latest news. It seems one of his captains decided to explore further north, just to see what was there."

"And to claim it for the empire, no doubt," Thomas Cromwell says, with a wry smile. "Fear not, Eustace, the place is big enough for us all to have a piece. When our two sides meet… there shall be the boundary between Spanish Americas and New English land. A happy solution, I think."

"Ah, yes. That would be a Utopian solution," Chapuys replies, nodding his head. "A race against time to see who can take the most. Perfect, save for one thing. The savages who think the land is theirs."

"Poor soulless creatures, who need to be brought into the church of the one God … whether it be Romish, or Protestant."

"Captain Santiago advanced almost two hundred and fifty leagues up the seaboard, until he met any kind of opposition."

"Not Governor Ibrahim and his men, I hope?" Thomas Cromwell says lightly, but curses under his breath. If that damned blackamoor has started a war, he thinks, the king will be furious.

"No, a great war band of northern natives, numbering some three thousand armed warriors," Chapuys tells his friend. "The captain, with only seventy soldiers at his disposal, decided to retreat back into the Floridas, rather than face them."

"Really?" Cromwell is amused at this. Spears against muskets, and the Spaniards take fright. "They ran away from a few hunting bows?"

"No, Thomas, they retreated in the face of a war band armed with the very best muskets available. English muskets, my friend. At least a hundred of them. You see why I am so angry?"

"Ibrahim would never arm the natives," Cromwell says, but he is not so sure now. The man is an adventurer, intent on cutting out an empire, and might think arming the natives against the Spanish a good idea.

"Admiral Santa Cruz was furious, of course. It seemed to be a blatant act of war." Chapuys is calmer now. "He sent one of our ships north, armed with cannon, and two hundred fighting men. It was his intention to capture your outpost, and take all of your people captive."

"Ah, I fear a 'but' coming on," Cromwell says, softly. It is one of those rare moments in his life where something has not gone to plan, and he fears the worse.

"But the English fort was gone… burnt to the ground. There were the remains of your people everywhere. They searched, but found no survivors."

"What about the ships?" Cromwell abandons all pretence that it is none of his doing. "There should be three ships… with cannon. How could they have…"

"Been overcome?" Chapuys shrugs. "Who can say. One craft was a burnt out hulk, and a second was drifting in the cove, quite deserted, but with its guns spiked. The third was gone."

"Gone"

"Like your dreams of empire, old friend," Eustace Chapuys says. "I trust you will explain this disaster to your king in the most flattering light possible?"

"Almost four hundred men and women, missing or dead," Cromwell says. "How could it be?"

"One ship seems to have escaped. Perhaps…?"

"Yes," Cromwell says. "Perhaps…"

*

Elizabeth Farriby's heart roars in her chest at the sound of footfalls on the stone flags outside her chamber within the Tower of London, and she wonders if they come to release, or burn her for the hundredth time. The door is unbolted, and Robin Crabtree is there, bearing a tray of food, and a flagon of watered Renish wine.

"Dear Robin," she says, but stops when she sees his face. He mimes for her to remain silent whilst he places the food on a table, and returns to the open door. He glances outside, then, satisfied he is not followed, he comes back to her and takes her hand in his.

"My sweet girl," he starts. "We must be careful for the nonce. Abraham Wake, the Torturer in Chief of the Tower, sends me word that Sir Richard Rich has put a spy amongst the guards. This is so that he might listen and report your words. I shall uncover the rogue, and see he is kept away from you, but we must watch our tongues for the moment."

"Then tell me the news at once, whilst he is absent." Elizabeth has only been in the Tower for eight days, but it seems like a year has slid by, and she is losing hope of ever seeing the world she left again.

"Your so called friend, Nell Gifford, has now recalled seeing your cat changing shape." Young Robin delivers the news with a blush, for it is plain that the Attorney General of England is behind this sudden new 'finding'.

"What?" The girl is shocked at so blatant a lie from her friend, and cannot understand what it is she must have done to so anger the woman. "Now poor Lucifer is accused."

"Yes… it is a most unfortunate choice of name for the animal, Mistress Elizabeth," Robin Crabtree says, with great understatement. "Perhaps a less contentious title might have been wiser?"

"He is as black as soot, and he has burning eyes," the girl says. "What else but Lucifer, or Satan would do? I had no inkling that naming my cat so would cause such a vile charge to be laid against me. What else can you tell me?"

"That the old woman, Jane is now thought to have been a witch," Robin says, "but it helps us little. Rich will just say you were in league with her."

"Poor Jane was just an old woman," Elizabeth replies. "She might have made up a few cures and such like, but she was no sorceress."

"Perhaps you are right," Robin says. He will keep the rest to himself for now, and hope that Sir Will Draper and his people can find their way to the truth, and so save the girl. In just a few days he has become smitten with Elizabeth, and will not allow any harm to befall her. "Though I have a plan, should the worse happen."

"To escape the Tower of London?" Elizabeth shakes her head in disbelief. "How comes it that Anne Boleyn could not escape her fate, yet I might?"

"We have friends," Robin says, softly. "Many of the gaolers, the torturer, and several of the guards captains are Draper men, and they can be relied upon to turn a blind eye at the right moment. If needs be, I shall come for you, and lead you to freedom. Though I fear we must flee the country, and never return."

"If I am with you...." Elizabeth leaves the words hanging, and Robin blushes with pride at her reciprocated affection.

"Forever," Robin Crabtree says. He kisses her then, and slips out of the chamber. As he makes his way back to his own quarters, Richard Rich's Sergeant at Arms, Toby Wilton, steps from the shadows at the end of the corridor and stares at his back. He shakes his head, and creeps up to the chamber door. In his state of reverie, Robin has quite forgotten to throw closed the heavy iron bolt.

Wilton grins at the amateurish young man's failing, then eases the heavy bolt into place. From inside, he hears Elizabeth Farriby stir, and speak out.

"Who is there?" she says, and Wilton fades back into the shadows. He has very precise orders, and will follow them to the letter, come what may.

*

"Well, sire?" Norfolk holds his breath, because he knows how precarious Henry's judgement can be. The man, Judas Plank, has spoken and been taken from the chamber. "What do you make of that?"

"Had I not heard it with my own ears…" Henry wipes at a traitorous tear which has appeared at the corner of one eye. "Every word sounded as if from Cromwell's own lips. It all makes sense now. I see how he dunned me with his support of another woman, and made me think him against Cleves."

"It was cleverly done," Norfolk admits, honestly. "He made you think the choice was yours, and led you to Anne of Cleves, like a horse to water. Even you, who called him 'friend' could not have expected such deceitfulness, Hal. The man has betrayed you. He spoke of you as if you were a simpleton."

"He wished me to marry into the Holy Roman Empire," Henry says, "and he has succeeded. I argued with him, and even commended him for being honest with me about his interest in the Burgundy girl. I smiled and let him make me look like … an utter fool."

"Shall I have warrants drawn up?" Norfolk asks.

"Warrants?"

"Cromwell deceived you, but he was helped by Holbein, and even Sir Rafe Sadler put in his pennyworth. As for your Royal Examiner's involvement… we must investigate further."

"No."

"But, sire…"

"No warrants. Not yet. I do not intend this matter turning into another scandal." Henry recalls how messy his break with Anne Boleyn became, and wishes to proceed in a calmer way. After all, Tom Cromwell has done nothing, but trick him into a politically sound marriage. "You will recall what happened when you wanted rid of Cardinal Wolsey, My Lord Norfolk."

"Sire, that was my niece's doing, with help from the Duke of Northumberland." Norfolk can feel the ground shifting, and struggles to bring the king back to the present dilemma. "We all know you were going to forgive the fellow."

"Damn it, I was!" Henry sees a way ahead. "Sir Rafe is a fine minister, and loyal to his king. As for Hans Holbein … the rogue was bribed, no doubt… well, he is a foreigner, and much admired by Emperor Charles. It would be unwise to arrest him. Let it be known I do not favour him any more, and that will hit him where it hurts. His commissions will dry up."

"Then what of Draper and Cromwell?" Norfolk fears he has worked hard for little return. "The Earl of Essex indeed! The man is a common blacksmith's bastard, and has shown his true colours. As for Colonel Will Draper… he is the son of a priest, and once brought news of Wolsey's death."

"Draper is loyal to me," Henry says. He recalls the time he saved him from an assassin, and how he helped keep secret the terrible mistake Henry made in marrying his mistress. "I have knighted him, with good reason, and he has kept my secrets well. If I had a hundred such men as he, I would invade France with impunity, sir!"

"Draper was Cromwell's man, Hal,"

Norfolk insists. "Tell him of your misgivings, and he will warn Cromwell. He would even raise his sword to defend the damned fellow. Tell me you are not going to forgive them all?"

"All, save Thomas Cromwell," Henry decides. He cannot allow Norfolk to think him weak. The truth is clear to see, and the ill named Judas Plank has damned his Privy Councillor with it. "I find that I must show him my displeasure."

"Then let me arrest him."

"You are too rough," Henry replies. "You would drag him to the Tower in chains, and have him tortured. Then the axe."

"And you would not?" Norfolk says, and immediately sees he has overstepped the line between king and lord.

"By God, you presume to think for me now, Norfolk?" The king roars to his feet, and smashes his fist down onto the table, sending the remains of the food scattering in all directions. "Tread carefully, old man, for I am still king in this castle!"

"Sire, I meant only to ask what you wish to be done," the duke simpers. "If we are not careful, Cromwell will be warned, and flee the country. He has friends in the Low Countries, and many Lutheran allies in Antwerp, Aachen and Ghent. He might escape, and raise arms against us."

"Thomas Cromwell would never do that," Henry tells the duke. "I know him too well. He saw that we must ally ourselves to Charles, against the French, and simply saw to it. His fault lies in conspiring to make it happen, despite my own thoughts on the matter. That is not a hanging offence, My Lord. Cromwell has had his way, at my expense, and I must accept that he did it for love of England… and of his king. We have drawn bows together, devised schemes against our enemies, and even brought down the Roman church together. The man loves me well, Norfolk, and I cannot bring him down for it."

"Then humiliate him," Norfolk says. "Let him be taken in, for questioning, and asked about his part in tricking you, Hal. If he lies, and denies it… then you must punish him, severely. If he admits it, and begs forgiveness, you might fine him, and remove him from a few of his positions. Put myself and Rich over him for a few months, and spurn his friendship, until he resolves your marriage dilemma."

"What, force him to save me from Cleves?" Henry smiles at the idea, and sees how Cromwell might be chastened by such a thing. "Have him report to you, and take away some of his responsibilities? Excellent. That will show him. Then I will make him have me un-married… howsoever it is done. Yes, Norfolk, I like it, and will have it so. He can be removed as head of my council first. That way, he must bow to his new master. Rich or Tom Audley will do for now. It is only temporary, after all."

"If he gets wind…"

"That is your task, Uncle Norfolk," Henry says. In his mind, it is all now a great jest to be played out, with Cromwell the butt of the joke. "How will you do it, without arousing his suspicions?"

"I have a man, sire," Norfolk says. Things are not going exactly to plan, but he is sure that Donne's arrangements will suffice to see the matter concluded well. "He tells me he can remove Thomas Cromwell's protection, and have him under guard without anyone finding out, until Your Majesty wishes. You might want to speak with Cromwell, or I could question him … without torture, and find out his own mind on things."

"His own mind?"

"Yes, sire. Cromwell always has a plan, and once he sees he has annoyed you, he will wish to reform himself in your eyes. If he truly loves you, he will admit his guilt, and offer restitution. You might wish to remove his new title, or throw him out of Austin Friars. You might even wish to have him spend a few weeks in the Tower of London. Not a cell, of course… but a nice suite on the upper floors?"

"Very well. Have your people arrange matters," Henry says to the jubilant lord. "Have Tom Cromwell detained at my pleasure. I think you will find his young men the match of any you have though."

*

"I have been with every girl in the entire house… twice now," Richard Cromwell grumbles. "It has been ten days now. When will this Rupert Donne fellow show up?" Mush Draper can only shrug his shoulders. He is tired of waiting to ambush the Duke of Norfolk's man, and longs to be back in the arms of his beautiful Venetian mistress, Isabel.

"Let us give it another two days," he says, "then we can go home. I dare say the bastard has been held up on business, and will show up after we leave. Lucky for him." The plan, to tether the man down, and beat information out of him is in tatters, and Big Jenny, the madam of the house is distraught at how events have come about. She is in the pay of Cromwell, and it is her information that has brought his best men to lodge in her bawdy house, to waylay the Duke of Norfolk's most dangerous agent.

"I'm sorry, lads," she says. "The fellow was so boastful about undoing Master Cromwell that I had to let you know. He was speaking of some great ruse, to bring Austin Friars low, and I feared for us all."

"You did well," Mush tells her. "It is just ill luck that we came at the wrong time. This Rupert Donne has a loose tongue, and that means he is not as clever as he thinks. We will catch up with him, and drag from him his wicked plots."

"But you have been away from Master Tom for so long," the voluptuous tart replies. "It is a wonder he has not sent for you."

"He does not know where we are," Richard says.

"No, we sought to do something without his direction," Mush confirms. "It seems that he and Will run our lives for us, and we seek to show them otherwise."

"Then who is looking after the master?" Big Jenny asks.

"Kel is there," Mush replies.

"Kel Kelton?" Jenny shakes her head in frustration at these two would be clever men. "Kel is in Devon, last I heard, with Sir Will Draper. Who is left with Cromwell, save a few wooden heads with daggers? Who is there to watch over him when he sleeps?"

"We will be back at Austin Friars in a few days," Richard says with more confidence than he now feels. His uncle will be furious with them, and they are returning empty handed. "Besides, Rafe Sadler is always about the place, and Miriam Draper has more brains than either of us … even together. My uncle is safe enough."

"Of course he is," Mush puts in, but there is a nagging doubt, which he cannot rid himself of. What if this Donne fellow spoke out, just so that word would get to Austin Friars? "How long has this fellow been coming to visit, Jenny?"

"Why, the last time was his third call," Jenny says. "He paid well for his pleasure, twice. Then he asked for me. I told him as how I never pleasured the customers personally … save you, Dick … but he offered double the money. When I spoke with little Maud, she told me he wanted nothing but a good beating, so I agreed."

"And it was only then, when he was with Tom Cromwell's paid agent, that he let slip his scheme?"

"Why, yes," Jenny says, and her countenance drops. "Oh, sweet Christ in Heaven, Master Mush, what have we done?"

"What are you talking about?" Richard Cromwell is, as usual, a little slower on the uptake, and cannot see that they have been tricked.

"Rupert Donne *knew* Jenny was in our pay," Mush explains to his friend. He deliberately let slip what he was about to her, in the hope that she would report it to us. He has drawn us away from the master, most cleverly. Perhaps he only hoped to weaken our defences, but instead, he has removed Cromwell's most loyal men."

"Why?"

"God knows," Mush replies, "but we must saddle up, and return to Austin Friars at once."

"It will be dark soon," Richard complains. "Must we ride through the night on so dangerous a road?"

"We must," Mush says, "and let us pray to which ever god you wish that we are in time."

"In time for what?"

"God alone knows," Mush says again. "And I fear he is not for telling us!"

*

Sir Will Draper, Colonel of the King's Royal Examiners Office, and commander of a crack troop of investigating officers, is almost bent double with sickness. The return journey, first by fast mount, and then by one of Miriam's most seaworthy cogs has been his undoing.

Even as the small craft ties up in the harbour, he heaves the contents of his stomach overboard for the fourth time. Beside him, Kel Kelton hides a smirk, and tries to seem useful to his senior comrade.

"I think it was that pork, Master

Will," he commiserates. "It did smell most peculiar. Then I dare say this choppy sea has not helped. Even our prisoners are feeling sick. Though that might be at the prospect of their coming end, what?"

"Sweet Jesus," Will moans. "If you do not shut up, I shall take my pistol, and shoot you, Kelton. I do so hate the sea."

"We have never been more than a half league off the coast," Kel replies, cheerily. "Though it has saved us days of riding again, and now we need only canter inland for a half a day. Shall I bring you something to drink, sir? Some beer, or a glass of mulled wine?"

"By God, but I *will* shoot you!" Draper cries, and swings a boot at Kel's fast disappearing backside. The sea is rough, and the pork, as Kel pointed out, was a little old and chewy. He wonders if it is time for him to take things easier. Now in his thirty second, or thirty third year, the King's Examiner in Chief feels confident that he has earned an easier life.

Miriam will be pleased at how he is thinking, and often begs him to take a less active roll. There is little need for him to continue working, as Miriam is worth a vast fortune, and they can live well for the rest of their lives. Yes, he thinks, it might be time. First, however, there is the matter of Elizabeth Farriby to clear up.

He is close to knowing it all, and need only re-examine the single witness in the case for things to fall into place. That Richard Rich will be furious goes without saying, and his full report, when submitted to the king, will cause an uproar. His findings will tear apart the base superstition still prevalent in Henry's court, and change the way men look at things in a serious way.

"Salt water, that's what you need," the cog's ageing captain mutters. "Sink down a full cup of that, and it will purge you out, good and proper. It never fails, you poor fellow."

"Sea water?" Will muses. He has drunk stranger things in his life, and feels bad enough to risk anything. "What the hell… hand me a cup!"

*

Elizabeth Farriby turns in her sleep, and senses that she is not alone. In the dark recesses of her mind, she hears a familiar sound, as a bolt scrapes, and a door, though well oiled, creaks. She keeps her eyes closed, yet can tell that someone is standing over her.

She half opens her eyes, and tries to make out the shape that is now kneeling beside her. For a moment, she thinks it is Robin, overcome by his passion for her, and unable to keep away. If he touches her, she knows that she will submit to his desires, and allow liberties beyond those normal to a gentlewoman.

"Mistress Farriby?" the voice whispers, and her entire body freezes in fright. The voice is not one she knows. "Do not cry out, I beseech you. Compose yourself, and listen to me."

"Who are you?" she whispers.

"No one of any importance, my lady," the man replies. "I come with some advice. Under no circumstances must you try to leave the tower. Is that understood?"

"But if I am to live…"

"Master Robin Crabtree cannot save you," he says. "He is known to favour you, and he is closely watched. Stay here, and you have a chance of living. You must trust me. I know you fancy poor Crabtree loves you, but that will not make doors open, and iron bars melt away. The boy means well, but cannot help."

"I do not understand. What is your part in this?"

"I have no part," the deep male voice says into the enclosing darkness. "It is only that I have looked upon you, often, these last few days, and find you to be … beyond my reach. Would that I was a Robin Crabtree, and able to plight my love for you, but I am not, and can only act unselfishly. Ignore any attempt to remove you from the Tower. Trust to God, and to Will Draper."

"You know Will Draper?" There is a noise, and the sound of a bolt being thrown. Outside, a big, well muscled man smiles at how he has managed things. The girl will stay put, until Will Draper returns, and then things can be brought to a head.

Toby Wilton drops a hand to the wicked dagger at his belt, and touches the lucky amulet at his throat. Soon, Will Draper shall come to the Tower, or summon the girl. Either way, he will be drawn closer, and Wilton can accomplish his task.

Twenty pounds in gold coins is a great deal of money, and to receive such a sum for one, simple, little murder is not something to be taken lightly. Soon, Sergeant Toby Wilton thinks… soon.

13   Revelations

The great chamber within Topham Hall is still set out to resemble a court room, and Sir Richard Rich presides behind the oak table, as both judge, jury, and senior prosecutor. It is an all too common occurrence in England for a trial to be judged by the very man who lays the charges, and something Thomas Cromwell's newest legislation seeks to eradicate.

For the nonce, Rich has the upper hand, and will both present, and judge the evidence, as he sees fit. Unable to have the accused brought to trial, he now decides to continue the trial in her absence. Sir Will Draper has shot his bolt. Gone now for almost ten days, he has stretched the king's patience, and the trial must go ahead without his report.

To the left of Rich, on low benches, Miriam sits quietly contemplating events, with Pru Beckshaw and the Reverend Farrall by her side. The troublesome apothecary, Marion Giles is nowhere to be seen, and the Attorney General breathes a sigh of relief. Her pointed questions about the new evidence given by Nell Gifford is a thorn in his side, and threatens his proposed relationship with the witness.

Once the trial is over, Nell swears

she will become his mistress, and allow him favours hitherto denied. He licks his lips, and contemplates the coming victory. That he will win is a foregone conclusion now, because, even if evidence is shown to be false, it is too late. Before taking his seat in court, Richard Rich has taken the boldest step of his career to date.

Summoning a trusted servant, he has penned a short message, which he has addressed to Sergeant at Arms Wilton, who is currently acting as a guard within the Tower of London. The note is unsigned, of course, but the wording is unambiguous. Upon receipt of the note, Wilton is to go to Elizabeth Farriby's chambers, and strangle her to death.

Sir Will Draper will be outraged, as usual, but quite unable to reverse the decision. If the girl is found guilty, as he intends, the sentence of burning can be carried out on her dead body, and if she be found innocent … an unlikely event… Rich can blame an overly enthusiastic underling. Toby Wilton will be reprimanded with one hand, and handed a fat purse of gold with the other.

"This trial must now proceed," Rich says. "The defence have been given ten full days to bring fresh evidence, and they have failed to do so. As the crown's witness has already given her statement, it remains only for me to consider the verdict."

"Not so, sir!" Miriam Draper leaps to her feet. "There is the evidence of the cat to consider. Mistress Gifford, I am told, has added to her original fatuous claims."

"Madam, you are showing contempt for this court," Rich replies, sharply.

"Just its judge, Sir Richard," Miriam snaps back. "Let us hear the woman's new charges. What have you to hide?" Rich realises that Miriam Draper is trying to show grounds for calling his verdict into disrepute, and sidesteps the trap. He will hammer in this final nail, and so damn them all.

"Call Mistress Nell Gifford … again," he shouts, and the clerk of the court disappears to fetch her. For long moments Miriam and Rich stare at one another, each showing their contempt for the other, then Nell comes in. She is wearing a new dress, bought by Rich, and looks the part of pure innocence. Rich waves her to the smaller table, which serves as a witness box.

"My Lord, you want more of me?" Nell says, and a secret little smile passes between the two.

"I do, Mistress Gifford," Rich says, pompously. "Pray speak of the cat. How did you come upon it so?"

"As I came into the room, Elizabeth had just leapt from her besom, and the cat

... the foul black creature, was writhing on the floor, changing its form."

"Outrageous!" Richard Rich says. "Such infamous goings on must be punished as the law demands. It is the verdict of…"

"One moment!" Miriam is on her feet again. "Has that been put down in the transcript of the trial?" the clerk, whose task it is to make a full log of everything that passes looks up angrily.

"Madam, I take down every word … even your own inappropriate utterances."

"Quite so, Master Channon," Rich says. "Your abilities are not in question here."

"Of course not," Miriam says, with a smile on her face. "I seek only to make sure everything is in order. In the absence of the accused, might I call a witness in her defence?"

"You have someone who can prove her case?" Rich asks, and he feels a little nervous until Miriam shakes her head.

"A character witness, sir," she says, and Rich nods his acceptance.

"If it mitigates the poor girl's actions … I shall allow it," he says magnanimously. "Bring this person in."

"Call Mistress Marion Giles," Miriam says, and the apothecary walks briskly to the witness table. Nell Gifford steps aside, and throws a glance at the judge. Rich shakes his head, as if to warn her to stay silent.

"What have you to say, Mistress Giles," Rich says. "Though I must caution you about wasting the court's time."

"I was asked to attend, with Sir Will Draper, the poultry farm of Jeb Buckley," Marion states, firmly. "It was obvious to see that the chickens had been poisoned with a distillation of *Belladonna*, mixed with another drug ... most likely to be *Monk's Head*. It was clear that this poison was poured into the feed bucket, whilst Jeb Buckley's attention was diverted."

"Then the witch, Elizabeth Farriby poisoned the birds," Rich states. "What other explanation can there be?"

"Jeb swears that it was Elizabeth who spoke with him the most, and that her friend, Nell Gifford, lingered nearby. I suspect that it was she who poisoned the..."

"Conjecture!" Richard Rich is red faced with anger. "Strike that from the record, Master Channon. I cannot allow such unsupported testimony, Mistress Giles. Have you anything else to say, before I pass sentence?"

"Yes, sir." Marion takes a paper note from her bodice, and unrolls it. "In company of Captain Beckshaw, Reverend

Farrall, I…"

"Your husband to be?" Rich says, and snorts with laughter.

" … visited the house of the deceased woman, Jane Townley." Marion consults the paper in her hand. "After a search, the captain found various items which are commonly used by those who fancy themselves to be witches. Amongst other things, there were concoctions of Monk's Head, Hemlock and Belladonna. It is clear that the woman was not a witch, and that she used these poisons for her own ends. In small amounts, they can effect cures, but in larger doses, they are all quite deadly."

"Then she was in league with Farriby," Rich says. "Witches often have creatures to do their bidding. It is easy for one in league with Satan to coerce the feeble minded into doing their foul business for them. The Devil seeks out the weak minded, and opens their hearts to his wickedness."

"She died from Belladonna poisoning herself," Marion Giles persists.

"Which means what exactly?" Rich shrugs. His mind is set, and he cannot, or will not, grasp the importance of this new testimony. "No, this is not admissible as evidence, madam. You merely delay the inevitable."

"One moment!" Miriam Draper is on her feet again. "I wish this on record, sir. It is our belief that Nell Gifford approached Jane Townley, and bought poison from her. She killed the chickens, then accused Elizabeth Farriby of witchcraft. Mistress Farriby was trying to help old Jane move to a better home, and Nell knew the old woman would guess what was happening, and speak out. So she poisoned the old woman too. Once reported to you, Elizabeth's fate would be sealed. I suggest, sir, that it is Nell Gifford who should be on trial here… not my friend."

"Suggest what you will," the Attorney General of England replies, stiffly. "You throw vile slanders at Mistress Gifford, without evidence. Nell Gifford has no motive, you silly woman. Why would the girl commit murder, and then accuse her best friend of witchcraft? What was her aim?"

"To get her burned, sir," Marion offers.

"Too fanciful," Rich replies. He is not a stupid man, and can see the one glaring hole in this ridiculous defence. "Why not simply poison Elizabeth Farriby? Why go to such elaborate lengths to have her condemned and burned at the stake? Can you answer me that, madam?"

"No, but I can." Will Draper has

slipped into the chamber, unannounced, and now takes centre stage. "I am just back from a visit to Devon, My Lord Attorney General. Ah, I see you flinch, Mistress Gifford. Have I touched upon a sore spot?"

"You are too late, Draper," Rich shouts. "The case is heard, and sentence will be passed. Elizabeth Farriby is a proven witch, and will die for her sins. It is the verdict of this court that…"

"The girl is innocent," Will says, coldly. "You asked my wife why Nell Gifford would entrap Elizabeth Farriby, rather than simply kill her. You also asked a most pertinent question … what was her motive? How could this girl possibly benefit from her friend's cruel death?"

"And you claim to have the answers?" Rich smirks, and waves a hand about the room. "Pray, do tell the court, Colonel Draper. We are waiting. I hope you are not wasting our time."

*

"See the horses are rubbed down and watered," Mush says as he slips from the saddle. It has been a long, hard ride, and he is tired. "Then send food into us. Richard and I will be in with Master Tom."

"The master is not here, Master Mush," the lad replies. "A summons came for him to attend an urgent council meeting."

"At Whitehall Palace, or Westminster?" Richard asks.

"No, sir," the lad tells them. "The messenger came very early, and spoke alone with the master. Then he came out, and demanded a horse for Master Tom. A right bloody minded sort of a fellow he was. A horse was brought, and off they went."

"What else can you tell me?" Mush asks.

"Nothing, sir… but the old blind man who spies for us was just coming in. I dare say he might know something."

"You mean Blind Dick?" Richard Cromwell's hopes rise, for the old beggar, even without his eyes, is one of their best agents in London. "Is he about?"

"Kitchens, sir," the lad replies. "Eating up his breakfast."

They go into Austin Friars, and make their way through to the kitchens at the rear of the house. A dozen men are at the table, eating, and they call out ribald comments to the newcomers.

"Blind Dick?" Mush calls, and a white haired old man, with milky eyes, raises a hand.

"Master Mush, I am here… for my sins," he says. "What is it I can do for you?"

"Master Cromwell rode out earlier,"

Richard puts in.

"Hello, Master Richard," Blind Dick replies. He can smell better than any man in the room, and has ears that can outdo those of a bat. "As I came into the courtyard, they were leaving. Master Tom was agitated, because of some hastily called meeting. He asked his companion why the council was called at Hampton Court, and why so urgently. The saucy fellow told him that he was but the messenger, and that his orders were from Tom Audley, the Lord Chancellor of England, and that there was talk of Spanish ships off the isle of Wight."

"Dear God... then it's war?" Richard asks, and Mush groans at all that he hears. In his heart he knows that no Spaniard would dare enter English waters, and expect to live long.

"I doubt it," Blind Dick says, "for his voice was not right. I think he was speaking an untruth. Besides, I know the rogue of old, and he will know more than he says."

"You recognised the messenger?" Mush asks.

"Of course. I could smell the stuff he rubs onto his head, and I never forget a voice. The last time I heard him was when the Duke of Norfolk came for supper. He stayed with the horses, whilst his master dined, and tried to bribe a couple of the stable lads. They told him to bugger off. I tell you, gentlemen … that Rupert Donne is a bad sort, and no messing!"

"Rupert Donne?" Mush sees it all now. Donne has stripped Cromwell of his best men, and lured him away. "Then he is about to try and ruin Master Tom. They are for Hampton Court Palace then, Dick?"

"Yes. From his tone, that bit was true enough," Blind Dick says. "I told your boys here about it, and they are for following the master, just in case."

"When did they leave?"

"About a half hour since," one of Cromwell's brighter young men offers.

"And yet you sit here on your arses, stuffing your stupid faces?" Richard is in a rage, and sweeps the table clear. "To horse, you useless bastards, and pray to God we are not too late, lest I skin you all alive!"

*

"The two questions are intertwined," Will Draper says. "Nell Gifford needed Elizabeth dead, but not under ordinary circumstances. She wanted her friend killed by the force of the law."

"Why would she?" Rich scoffs, but he is worried what Will Draper has up his sleeve.

"To distance her from the deed, and to make sure suspicion never fell on those whom she serves," Will says. "I knew Elizabeth to be innocent, and could not see any reason to speak against her, as Nell did. Then a friend, Rafe Sadler, mentioned how briefly the girl had lived here. He wondered where she first hailed from, and that set me thinking."

"Does it matter where a witness is born?" Rich says. "This does not alter my decision, Colonel Draper."

"I recalled her say something about coming from a place in Devon," Will presses on. "Then I remembered what Rafe said about the inheritance. The details were being handled by a reliable man who hailed from Exeter. Sir Josh Benson employed this lawyer, Edwin Carmody, to handle his estate. So, I had two points of reference leading me to Devon. What if…"

"What if the moon is cheese," Richard Rich sneers, but nobody laughs.

"What if Nell Gifford was known to Carmody?" Will says, and the girl begins to pale. "What if she knows him, and knows about the will? It left everything, bar a few small bequests, to his illegitimate daughter, Elizabeth."

"Bastards cannot inherit." Rich knows his law, and sees a flaw in Will's reasoning. "She should never have come into it."

"If the bastard is named, and there

are no better claims, she is entitled," Will says. "Now we come to the interesting part of our tale. Edwin Carmody is a pillar of the Exeter community, and is even held in high regard by the king's council, who he helped last year. He is a fine fellow, who endows alms houses, and pays for church roofs."

"This fellow seems like a grand sort… a philanthropic man, intent on bettering the world for his fellow man," Rich says. "Where are you going with this … this diatribe, Draper?"

"Why, to the truth, Sir Richard," Will says. Then he explains how he visited the lawyer, and found him to be honest in most ways, save when Nell Gifford was mentioned.

"I told him that Nell Gifford was taken prisoner, suspected of trying to poison one person, and accusing another falsely." Will stares at the girl then. "From his look, I knew two things. Firstly, he knew the name Gifford, and secondly … he was shocked that Elizabeth Farriby was not in chains, accused of witchcraft."

"But she was," Rich says, somewhat confused. "Why say otherwise?"

"I lied," says Will Draper. "After meeting him, I sent my companion, Kel Kelton, to Barnstaple, whilst I investigated Nell Gifford's past."

"I see." Richard Rich can sense some hard evidence is about to come out, and he decides to remain silent until all is known. It is too late, of course, as Toby Wilton will have the order in his hands by now, and will silence the girl.

'Even if she is innocent, I shall blacken everyone's character to the king', he thinks. Draper, he knows from Norfolk, is already under some suspicion. "Do go on, sir. I am a fair minded man, as you know, and I am willing to listen to your evidence with an open mind."

"Of course, Sir Richard," Will says, with a wry smile. "I expect nothing less than probity from you, and know you will accept my offering openly."

"Your servant," Rich mutters. Apart from being a close ally to the Duke of Norfolk, he also sends generous gifts of money to his man, Rupert Donne. Because of this, he has just found out that there is a plot afoot to damage Thomas Cromwell, though he has no firm details. He has the choice of keeping quiet, or letting Thomas Cromwell's camp know. In the former case, Cromwell might well triumph again, and frown on him, but in the latter event, if Cromwell survives, he will owe Richard Rich a huge favour. "What has Barnstaple to do with this business?"

"Most of the town, and the surrounding countryside is… or was… owned by Sir Josh Benson," Will continues. "It is where the lawyer, Edwin Carmody, was born, and where he squandered away his misspent youth. Kel Kelton found out that Carmody was a rare young man, in that he did not desert the young woman he swived. A child was born, in secret, and the woman's good name was thus saved. She later married someone of her own high station, and had two more children. Both died in infancy, but her hidden son thrived under the watchful eye of his father."

"I see." Rich does not, of course, see, but does not wish to seem out of step. In the corner, Nell Gifford is white with fear.

"The lady in question was Amelia Benson, sister of Sir Josh," Will Draper tells a hushed chamber. "The boy was born just a few weeks after Sir Josh Benson's own mistress had given birth to a daughter … known to us here as Elizabeth Farriby."

"Then he was also a bastard… and one with less rights than the elder one?" Rich chances.

"Just so," Will replies. "Though it did not really matter, as the Benson family had many legitimate branches. Montagu, the younger brother, and his two sons stood in line. For years, Carmody worked as Benson's lawyer, and helped him become a very rich man indeed. Now and then, he would throw a scrap to his secret son, Lucas. He helped him gain positions on charitable boards, which brought in small salaries, and saw he was well educated."

"A good father, in fact," Rich says. "How comes he to be so embroiled in this present case?"

"I suspect it was just idle talk… a man passing the time of day with his hidden son," Will continues. "He mentions the child's birthright to him, and it festers in the boy's mind. Lucas sees that, but for a wicked twist of fate, he might inherit a vast fortune. The years pass, and Lucas grows into manhood. Then Montagu dies in what everyone thinks is a hunting accident. His son, Walter, is killed by a stray crossbow bolt, whilst hunting, a year or two later. Then Daniel is waylaid in Cornwall and murdered… seemingly for his purse."

"Good God, such infamy!" Sir Richard is shocked, and can see the prospect of bedding Nell Gifford dwindling away.

"The purse had but two pounds and some coppers in it… a fact *known* to Edwin Carmody. Thus I realised that it was Carmody who had intimate knowledge of the murder, or he had pressed his son into the wicked crime. With all three men dead, the way was now clear to have his son inherit.

Amelia, most obligingly, died of the sweating sickness, and her old husband went with her to the grave. Both children had already died in infancy."

"An unlucky family history," Rich offers.

"Not simple bad luck, sir." Will Draper gestures to the closed doors. "My man, Kel Kelton, stands without, and has both Edwin Carmody and his son, Lucas, in chains. Once the Benson clan were all dead, the lawyer would reveal the existence of Lucas, and furnish proof that his mother was a Benson. The father was to remain anonymous, of course, lest suspicion was aroused… but Lucas would assume the name Benson, and inherit almost a half million pounds in land and property."

"But what of Elizabeth?" Rich asks. As the older of the two, and as she was specifically named in the will, she could argue a case for herself, and most likely win it. It makes no sense, sir!"

"Edwin Carmody had no idea she existed, until after the murder of the Benson family. It was only when old Sir Josh realised he was alone in the world that he told Carmody of his illegitimate daughter. It was whilst he was settling houses on his many mistresses, and Carmody must have been shocked, even horrified at the revelation. So many deaths, and all for naught.

He met with Lucas, and told him what had come about. The young man was all for riding to Topham Hall, and killing Elizabeth, but his father stopped him."

"I see." Rich is stuck in a rut, and can only hope the agony is over soon. "Then what?"

"If Elizabeth died, suspicion would fall on whoever stepped up to claim the inheritance. Also, should she die, all sorts of cousins and other relatives might turn up, and make a claim. It was a mess, until Carmody came up with an answer. Nell Gifford."

"Nell Gifford?" Rich wilts a little more.

"Nell is the lover of Lucas." Will watches Sir Richard Rich's face drop. "She agreed to visit the village and, over some months, befriend Elizabeth. Once they were close, Nell was to accuse her of witchcraft. Carmody knew how quickly witches were found, and burned… often without any trial, or even an investigation. With her executed, the estate is ownerless. No relative of Elizabeth would be considered, because she was a witch, and might have gained the inheritance through the black arts."

"Of course. What a devious plot," Rich says. "If you have the proof."

"I have, sir. Both Carmody and his son have made statements. Under the weight of evidence, they shall throw themselves on the mercy of the court. As for Nell … she has proved herself to be a black hearted wench. Not only did she poison the chickens, but she also killed an old woman to keep her silent, and accused Elizabeth of witchery."

"I am innocent!" This cry, from Nell Gifford makes them all turn to her. "They tricked me into it, My Lord. Save me, and all will be as you wished."

"Enough!" Will silences the crying girl. "You have done murder, girl, and tried to pervert the course of justice. Had Sir Richard Rich found Elizabeth guilty, he would have condemned an innocent girl to a horrible death. You lied about her. When out, you poured some of the belladonna into the feed, and used the rest to silence poor Jane Townley."

"It was she!" Nell has one last try. "She was a witch, and used her magic on us all."

"She was a lonely old woman, who used simple country things to make remedies for her fellow villagers. She cured toothaches, and eased stomach cramps. She sold you the potion, thinking it for some ailment, but when she heard about the chickens, I think she confronted you. It was then you poured the rest of the poison into her drink. Once done, you left, and waited for her to sip the watered down beer we found in her house. One swallow was enough to kill her. Jane Townley died in agony, to save you from being exposed."

"And you have sworn statements?" Rich is dubious, because his own men often have to resort to torture. "How so, without putting them on the rack?"

"We put them in separate rooms, and told each one that the other was swearing against them. Once the son thought his father was accusing him, he told his tale. The father, upon hearing how his bastard son was dunning him, told another version. Each man is condemned by their own words, without the need to break their bones, Sir Richard."

"Then this case is …" Rich cannot think straight. Then a sudden thought comes to him. His presumption of the guilty verdict has caused him to send word to Wilton. The girl is already dead, along with her would be lover. Now he must explain to Draper, and avoid an unpleasant scene.

"Over." Will Draper signals for one of the guards to take Nell Gifford into custody. "Elizabeth Farriby is innocent, and the real culprits await your pleasure, Sir Richard."

"They shall both hang," Rich promises.

"Nell Gifford is as guilty," Miriam says.

"She will suffer the same fate she wished on Mistress Farriby," Rich promises. "Mistakes have been made, but we must get over them, and allow these unpleasant things to be forgotten."

"Then you will release Elizabeth at once?" Miriam asks.

"Ah … yes… of course." Rich is in agony, and wants only to escape the confines of the courtroom, but a big oaf of a soldier stands in his way. He throws out a hand, as if to brush the man aside, then realises who it is. "Wilton?"

"At your service, sir," Toby Wilton says.

"You are meant to be at the Tower," Rich is shaking with fear, and can only resort to the stutter he has fought to master for years. "W-what the d-devil are you d-doing here, man?"

"Orders, sir," Wilton replies. "From Colonel Draper."

"What orders? You are m-my man, sir!"

"Bless you, but no, sir," Wilton replies. "I was made up to sergeant in Ireland, by the colonel, when he was still only a wet behind the ears captain in charge of buying horses. When I joined your service, it was at his request. He thought you might turn out to be a rogue. And so it was, sir. I mean to say, offering me forty pounds to kill him… and then have me keep an eye on Mistress Elizabeth. I received your order, right enough, but I was already here." He steps to one side, and Elizabeth Farriby is revealed. She curtseys to Rich.

"Good day, Sir Richard," she says. "How long do you need to get off my property?"

"Mistress … I am so pleased to see you," Rich says, honestly. He has been fooled by the King's Examiner again, but in this case, it has saved him from embarrassment, or even physical harm from Will Draper. "May I return this lovely house, and lands to you, with my most humble apologies for the inconvenience. I hope the Tower was not too uncomfortable?"

"Not at all," Elizabeth says. "In fact, it has given me a most interesting dilemma."

"How so, madam?"

"I appear to have two suitors," Elizabeth tells the cowed Attorney General of England. "Master Robin Crabtree is poetic, and rather pretty, but Toby Wilton is older, and more … physical. I am now able to consider both proposals at my leisure. Good day to you, sir, and have a safe journey back to London."

Rich bows, and catches Will Draper's sleeve as he passes in the outer corridor. The big King's Examiner frowns down at him, and pulls his arm free.

"A moment of your time, Will?" Rich asks. "I assure you, it will be a moment well spent."

"You almost execute an innocent friend of mine, then send orders for her murder," Will Draper says. "This best be good, or I might just kill you, and then pull out your stinking innards with my knife."

"I was dining with the Duke of Norfolk last week," Rich says. "He speaks of nothing else but bringing down your old master."

"What of it?" Will sneers. "Norfolk is an old fool, and Tom Cromwell is big enough to look after himself. This is not news to me."

"Norfolk spoke of a special fellow in his employ," Rich continues. "A man who can bring your friend Cromwell down onto his knees. The duke was not in the mood to give me details, but Rupert Donne was open to a hefty bribe. It seems that something will happen today… at Hampton Court. The king has called a special meeting of the council, and that always bodes ill for someone. I have begged off, because of this trial… but have no wish to see Thomas Cromwell caught out."

"You hate us all," Will replies.

"No, I simply look to my own self, Draper. I just wish to retain my power, and that means I must sit on the fence between the two. If Cromwell comes out of this day still at the helm, remind him that I warned you."

"When is this damned meeting?" Will Draper demands.

"Now," Rich confesses. "I could not warn you sooner… not whilst the trial was going on."

"You spineless coward," Will sneers. "If I ride at once, I can be at Hampton Court within a half hour. You best pray I am in time to warn Cromwell!"

Sir Richard Rich watches Will Draper run for his horse, and smiles to himself. He might have lost this latest little scuffle, but he is confident of winning the next… and that next could well be the struggle for control of England.

14 The Trap

Rupert Donne is close to the success he has craved, ever since being a small child and scavenging along the Thames river bank. Growing up in poverty has twisted his soul, and his avowed intent is to live out his life in splendour. He has watched the Cromwells and Norfolks of this world prosper, seemingly without effort, and aims to do the same, at whatever the cost.

At the age of eleven he discovered how to steal from drunks coming from the whore houses in Cheam, and at twelve he had killed his first man, who had awakened and caught him at his work. The knife had slid home, easily, and Donne's future life of crime was settled on. From murder, it was an easy step to informing, then to finding information, even when it did not exist. In his twenties, he had come to the attention of one of Norfolk's stewards, and a couple of years later, he was known to the duke himself.

Now, he was embroiled in the greatest plot ever to be made, and would come out of it as a knight of the realm… and right hand man to the most powerful man in England, after the king. Once set on the road to destroying Cromwell, no other crime would ever seem beyond his reach.

One day, perhaps soon, Norfolk would ask him to do treason against the king, and he was more than ready. After all, one man is much like another, and they all must die one day.

For now, he is impatient to deliver his companion to the council meeting, and urges him on. For an older man, the stocky Privy Councillor sits a horse well, and he rides like a man used to long hours in the saddle. In truth, Thomas Cromwell's abilities are but the memories of his days spent as a boy soldier in the northern states of the Italian peninsula. In Genoa, he learned how to fist fight from the wild rogues around the harbour, and the Venetians taught him how to fence and throw a well balanced knife.

A single act of bravery, whilst fleeing from enemy cannon, was enough to put young Cromwell on the way to success. A life saved in the desperation of flight placed him in the company of a wounded officer called Gritti, who would become Doge of Venice, and lay the foundation of Cromwell's later life. Chances, he muses, must be taken, and lessons are there to be learned.

Old habits die hard, and good old habits can keep a man alive in a tight situation. That, Cromwell knows, is why he still carries a concealed dagger up his loose fitting sleeve. The blade he now carries is a jewelled creation, said to be the dagger used by Saint Longinus to wound Our Lord. It is considered to be a valuable relic, but it is designed to kill, swiftly, and with surprise. He thinks the man with him is a Norfolk creature, and he wishes to take no chances.

What is it that is so urgent, Thomas Cromwell thinks to himself. This garbled story about Spanish fighting ships in the Solent does not ring true, and the man who brings such disturbing news is a familiar of the Duke . He leans back in his saddle, and the horse slows down from the gallop. Cromwell watches the messenger gain some distance, before he realises, and then he also slows down.

"Sir, we really must not tarry on the road," Rupert Donne calls back to his unknowing quarry. Tom Cromwell affects a harsh wheezing voice, and pats his horses sweaty neck. They are still weaving through the narrow streets of the city, and making their way westwards.

"My poor old horse is tiring, young man, and I am not as fit as I once was, Master … I did not get your name, sir…"

"Donne, sir," the man says.

"And whose man are you, Master Donne?" Cromwell asks of him. Everyone, save the king, belongs to someone, and the master and servant relationship is the very foundation of the modern day Tudor society.

"I am merely a steward on the Arundel estates, My Lord Essex," Donne says.

"Oh, do not call me by that infernal name," Thomas Cromwell tells him. "I so dislike the idea of having such a noble sounding title. It gets between me and those who serve me. Though such young men are in short supply today."

"Called away on business, perhaps?" Donne says, casually, and Cromwell sees how things lie. Mush and his nephew are drawn off on some silly errand, Rafe Sadler is nowhere to be seen, and Will Draper, one of the rocks upon which he has built the edifice of Austin Friars, is away defending some poor innocent girl accused of witchcraft.

"Never mind," Thomas Cromwell says. "Even when I am without my own sworn men, I am completely safe from harm."

"Sir, I mean you no hurt," Donne tells him, which is, in a strange way, the truth of things. "I am assigned only to fetch you to a council meeting. But my curiosity is aroused, My Lord Cromwell, and I wonder how can you claim to be safe from attack?"

"I have an unseen shadow," Thomas

Cromwell says. "My friend … one of my best friends… thinks he is being clever. For some time now, he has had me closely followed by one of his best agents. This man owes me his life, and would kill anyone who dared harm me."

"Really?" Rupert Donne looks back down the crowded road, and spends long moments watching the milling mob. There is no sign of anyone following, and he smiles to himself. "Then the fellow is a master of disguise. You are lucky to be so well guarded, my dear sir. Now, shall we ride on?"

The two men kick their mounts into action, and set off at a steady trot. They will reach Hampton Court sometime in the mid morning, Cromwell thinks, in plenty of time for the very special Privy Council meeting called by an exultant Duke of Norfolk.

Behind them, a lone figure emerges from a shadowed side street, and mounts up again. He is perhaps just too far away to save Tom Cromwell's life, but close enough to then cut the throat of any would be assassin.

*

"What is it?" Eustace Chapuys looks up from the long report he is compiling for the emperor, and waits for little Piper to speak up. The child, he suspects, is one of Cromwell's minions, but he pretends to be the ambassadors servant, and draws two small wages for his double dealing.

"Message from that Old Blackheart, Your Lordship," Piper announces. He clicks his heels and bows, just like the gentlemen of the court he so wants to join, one day. Chapuys sighs, and puts down his goose quill. The lad is insufferable, but has a way about him that endears him to you. The ambassador can do nothing but smile, and chide him, but gently.

"Do not call Señor Gomez 'Old Blackheart'," he says to the boy. "Señor Alonso is a man of honour, and they are few and far between these days. If he has a reputation for doing evil, then it is a false one. Nor must you call me 'Lord' or any such title. I am an ambassador, and bear no other appellation."

"As you wish, *Master* Chapuys," Piper replies, pertly. "Shall I say what the *most honourable* Alonso Gomez says, or not?"

"Speak, boy, or I will have you flogged."

"Only a lord can order that," the lad jests. "Gomez was lingering around Austin Friars, like you told him… and Cromwell went off for a ride."

"Yes?" Eustace wonders at this news.

"As Master Cromwell is supposed to be at home for the entire day, Gomez thought it odd that he should go off, with but one companion. He sends me to tell you he is following, in case there is mischief afoot."

"I see. This man with Cromwell… is he known?"

"Not to me, sir," Piper tells his master, "but Blind Dick knows him to be a cursed Norfolk man. Mush and Richard are back, and rousing all the Austin Friars lads to arms. They are riding off to Hampton Court Palace, even as we speak."

"Then there is something going on," Eustace Chapuys decides. "Have the stable saddle my horse. I must ride to Hampton Court myself, pretending to some mis-remembered meeting there, and try to sniff out what is about to happen."

"Right away, sir. Two Horses." It is a statement of fact, rather than a question. Alec Piper is a scrap of a boy, who thinks he might be twelve or thirteen years of age, but has only the recollections of an old woman at the foundling home Thomas Cromwell has endowed. He is a child of the gutters, but he can ride a horse well enough, and has been taught how to use a Spanish throwing knife by Mush Draper. If Ambassador Chapuys is riding into trouble, on behalf of Cromwell, then he must ride with him.

*

Miriam Draper raises her glass and offers a toast to Elizabeth Farriby. Pru Beckshaw and Marion Giles follow suit, and then they drink one another's good health. The charge of witchcraft has been, grudgingly, dismissed by Sir Richard Rich, who has gathered up his retinue, and set off for Hampton Court Palace.

"It is his intention to arrive much later in the day," Pru says, with a far away look in her eyes. "He seeks to avoid a great fall, yet the darkness will sweep over us all."

"Pru… what is it?" Miriam asks. The younger woman shakes her head.

"Did I speak?" she asks.

"Yes, of darkness," Marion Giles tells her. "Let us hope that it is Rich who falls into the dark."

"Richard Rich shall die in his own bed." Pru announces this as a fact. "He is a villain now, and for all time. His punishment shall be the burden of guilt he must carry to his grave."

"You must have shame to know guilt," Elizabeth puts in, "and he has none. Still, I am recovered, and my wealth restored to me. Indeed, it seems I am to be richer by the ten fold. I must thank God, and your remarkable husband for that, my dearest Miriam."

"Will did his duty," Miriam replies. "Had he found against you, your end would be reached. I thank God you are innocent, my dear, but please do me one favour."

"Name it."

"Stop speaking to your cat in such a *familiar* way," Miriam says, and they all laugh at the clever play on words. "I fear that Lucifer must become 'Tabs' or 'Fluff', if only to avoid future suspicion!"

"Mistress… forgive me but…" It is the old servant, Michael, and his visage is drawn and angry. His hands are trembling, and he wrings them, as if wishing to choke the life from someone.

"What is it, Michael?" Elizabeth sees the old servant's clear distress, and wonders what can be causing it.

"The Attorney General has left you a dreadful gift in the far meadow," Michael replies. "He has chosen the finest oak on the boundary, and hanged two men from it. It is Edwin Carmody, and his son. The guard says they are to swing there for a week, to deter others from a life of crime."

"He has hanged them both, without trial?" Miriam asks. The very act flies in the face of English law, and harks back to the bad old days when the barons could punish at will, without recourse to a judge and jury.

Thomas Cromwell will be enraged, not at the punishment, but at its arbitrary nature. Sir Richard Rich has stepped outside the very law he is meant to uphold.

"They both confessed," Michael says. "Lord Rich says that was enough to dispense with the trial."

"What of the girl, Nell?" asks Marion Giles. She knows Rich had designs on the girl, and cannot help but think he will use his power to make her surrender to his lust.

"Dead." The single word hangs heavily in the chamber. "The soldier told me she took poison … the same she used to kill Jane Townley. It was that, rather than be burnt alive, I suppose. It seems she and Lucas were lovers, and the sight of him kicking on a rope was too much for her poor mind. The fellow says that Rich stood by, white faced with horror, and watched her die in agony."

"Wait for the guard to leave, then cut them down, and have them… all three… buried decently," Elizabeth Farriby tells the old man. "I cannot have bodies picked over by the carrion birds on my land, and besides, I thought Nell Gifford to be a friend of mine. Take dear Toby Wilton with you. If the soldier is still there, he will chase him away for us."

"Dear Toby?" Marion asks with a

raised eyebrow.

"He is so sweet," Elizabeth says. "Then again, so is Robin Crabtree. I fear the final choice between the two is going to be far too much for me."

"Make sure neither one of them can lay hands on your wealth," Miriam advises. "Let me open an account with my Antwerp bankers for you. Then you shall be safe to marry whomsoever you might settle on."

"I thank you, my dear friend," Elizabeth replies. "Your advice is always welcome."

"Unless it is to invest in the New Found Land," Miriam tells her, ruefully. "That escapade has cost me a pretty penny."

"And many lives lost," Pru reminds her. "Though all is not doom and gloom, for there is one who will *come from the darkness, and bring light*."

"Thank you, Prudence," Miriam says, sourly. "Would that your famous predictions were easier to understand!"

*

"We should dismount here, sir," Rupert Donne says, "and walk the rest of the way. The streets are narrowing." He slides from his horse, and takes Cromwell's mount by the bridle.

"What trickery is this?" Tom Cromwell asks. "We are for Hampton

Court, and that lies well beyond the river, sir."

"My apologies for the deceit. We are due in Westminster Palace, my Lord Essex," Rupert Donne replies, with a smirk. "That tale about Hampton Court Palace was but a way of stopping unwanted followers from tagging along on our tails."

"Then there is no meeting?" Cromwell touches the jewelled hilt of the concealed dagger, and contemplates thrusting it up into the fellow's ribs, but needs to know what is afoot first.

"There is, sir," Rupert Donne tells him. "Though it is at Westminster Palace, rather than Hampton Court. It is a secret council, ordered by the king himself, and outsiders are not welcome. Your people were not invited, and I was told to keep them at arms length. My orders are quite concise, and from the highest authority."

"Then let us turn left at the next corner, and come upon the palace from the main entrance," Cromwell says. "It will be quicker for us." In fact, this entrance is guarded by Master Chaney, a captain of the king's archers, who is also in the employ of Austin Friars. A crook of the finger will bring him running, along with a half dozen armed men, and his presence will provide security enough. Once in the presence of the king and his council, no man will dare raise a hand against Cromwell.

"As you command, Lord Essex," Donne replies in an off handed way. "It is all the same to me. I am to deliver you safely, and that is my duty done. I am not welcome in such exalted circles."

"You connive with Norfolk well enough," Cromwell says.

"As Draper does with you, sir," Donne replies, quite tartly. "I fear it is the lot of we lesser men. Were I of independent means … I might well consider a change of master."

"Indeed?" Thomas Cromwell dislikes the fellow, but that is no bar, for most of his best agents are devious, underhanded, and quite deadly. "Then perhaps we should talk, one day?"

"At your service, My Lord Essex," Donne replies. If today does not go well, he sees that he might easily change sides, and prosper at Norfolk's expense.

*

The council chamber within Hampton Court is smaller than Whitehall's, and less ornately decorated than Westminster Palace's great Star Chamber, but it is furnished with a long oak table, and enough chairs to accommodate every Privy Council member. Today, it is populated by no more than a half dozen men, and each of them sits, bemused by their precipitate summons.

The door opens, and another couple of council members straggle in, cursing the unexpected call to meet.

Sir Rafe Sadler, who has recently been raised in rank, is the council's newest, and most youthful member, and he cannot think why a meeting has been called at such very short notice. With him, rolling dice in his cupped hand, is Sir Tom Wyatt. The poet is a member of the council because Henry likes him for now, and seeks to bring some gaiety to otherwise drab meetings. On this morning, he sighs, and wishes the servants would hurry along with the usual refreshments. He has missed his Austin Friars breakfast for this meeting, and is not best pleased.

"Poor Suffolk looks quite exhausted," he whispers to Rafe, who smiles and nods in understanding.

"He has a vibrant new mistress," Sadler informs his poetically inclined friend. "She is not yet twenty years of age, and she wears poor Charles out with her constant amorous demands."

"I should offer to help him out," Wyatt sniggers. In truth, he has already done so, without Suffolk's knowledge, and he can agree that young Lady Eunice Soames is definitely '*vibrant*' between the bedsheets. "Then again, the archbishop is not looking too happy either. The damp

Canterbury air must disagree with him."

"Archbishop Cranmer must have ridden through the night to get here," Rafe replies. He is perplexed by the inconvenience of it all, especially to the ageing archbishop. "I was at Whitehall when I received the order, and few here were close by. Cumberland and Derby were hunting in Kent, and My Lord Worcester was visiting his youngest sister in Hertford. As for the others..." The king's minister pauses, and glances about the chamber. His face clouds over, and he puts a hand to the knife hanging at his side. "Oh, Sweet Christ on the Cross!"

"What is it?" Wyatt sees the movement, and checks that his own blade is loose in its bejewelled scabbard. It is the only weapon allowed them in chambers, and he wishes now for a brace of primed pistols, or a sharp sword. "What do you perceive that I do not?"

"Look about you, my friend." Rafe nods towards the far end of the table. "John De Vere, the Earl of Oxford, is here. He is a good friend of Thomas Cromwell. As are we both... and then there is the Duke of Suffolk. Old Cranmer bears my master no malice, and the others are all in Cromwell's debt, one way or another."

"So?" The poet sees no harm in the chamber being full of friends. It makes a welcome change from having to watch his back.

"Where is Norfolk?"

"The old fool always comes in last," Wyatt says. "He fancies that it makes him seem better than the rest of us."

"Then where are the two Seymour brothers?" asks Rafe. "Or that little shit Harry Howard? The Earl of Surrey is Norfolk's own dog, and so never far from his father's side."

"By God, yes!" Tom Wyatt scours the room with his eyes, and starts to colour up in anger. "The Lord Chancellor is absent too, as is Bishop Gardiner, and that crawling bastard Rich. What is going on?"

"This is no council meeting, Tom," Rafe says. "It is a gathering of all Tom Cromwell's closest friends on the council. Can he mean it to be thus? Has Cromwell brought us here, in conclave, and excluded his enemies?" In answer, the chamber door is thrown open, and Will Draper enters, with Mush and Richard Cromwell at his heels. He looks about him, and comes to the same conclusion that has so worried Rafe Sadler.

"Treachery!" Will cries, and the chamber falls silent. "We are lured here, gentlemen… and not by the king. This is Norfolk's doing. I was told Cromwell was here."

"His friends are," Tom Wyatt says. He stands, and beckons to Charles Brandon. Suffolk comes to them, with a confused look on his face. "Charles, where is the king?"

"Arundel, with his new falcon," Suffolk replies. "He bade me come here today, and chair this council meeting. I do not understand why so many are absent. Surely, Norfolk and the rest must know of the meeting?"

"What was the purpose of the meeting?" Rafe asks.

"Why, to discuss the latest news from the New Found Land, and see how we can recover from the financial blow."

"There is no financial blow to recover from," Will Draper says. "The Draper Company stand surety, and will recompense His Majesty, and add the profit he thought to make. There is nothing to talk about, Charles."

"Oh, he did not … I thought him my friend… why would he then tell me this … untruth?"

"We have been duped," Will explains to those council members present. "Mush and Richard were drawn away from Cromwell, then sent here. I was told to come here, rather than Westminster. I wager that Norfolk and his followers are there now, holding a meeting in our absence."

"What about my uncle?" Richard asks.

"He is not here, yet he left Austin Friars before you," Will Draper says. "I can only think he is taken to Westminster … a prisoner of our enemies, or assassinated. Norfolk is finally making his move."

"How so?" Mush is outraged at the idea. "There is nothing Master Tom can be charged with. He is the king's man, and as loyal as can be."

"Norfolk must feel confident," Suffolk puts in.

"He is with the king a lot, these last weeks," Tom Cranmer, Archbishop of Canterbury chimes in. "Henry wants rid of poor Anne, and thought Tom Cromwell would have her sent back to Cleves. I spoke with Cromwell, and he is very much set against an annulment… as is my church. The Duke of Norfolk plays the part of Satan in the Wilderness, and whispers in the king's ear."

"Then you think Norfolk is trying to gain control of the council?" Will asks. He can see no other explanation, and fears Cromwell's faction have been wrong footed.

"Why not?" Cranmer replies. "If he puts forward a resolution, demanding the king is divorced, and it is voted through by his rump council… you see … Henry will back him, and Cromwell must agree, or lose his rank."

"What can we do?" Suffolk asks. "Can we not declare this spurious council meeting to be illegal?"

"It needs only a simple majority of those present," Cranmer tells him. "With Norfolk, Surrey, and the two Seymour brothers pushing the motion, they will gain that, and carry the day."

"Then let us ride to London, and put an end to this business at once," Richard insists. "I have thirty armed men with me. We can arrest Norfolk, and let my uncle protest to the king. Once Henry sees that the duke means to steal control of England, he will come to his senses, and have the old rogue arrested."

"That will not do," Suffolk says. "The great lords take it in turns to garrison the city and the Tower. This month, it is Norfolk's task, and he has a thousand soldiers all about the place. I can raise twice that number within the day, but that means we must storm London, and risk a civil war."

"Would you go so far?" Will asks.

"Without Henry's written permission?" Suffolk shakes his head. "I will not be the man who starts the next civil war. If Henry bids me… I would fight my way into the city, and hang Norfolk by his heels, but he is keeping out of sight. Arundel is Norfolk's castle."

"Then the king is stepping aside, and waits to see who will come out on top," Will concludes. "Mush, stand the men down, but send agents into the city. We must find out what is going on, and where Master Cromwell is."

*

Alonso Gomez sees Thomas Cromwell dismount, and does the same. The man with him seems to offer no threat, and they set off down a side street. The Spaniard guesses where they are heading, and runs to get ahead of them. It is market day in Westminster, and the close set streets are tightly packed with beggars, jades, vagabonds, knife grinders, hooky men, sweeps, hawkers, stall holders, and customers, eager to buy in the week's provisions.

Gomez slips through the throng, and is able to get within a dozen feet of Thomas Cromwell without being noticed. He watches as the two men approach the main entrance of the palace. Thomas Cromwell pauses at the door, and the man with him puts a hand to his back, as if about to urge him inside. The king's minister raises a hand in greeting, and a big, rough looking fellow, clad in uniform red, comes over to him.

"Good day Chaney," Tom

Cromwell calls. "It seems I am to attend a council meeting today. What do you know of it?" Alonso Gomez watches as the big soldier salutes Cromwell, and waves for him to step inside.

"My Lord Norfolk, and some of the rest of them, are already within, Master Cromwell," the captain of the king's archers informs him. "Though His Majesty has yet to arrive."

"Most odd," Cromwell says. "Master Donne, your services are no longer required. Captain Chaney will escort me to the chamber. Captain… if you please?"

"My honour, My Lord Essex!" Captain Chaney bows, and throws Rupert Donne a look of contempt. "Be off now, fellow. You are not permitted within the palace without a signed warrant."

"I was told to …" Rupert Donne attempts to argue, but the big man steps between Thomas Cromwell and himself, and glowers at him, fiercely. Norfolk's man sizes him up, and considers the chances of making him give way. "My master will vouch for me."

"Is he here?" the captain of the guard asks.

"He is inside," Donne insists. "You have but to ask him."

"Not here though?" the big soldier says, and grins.

"No, not here... but I insist..."

"Insist, do you? Bugger off, you little turd," the captain of the guard growls at him. "Before I kick your arse into the river." Then both he, and a grinning Cromwell, step inside. Alonso Gomez waits for a moment, until Rupert Donne walks away, then turns about, ready to return to his own master. He has no idea that Eustace Chapuys is already galloping to Hampton Court, and that he has just allowed Thomas Cromwell to walk into the spider's web.

15 The Fall

"Slimy bastard," Captain Chaney mutters as he, and some of his men, escort Thomas Cromwell to the council chamber.

"You know him?" Cromwell asks.

"I do, sir," the captain replies. "He is the Duke of Norfolk' special man. They say he can torture a confession from Jesus Christ hisself... pardon the blasphemy, sir... and that he is the bastard child of Satan's whore."

"Yet he comes as a messenger?" Thomas Cromwell ponders this latest twist, and wonders why there is so much secrecy about this particular meeting. The tale about Spanish ships raiding is too far fetched to be true. It would take a veritable host of war ships, and many thousands of troops to breach the English defences. Besides, with the new marriage, the emperor has no reason to go to war with his new ally.

"Here we are, sir," the big captain says. "I shall stand guard, with these fellows. Should things not go well, we will be on hand."

"What do you know, Chaney?" Cromwell is alarmed now, for it seems that everyone knows something he does not.

"Nothing, sir... save I am ordered

to escort councillors here, and stand guard," Captain Chaney says to him. "Though the duke seems to be in fine spirits, as does his son, that piece of worthless scum, Surrey."

"Then they mean to try and best me again" Thomas Cromwell says, softly. "Will they never learn?" He takes a deep breath, throws open the chamber doors, and strides in. He crosses the length of the chamber, and stands at the head of the broad table.

It is customary for Norfolk and his few followers to huddle at the base of the table, from where they can fire off complaints about all he suggests, but today, he sees that Norfolk is sitting to the right hand side, flanked by the two Seymour brothers, who look sheepishly at him. His son, the worthless Earl of Surrey is close by, grinning like an idiot who has found a farthing.

"Ned, Tom…My Lord Chancellor… Norfolk…" Cromwell nods to each in turn, and becomes aware that none of his closest colleagues are currently present. "Must we then wait for the others?"

"We have a quorum," Ned Seymour replies, coldly. Tom Audley shifts in his seat, and coughs, whilst Bishop Gardiner looks at his hands. They have both been hoodwinked into coming, and only now see that they have been used in a most dangerous way.

"Not one to my liking, Ned," Thomas Cromwell replies. "We must wait upon the rest coming, I think. They shall be here shortly, I presume?"

"I fear not." The Duke of Norfolk speaks for the first time, and gestures towards the chamber doors. It is only then that Thomas Cromwell sees he is at a disadvantage. Sir John Russell, whom has long been in his employ, steps across the door, and puts a hand to his sword.

"Weapons… in this, the Star Chamber, Norfolk?" Cromwell says. "Are you mad, to so defy convention?"

"A precaution… enacted for safety's sake, *Milord* Cromwell," the duke returns. "Now, I call this meeting of the council to order."

"That is for me to say, sir!" Cromwell snaps, and goes to take his seat at the head of the table. In the absence of the king, he is the senior man, and entitled to sit in that place. It is vital that he keeps order, even in the face of such odds against him. He must take his place, and use the force of his personality to halt whatever is afoot.

"Do not sit down there, Cromwell… it is no place for the likes of you," Norfolk sneers. "Traitors do not sit with gentlemen!"

Thomas Cromwell remains standing. He glares at each man in turn, and then at Sir John Russell who guards the inner door. Russell returns his gaze, evenly. It is this that most hurts him.

"Russell … you will go far," he says. "I see you have learned the art of betrayal all too soon." Russell remains stone faced. He has been drawn into this escapade at the last moment, and has not been told that his master was to be arrested. Norfolk believes a generous purse will buy any man, and Russell knows his presence will be seen as a wicked disloyalty. "What calumnies will you lay against me, Norfolk? I cannot think of one charge that will stick to me, and the king knows it to be so. If nothing else, he is a just monarch."

"Bribery, perjury, sedition, the subordination of witnesses, and treason," the Earl of Surrey chimes in with. He is a pale imitation of his father, Norfolk, and a drunkard and a libertine. His hatred of Will Draper, and Cromwell, is well known. Norfolk throws him a glance of complete contempt. Despite forbidding him to speak, the young fool has given Cromwell ammunition.

"I have bribed many," Tom Cromwell retorts. "The amounts are well documented … as are the names. I do recall My Lord Norfolk taking a sum for betraying Robert Aske a few years ago, and a certain clergyman in this council, who took money from the treasury to vote through a decree against the Roman church." The duke is stunned by his minor treachery being known, and Stephen Gardiner blushes with shame.

"You perjure yourself," Surrey throws back, his voice crackling with hatred.

"Like Harry Percy and your own father, when denying the Boleyn whore's infidelities, or Richard Rich reporting imagined conversations? Or, perhaps, when you, Tom Audley, spoke against Sir Thomas More?" Thomas Cromwell is in a passionate rage of his own now. "As for the subordination of witnesses… look to Richard Rich once more… who has not the gall to show his face here today."

"Enough, I say!" The Duke of Norfolk stands up and, rather melodramatically, stabs an accusing finger at his old enemy. "The king will swear out a Bill of Attainder against you, Cromwell."

Arrest and conviction, without need of a trial is, on the face of it, the perfect avenue for Norfolk to choose. It bars Thomas Cromwell from appearing in a court of law, and stops him from offering any defence to the false charges brought against him. The duke, however, has chosen his words most unwisely, and Cromwell pounces.

"*Will* swear?" Cromwell sees a chink of light, and leaps on it like a ravenous wolf upon a lamb. "Then he is not yet turned completely against me, Lord Norfolk, and you have made a false move."

"We know about Holbein," Norfolk says, coldly. "You are betrayed with your own words, sir."

"Then I am condemned already, and cannot argue against the charge of treason," Cromwell snaps. "Brought low, by a dog and his gutter born whelp!" This last is said against Norfolk and his loathsome son. The Earl of Surrey, like his father, believes himself to be of better blood, even than the king, and such a slur against him is enough to drive him to distraction.

Thomas Cromwell is standing, almost toe to toe with the Duke of Norfolk, with his back to Henry Howard. The hate filled earl sees his chance of swift revenge, and draws the dagger from his belt. He rushes forward, intent on driving the sharp blade up into his mortal enemy's back. Stephen Gardiner, the utterly ashamed Bishop of Winchester, sees the movement and, in memory of the friendship he once had with Tom Cromwell, thrusts out a foot.

Henry Howard, Earl of Surrey, trips over the extended leg, and crashes, heavily, to the floor. The unsheathed knife clatters away across the flagstones, and the Privy

Chamber falls into a deathly silence. But for Stephen Gardiner's prompt action, murder would have been done in the king's palace, and the infamy of the deed would never go away.

The Duke of Norfolk realises how close his son has come to ruining everything, and in a fit of temper, he snatches Cromwell's chain of office from his neck, and cries out for help. Captain Chaney bursts in, sword drawn, with two burley archers close behind him.

"Arrest that man, captain!" Norfolk screams. The soldier stands, bemused, and sees Surrey crawling towards his father on all fours. He is whimpering, and a double edged knife lies close to his hand. He signals to his men, who leap forward, and snatch the dissolute young earl up into their strong arms. Young Howard yelps in fear, and tries to twist away from their vice-like grips.

"Be still, you filthy murdering dog," one of them says, "or I'll brain you where you stand!"

"No, you oafs!" The Duke of Norfolk is almost purple with rage now. "I mean *him*. Thomas Cromwell!" Chaney sees that the duke means it, and signs for his men to let Surrey go. They release him, and he crashes to the floor, heavily, where he curls into a ball, and groans.

"You mean Master Cromwell?" Captain Chaney asks, with a deliberately puzzled look on his broad face.

"Yes… Cromwell!"

"You want us to take *the* Earl of Essex into our charge, My Lord Norfolk?" Chaney says the words with deliberate care. To make a crass mistake now might prove fatal to his career, and so he insists on absolute confirmation of so outrageous an order. "Is there a warrant for his arrest, sir?"

"A warrant?" Norfolk is almost gasping with rage and frustration. "What are you talking about… you addle brained fool?"

"I can only make an arrest within the confines of a royal palace if in possession of an official warrant," Captain Chaney replies. "It must name the accused, clearly, and be signed by a responsible member of the inner chamber… or the king hisself, Your Lordship. It is usual for the senior council member to sign for the king. In this case, that would be the Earl of Essex, milord."

"Are you mad… you pox ridden dog?" Norfolk yells. "How can the bloody man sign to have himself arrested?"

"I grant you that it is a real puzzle, sir," Chaney offers, stone faced. "Might the matter not wait until a *full* council is present?"

"Arrest Tom Cromwell at once, you bastards!" the Duke of Norfolk cries, and his spittle splashes onto his beard. This crude demand is unambiguous, and Chaney sees himself caught in a cleft stick. If Cromwell now demands the duke's arrest, he is undone. For a moment, he hopes Cromwell resists, and counter charges Norfolk, for he has a mind to protect his Austin Friars master, and sort out the awful mess later, but the Privy Councillor does not speak. Instead, he steps forward, and places himself between the two archers.

"My Lord, if you…" the big man is ready to support Cromwell, but he is silenced by a raised hand.

"Hush now, Master Chaney," Cromwell tells him. "Do your duty… as I have always done mine. The law will take its course, and justice shall be done."

"Master Cromwell, at the request of one third of the Privy Council, I am arresting you on the charges of…" The captain realises that he does not know the charges, and he still has no written warrant to serve.

"Sedition and treason," Norfolk says, as he gloats over his triumph. "Let's see you wriggle out of this one, blacksmith's boy!"

"Yes," the Earl Surrey simpers from the floor, "let us see what you do now… agh!" Bishop Gardiner, unable to restrain himself, kicks the young man sharply up the arse.

*

"What news?" Will Draper asks, and the messenger almost bursts into tears. James Lower, one time falconer to the Duke of Norfolk, and secret agent of Austin Friars has galloped from London with the latest happenings, and can scarcely believe how swiftly things have moved.

"Master Tom is taken, sir," Lower reports. "Captain Chaney was called upon to arrest him in the chamber. He tried to avoid the duty, but Norfolk insisted. He and Surrey were there, along with Tom Audley, the Seymour brothers, and Sir John Russell."

"What's this… John Russell, you say?" Mush asks. He is collecting names for his own list of retribution, and his erstwhile comrade's name will now go onto it. "What was his part?"

"He held the inner door, whilst they conspired to condemn the master," James Lower continues. "Norfolk's people are already going about London, trying to find Cromwell's wealth. They will strip Austin Friars to the bare bricks, I fear."

"Not so," Will says. "We feared as much, and have set our own plans into action. My wife's people are at Austin Friars now, removing every item of value they can. It will go into storage, until Master Cromwell is freed, and restored to his proper position."

"As for the money…" Mush grins. Miriam has long handled Cromwell's real wealth, and it is all safely abroad, save for some ready cash for bribes and wages, amounting to less than twenty eight thousand crowns. "Neither the king, nor Norfolk will see a single penny. What they can lay hands on is already owed to the treasury. Master Tom is a wily old bird. When he returns to us, we shall laugh about this!"

"Where is he now?" Richard Cromwell asks.

"I am not sure," James Lower tells the younger Cromwell. "I had my news from one of Chaney's archers, and I watched them put the master in a boat. It is one of Lady Draper's barges, and the crew seemed to be sympathetic to him."

"Then he is not in Norfolk's hands. Eventually, they will take him to the Tower," Will says, "and that will suit us very well."

"Norfolk has sent his own men to the Tower of London, with orders to replace any who favour you, Colonel Draper," Lower tells the gathered company.

"Enough will remain," Will replies. "They will guard him from assassination, and see he is not maltreated."

"Then your task is made harder." Eustace Chapuys has just arrived, with Alonso Gomez, who has caught him up on the road. "If he is in the Tower, escape is unlikely."

"Thank you, Eustace," Will says, "but some of my men are well embedded, and enough might remain for our purposes."

"That is for you to know, of course," Eustace Chapuys replies. "For my part, I can only do that which I promised your master, some time back. I promised to make sure all are welcome within the empire. My master, the emperor, is a forgiving soul, and will welcome any who wish to slip away to the continent."

"I am sure it will not come to that," Mush says. "How can they find Master Tom guilty of anything? What crime has he ever committed, that was not for the king's benefit?"

"It is all about Cleves," Richard says. He is slower than the rest, but his mind grinds on to the right answer in time. "I knew he should not have pressed Anne onto the king. It was a mistake to make her … too pretty."

"Henry would not bring down his best minister over such a trivial thing," Rafe Sadler tells them. "If a marriage is made, it can be broken. All he needs to do is insist, and the king shall have his way. Master Tom would never stand against him at the last. He would go to Anne's people, and come to some arrangement."

"Then what has caused this upset?" Mush asks.

"I told you," Richard Cromwell insists. "It is all about the portrait. You see, Hans Holbein altered it to favour Cleves … at my uncle's bidding. If Henry has found this out, he will be furious."

"He might strip Cromwell of a few titles… even fine him heavily, but not this."

"Then Norfolk has gone too far," Rafe concludes. "He has overstepped his authority, and that means we can persuade Henry to reconsider. Once he sees that old Tom Howard is going for a charge of treason, he will put a stop to it. Remember how much he regretted Cardinal Wolsey's death?"

Of course, they think. The room falls silent, in contemplation of the past few hours' unexpected events, and they all see now that it is nothing but a minor squall. The king values Thomas Cromwell above Norfolk, and knows not to go too far.

"We must get to Henry," Rafe Sadler says. "Explain to him how Norfolk has misused his power to arrest Cromwell. We must make him see that he could lose his best minister, because of the hatred

Norfolk holds for him."

"Yes, you must follow every avenue," Will Draper says. "For my part, I will investigate this entire mess, and see where we can act to best help Master Tom." He looks about the chamber, which is now crowded with the young men of Austin Friars, and those who have reason to dearly love Thomas Cromwell. "Before we start, I must ask you all an important question. Do any of you here wish to take ship for Antwerp? If so, then go now. You will not be thought ill of … but the ticket is one way. Well?" Not one man moves. "Good fellows, your loyalty does you proud. Then let us get on with the business at hand. Master Cromwell is innocent, and we must contrive a way of saving him!"

*

The river is as calm as he has ever seen it, and Thomas Cromwell has no trouble stepping into the broad beamed boat. The man at the tiller bows to him, and points to a well padded seat. As Cromwell goes to sit, the man whispers to him.

"This is Lady Miriam's boat, Master Cromwell. She always bids those in her employ to offer any help we can to Austin Friars fellows, sir," he says.

"Thank you, but…"

"One word from you, sir, and your guards will go over the side. She commands me, in such circumstances, to say that she *always* has a fast cog waiting at Wapping. It can be in France within the day, or take you to wherever your heart desires."

"Tend to your boat, young man," Thomas Cromwell replies, softly. If it is suspected that Miriam Draper has conspired in his escape, her fortune, her life, and that of her husband, and children, will be forfeit. "Let me steer my own course. Can you get a message to my family and friends?"

"Speak, and I will remember it," the boatman tells him.

"Have my people look to themselves. Tell Miriam to see my fortune is spread about wisely, and save my son, Gregory."

"One of my rowers has already run to your house, sir. If Master Gregory is about, he will warn him of the danger. Then, should he wish, he can be taken aboard Lady Miriam's cog," the lad says. "It is but a few minutes journey downriver from Austin Friars."

"Enough whispering, if you please, Master Thomas," Captain Chaney calls to them. Then he approaches, and drops his voice. "I must not let you speak with anyone, sir, by order of the damned duke. This poor fellow is no-one, of course, rather than anyone … so he does not count." He turns his back on the pair, and signals for the remaining rowers to take oar. The broad beamed craft eases from the jetty, and edges out into the calm Thames. On the shore, a carter waits until the boat is underway before beckoning a street urchin over to him. He presses a halfpenny coin into the boy's grimy hand.

"Master Tom is under arrest," the man tells the lad. "Run to the Lincoln's Inn law courts, as fast as you can, and find Barnaby Fowler. Warn him what is afoot, and then attend upon him."

"What of Draper House?" the lad asks. "Lady Miriam is away in the country, but her household should be warned as what is afoot."

"I shall take a boat down river," the loyal agent tells him. "It might be best for them all to go into hiding for a few days."

"Master Tom will sort the bastards out," the lad says, and takes to his heels. The idea that Thomas Cromwell might be fallible does not cross his mind, and that he might be bested by Norfolk is, to all his people, a quite absurd thought.

*

Thomas Cromwell continues to whisper his instructions, whilst the smooth river flows by, until the boat suddenly swerves from its hitherto linear course. The king's minister looks up then, and sighs. The boat is butting up against a stone wharf he recognises very well. It is the self same spot where he sent Anne Boleyn to meet her fateful end.

"Master Cromwell, I am Robin Crabtree, the Assistant Warden of the Tower of London," a voice calls from the flagstoned landing. "Pray do let me help you ashore, sir, and through to your chambers. A mutual friend thinks you might appreciate the late queen's accommodation. It is well furnished, and overlooks the river."

"A mutual friend?" Thomas Cromwell smiles, and nods at the news. His last days will be comfortable, at least. Though he might have many such friends looking out for him, they will not be able to keep him alive. "I thank you, sir. Pray give me your hand, and I will give myself into your care."

Thomas Cromwell, Earl of Essex, steps ashore and looks about him at the formidable stonework of the Traitor's Gate. It is meant to make grown men weaken, and scare confessions from those condemned to enter through it. Though feeling no fear, he cannot fight an air of melancholy which seems to seep out of the stone walls, and into his heart.

"This way, Master Cromwell," Robin Crabtree says. It has been an eventful week for him, and he is pleased that he was able to release Elizabeth Farriby, and so make his best chambers available for so honoured a guest. "You are to be treated well, but denied writing materials… by order of the Duke of Norfolk."

"Ah, I did the same to poor Sir Thomas More," Cromwell recollects. "The duke has a good memory."

"Better than mine, I fear," Robin says, softly. "For I suspect I might have left paper, ink, and quill in the desk drawer."

"Bless you, my young friend," Tom Cromwell mutters. "Do not put yourself in harm's way on my account."

"I owe my high office to you, sir," the young man replies. "It was Master Rafe Sadler who recommended me, after my father died, and left us in dire financial straits."

"Crabtree, you say?" Cromwell thinks for a moment. He recalls a wastrel father, and a pretty widow with three children to feed. "Yes, I believe I know the name. Your father worked for Miriam Draper… in her counting house at Cheam. He served her very well, young man."

"He did, sir, but the good pay was his downfall, and he quickly drank himself to death," Robin confesses. "Your help has made me into a better man than he, and I hope I am more reliable, and more sober than my father."

"He was, despite his failings, a most honest man," Thomas Cromwell says. "Miriam Draper commended him to me once as being trustworthy. I used him to convey certain secret monies to my agents. It was a shame he took to strong drink the way he did."

"May I serve you just as loyally," Robin Crabtree says.

"My dear Robin, you are a man with a future," Cromwell tells the young gaoler, "and I am a man with a past. Do not let the one be ruined by the other. I thank you for your kindness, but tread warily, and give them no cause to suspect you."

"They do not frighten me at all, sir." Crabtree means it, with all the fervency that comes with youth.

"They should, boy… they should!"

Robin Crabtree is young, and thinks himself invulnerable to the plots and dirty deeds of the court. He is already in a position of some authority, and commands a good salary, which also leads him to believe his suit with Elizabeth Farriby might bear sweet fruit. The time will come, soon, when he realises how fickle love can be, and that the girl he fell in love with cannot repay the depth of his emotion.

Even as he escorts Tom Cromwell inside the forbidding walls of the Tower of

London, she is accepting the ardent proposal of Captain Toby Wilton.

*

"See?" the steward taps the king's shoulder, and points into the clear blue sky. "Up, and to the left, My Lord."

"Good fellow... well spotted," Henry says. "He pulls the small hood from the head of his favourite falcon, and raises his arm up above his head. The bird leaps into the sky after the wood pigeon, and the hunters hold their breath. It has been a poor day's sport, and the king is in need of a success to boost his spirits.

"Sire." The same steward nods to the tented pavilion that has been erected on the nearby knoll. A messenger is just reining in his winded horse. The king frowns, and looks back to the sky. The falcon suddenly stoops, and misses its prey.

"Damn and blast it!" Henry explodes. "That damned bird is worthless. I rue the day Norfolk gifted it to me. Bring the fellow to me, Hoskins." The steward, whose name is actually Amos Enderby, runs off to fetch the man, well contented to be so misnamed. If anything goes amiss, it is Hoskins ... a rogue hanged a couple of years before... who shall carry the main blame.

"Well, what is it?" Henry must feign surprise when being given the news that the Earl of Essex, Tom Cromwell, is charged with misleading the king in the matter his most recent marriage. He must show some anger, then demand the fellow is stripped of his titles. Not all, of course. Perhaps, Henry thinks, he might stop him being in charge of the Court of Augmentations, or discharge him from being the Master of the Crown Jewels. Then there is the money. Norfolk says Cromwell is worth at least a million pounds, and should hand half over to the royal treasury.

"Your Majesty, I come from Westminster, and there is grave news." Sir John Russell is covered in dust from the road, and is exhausted from the fast gallop. He bows, and dusts himself down, as best he can.

"Russell… is it you?" Henry says, bemused at so high ranking a messenger being sent. "What is this news you bring to me so urgently?"

"The Earl of Essex has been placed under arrest, by the Duke of Norfolk," Russell reports. "Even now he is languishing in the Tower of London."

"Such melodramatic words, Sir John," Henry chides. "The fellow has wronged me, no doubt, and must be admonished. I must ponder on what punishment to inflict upon the rascal."

"Sire, there can be only one punishment for treason," Russell replies, and the king almost reels back in surprise. He looks about him, as if seeking advice, but there is no one there he can trust.

"Treason?" he asks. "How can this be so?"

"I had the great misfortune to be there, Your Majesty," Sir John Russell tells the king. "It was the Earl of Surrey who charged Master Thomas with both sedition, and treason."

"What right has Surrey to say such a thing?" Henry demands of those few courtiers who have accompanied him to Arundel. "I made it clear to Norfolk that Cromwell was to be taken down a peg or two. The shambling great oaf has misunderstood me."

"Or chosen to deliberately disobey, sire," Russell says. It is a small thing he does, but he hopes it will help Thomas Cromwell out, and make clear his own continuing loyalty to Austin Friars. He does not, after all, want Mush Draper coming after him with a dagger in his hand. "He made Captain Chaney, who commands the household guard today, arrest Master Cromwell, even though no official warrant was issued. Then he ordered him to take his prisoner to the Tower of London, upon his own authority."

"Norfolk's *own* authority, you say,

sir?"

"Many in the chamber were unhappy at Norfolk's usurpation of your authority, but only Bishop Gardiner tried to intercede. He stopped Surrey from stabbing Cromwell in the back." Sir John Russell watches as the king's face reddens to a shade akin to the stubble on his chin. "I knew this was not of your doing, and rode here, as fast as I could. What are your orders, sire?"

"Orders, you say?" Henry glances over his shoulder, as though he expects the faithful and reliable Tom Cromwell to step forward and issue instructions to all and sundry. "Yes… orders, of course. Norfolk has arrested Cromwell, you say?"

"Sire… he is in the Tower of London," Russell urges. "Your First Minister is locked up in a cell, and at the mercy of his greatest enemy. If you do not act, at once, I fear some terrible outcome that might well blight the honour of the great house of Tudor."

"Yes, I must act," the king murmurs to himself. It is a strange feeling for him to be alone, and unable to seek advice from his ablest advisors. "Where is Rafe Sadler… or Tom Audley?"

"One is at Hampton Court Palace, and the other is detained at Westminster, sire," Russell replies. "Norfolk seeks to keep your best men apart from you, for now."

Henry sees that he is quite by himself, and must make his own decisions. "What would Cromwell do, I wonder?" he says.

"Send orders to the Tower, staying any further action against Master Tom," John Russell insists. "Make it very clear that Cromwell will not be executed arbitrarily."

"Why would he?" Henry says, dumbfounded at the suggestion. "There has been no trial yet, has there?"

"The Duke of Norfolk says you will sign a Bill of Attainder against Master Cromwell, and there will be no need for a trial." Sir John Russell sees that the king is wavering, and presses on. "You must stay his hand, and insist on a fair hearing for the Privy Councillor. Thomas Cromwell is no traitor, sire."

"He lied to me, Russell."

"Of course he did, Your Highness," Russell admits to the king. There is little point in denying the fact, and there is a plausible explanation for Cromwell's actions. "The minister misled you, though only to spare you having to make an unpalatable, or ignoble decision. His actions were for your own good."

"My own good?" Henry barks with

laughter, but it is tinged with indignation. "He would tether me to this Flanders Mare … for my own good? No, sir… that will not do. I will do as you recommend, and stop Norfolk executing him out of hand, but I must have a full answer as to why he acted as he did. Did he think me a child, unable to make up my own mind? Have a scribe make out the required order, and you shall ride to the Tower with it."

"Thank you, Your Majesty." Sir John Russell bows low.

"I admire your courage, Sir John," the king tells him. "A lesser man would have kept silent in my presence. In the times to come, I shall count you amongst those few I can rely on."

"You honour me, sire." Russell heaves a sigh of relief. By this day's work he will secure not only his life from a vengeful Mush Draper, but advance himself in the king's eyes. "Pray, let me take a fresh horse and gallop… lest Norfolk acts precipitously."

"Yes … ride, sir." Henry watches Russell go off in search of a scribe, and turns to his steward. "You … Hoskins… retrieve my falcon, and pull its neck. It has served me badly."

16 Aftermath

"Dear God in Heaven, is that you, Harry?" the startled Baron Cedric Haricourt asks of the bedraggled figure that falls through his door. "What ever has become of you, sir?" Harry Howard, Earl of Surrey, is gasping for breath, and spattered from head to boot with mud and horse dung. He is crying with both rage and fear.

"They chased me, Cedric," he gasps out. "The filthy rabble threw shit at me, and chased me through the streets, like a common felon. My men fled in terror, and I thought those dirty dogs were actually going to tear me apart!"

"But why?" Haricourt is little more than a casual drinking friend of Surrey, whose house is close enough to Westminster Palace to provide a temporary safe haven. "What have you done to provoke the mob to such a fury?"

"Nothing!" Surrey whines. "It is all my father's doing. You know how he loves to intrigue against everyone, and plot their demise, don't you? He has had Tom Cromwell arrested, and …"

"Dear Christ!" Haricourt is dismayed at the news, and hurriedly calls for the servants to bar the doors, and all the ground floor windows against attack by the incensed commoners. "Is he then completely mad? With Thomas Cromwell gone, we are all ruined men."

"What are you talking about, Cedric?" Surrey is calming down, now he is in no immediate danger of being ripped apart by an angry mob. "The man is a criminal, and deserves all he gets. Father will see him off, and no mistake!"

"Can you not see what your father has done?" Haricourt asks. "With him in prison, business and commerce will suffer, then the banks will grow fretful, and call in their loans. I owe Austin Friars alone over a thousand pounds, at four percent. They have my house and the dairy farm in Dorset as surety. If they call in the loan, I shall lose half my wealth at a stroke. You must live beyond your means, Harry. What about your own debts?"

"Twenty thousand pounds, I owe. But I am with the Antwerp branch of the Schuster and Levi Banking House," the Earl of Surrey replies, with a happy grin. "Their head office is in Vienna, and they have my estates as surety against the loans. English politics do not worry them. I am safe enough."

"Really? Enoch ben Levi's eldest son is married to a second cousin of Miriam Draper," his friend tells him. "Draper and Cromwell own a two thirds interest in the banking house. I tell you, Surrey… we are all in peril now, thanks to the high handedness of your mad bloody father. The duke may ruin us all by his dangerous actions. Leave my house."

"Leave … what, now?" Surrey gulps in horror. "The mob may still be waiting."

"You have moved against Thomas Cromwell, and the Austin Friars set, Harry," Haricourt says, firmly. "I dare not shelter you from harm, in case they find out, and act against me. Good day, My Lord Surrey. I suggest that you take the back door, and run like hell!"

*

The Duke of Norfolk's men have stolen what they could from Austin Friars, and nailed a pronouncement to the front door. The great house is confiscated, in the name of the king, and will be put to some other public use, it says. Mush tears the parchment down, and rips it into two.

"I'll kill Norfolk," he says, with such intensity that his men fear for his mind. He returns to his horse, and is about to mount it when Sir John Russell canters into the courtyard. The sword is in his hand in a moment, and it is only the document, held out like a shield that stops the young Jew from killing the man on the spot.

"Orders from the king," Russell

shouts. "Read it, Mush, and you will see I am no traitor. I did not know my part in this, and Norfolk told me only to stand guard. I stand by doors, and await orders from my betters. It is what I do, my friend. I did not realise that it was Cromwell who was in danger."

Mush snatches the order from his outstretched hand, and reads it through, twice.

"By order of King Henry of England, France and Ireland," he announces to his men. "His Majesty wishes the said Thomas Cromwell, Minister of the Crown, to be detained at His Majesty's Pleasure within the confines of the Tower of London. Every kindness is to be shown the Earl of Essex, until such time as he may be granted a fair hearing, concerning the matter of the king's current marriage."

"Thank God!" Richard Cromwell says. "Then my uncle is safe from Norfolk's revenge."

"For now," Mush says. "You have done well to come here, Russell. I see that I was wrong to suspect you and, upon my honour, I bear you no ill will. Deliver this order to Robin Crabtree at once, and see my master is well cared for. Speak to him, if you can. Tell him that we are making our plans, and will have him back home as soon as we can manage it."

"Of course I shall," Sir John Russell says. "Are you thinking of taking him by force?"

"I have sixty men, and half the Tower's force are Will Draper's agents," Mush replies. "It is a possibility."

"Then let me forewarn you, my friend," John Russell tells him. "The Duke of Norfolk has replaced Master Crowforth … the king's armourer … with his own fellow. He has control of every musket, sword and cannon in the place. The duke is an old soldier, so he expects you to come at him head on. He thinks you will attempt some foolhardy escape, and has two companies of Light Horse stationed in the city for such an eventuality. Storm the Tower, and he will enfold you with his cavalry, and score an easy victory."

"I see. Then we must find another way of saving Master Cromwell," says Mush. "I will not have him languish over long, even if it is 'at the king's pleasure'."

"This order effectively saves his life," Russell says to his comrade. "Let Rafe Sadler and Will Draper work their wiles on the king, and get him to soften his heart. They must remind Henry of all the past services done by Cromwell, and the past failings of old Norfolk. That way, Cromwell shall go free, and the Duke of Norfolk will be ruined at last."

"You talk good sense, my dear Russell," Richard Cromwell says. "Ride, and do your very best for my uncle. Tell him we are his loyal servants."

Sir John lingers long enough to drink down a pint of weak ale, then climbs back into the saddle. He wishes to safeguard his own position well enough, but cannot shake off the ingrained loyalty that has come to tie him to his friends at Austin Friars. He is a little surprised at his own sense of worth these days, and puts it down to the almost magical influence of Tom Cromwell and his ill assorted gang of young men.

As he spurs his mount into action, Mush waves him off and turns back to the house. It is a pale shadow of its former self, and the stripped walls and general untidiness make him think of how transient life can be. Great today, and gone tomorrow. It is a phrase often quoted to him by Cromwell, as a way of ensuring that they remain always on their guard.

"Where is Suffolk?" he asks.

"Gone back into his own county," Richard says. "He thinks there might be war, especially if the Duke of Norfolk tries to push things too far. His yeomanry are the best in England, and he seeks to raise them to arms, but quietly."

"How many men has he?" Mush

asks.

"Not counting the twelve hundred foot, and two hundred horse he has just shipped to Calais," Richard replies, "I would guess at about eight thousand. He can muster another five hundred horse from the gentlemen who populate his estates. They are not trained cavalry, but they will follow Suffolk."

"Norfolk has ten thousand men, many who have fought against the Scots, and the northern rebels," Mush says, "and he might have the support of the Seymour family now."

"Ned Seymour wants his own power," Richard tells his friend. "He will not let Norfolk have it all his own way."

"Will he join us then?" Mush asks. He does not understand these English gentlemen the same way Richard Cromwell does, and is never quite sure who can be trusted.

"No, he will perch on the fence, and wait to see how things progress," Richard explains. "besides, he can only raise about a thousand men. Not enough to start a civil war… but enough to sway the outcome, perhaps."

"We should write to him," Mush muses. "Offer him something for his support. It is what Cromwell would do, I think."

"My uncle has been caught out," says Richard. "He is not the man he once was. Ever since Queen Jane died, he has only played at running England."

"Did he love her so much?" Mush asks.

"Like a daughter, I suppose," the younger Cromwell replies, unknowing of the real facts.

"Then let us hope Henry recalls those happier days, and remembers that it is because of Master Tom he has a son to rule after him. There is nothing more dangerous than the gratitude of kings."

"No, Uncle Thomas often said as much," Richard says. "You must never remind the king that he is in your debt… but drop a few hints, and let him work it out for himself."

"Then let us start dropping hints," Mush tells his friend. "For the clock is ticking, and Master Tom is on borrowed time!"

*

"I want Cromwell dead by morning," Tom Howard, Duke of Norfolk says, as he slices himself a cut of ham.

"Then you must get the king to sign his death warrant," Rupert Donne says. "With a legal warrant, I can do as you wish."

"Henry is in Arundel," Norfolk sneers, "keeping his hands clean. He will not be back for a week."

"He is on his way back to Whitehall Palace, by river, even as we speak," Rupert Donne informs his master. "My agent sends word that he is coming by water, and he wishes answers."

"Answers to what?" Norfolk has an uneasy feeling in his stomach. The mob have chased his son through the streets, and some have even hurled mud at himself, and shouted abuse. It seems that Cromwell was well liked by the rabble, despite his high office.

"He wishes to know why Tom Cromwell is taken for treason, and not some lesser charge," Donne says. "The king thinks to scold the fellow, not cut off his head."

"Then he is a fool," Norfolk says. "Cromwell is a danger to the crown."

"Cromwell does not have ten thousand armed soldiers at his disposal," Norfolk's agent reminds him. "Henry might see that as a rather pertinent point."

"The man is a liar, and he has spoken against the king."

"Over which queen to choose?" Rupert Donne shakes his head. "He values the man, and you must discredit him, beyond redemption, or face the consequences."

"Consequences?" Norfolk laughs at

the very idea of him having to face anything. "I am the Duke of Norfolk, fellow!"

"And what was Buckingham the lord of?" Donne snaps back at him. "The duke upset Henry, and paid for it with his life. Then there was old Cardinal Wolsey. He loved the man, yet let him be humiliated unto death. My Lord… forgive me… but he does not even like you over much."

"You saucy rascal!" Norfolk thinks he might well box Rupert Donne's ears for his impudence, but sees the truth in what the man says. Besides, Donne is the most vicious killer he has ever met, and not a man to trifle with. "Tell me what I must do."

"Make it so that the king cannot reprieve Cromwell."

"How can that be done?"

"Remind him that Tom Cromwell lied to him, at every opportunity. Make the king suspicious of how close he is to Will Draper, and how he curries favour with Charles Brandon. Warn him that the Duke of Suffolk has a large army, and currently holds Calais with his own men. Hint that he holds the *Calaisis* region for Cromwell, and not for the crown."

"Yes, of course." Norfolk's mood brightens. "If Henry thinks Cromwell might escape to Calais, and rally Suffolk to his cause…"

"Just so," Rupert Donne says. "Warn the king that Draper's men run the Tower of London, and remind him of the warm friendship between Thomas Cromwell and the King's Examiner over these last ten years."

"I shall do as you suggest, but will it be enough to make my treason charge stick?" Norfolk is worried that his old enemy might wriggle away, and return to Whitehall, even stronger.

"Ask Henry who first came to him with accusations against Anne Boleyn," Donne continues. "Ask him whom it was who recommended Will Draper be raised to the knighthood, and why that same man was in France last year."

"Why was he?" Norfolk asks.

"To treat with King François, of course," Donne says. "Let Henry see that Cromwell is friends with the emperor *and* the French king. Ask him why Eustace Chapuys lives next door to Cromwell."

"Chapuys.. Who is that?"

"The Holy Roman Ambassador."

"Oh, the little frog?" Norfolk nods with enthusiasm. He is beginning to see that a mud throwing exercise might just do the trick. "Yes, that is odd, isn't it?"

"Then there is your own safety to consider."

"My own…?" Norfolk is so taken

with ruining the Cromwell faction that he has quite forgotten that the man has many dangerous friends. "What do you know, Master Donne?"

"Nothing for certain," Donne replies. "Though Mush Draper will wish to kill you, of course. Then there is the King's Examiner himself. I dare say the colonel would not mind one jot slipping a knife into your gut."

"Dear God, but I must have more men about me," Norfolk says. "Have a dozen fellows armed and…"

"Which dozen fellows?" Donne asks. "Cromwell has agents everywhere, and the men set to guard you could be in his pay."

"Then what must be done?" Norfolk demands. He is used to things being taken care of, and wishes Rupert Donne would give him answers, rather than suggest problems.

"Press for Cromwell's execution," Donne informs his master, "and I will attend to the Draper family. Tell Henry that they have already started to strike back. Tell him that Judas Plank, the witness against him, is dead."

"Is he?" Norfolk asks. "I do not recall giving that order."

"He was waylaid, and murdered by two men, after meeting with the king. They stole his reward money."

"Good God!"

"A witness describes them as being big, violent looking fellows, dressed in black, and with a red 'C' pricked out on the sleeve and breast."

"Cromwell's own livery?" Norfolk is taken aback. It does not occur to him that the story is a complete lie. The murder of Judas Plank, and the stealing of his gold had been the plan, but Rupert Donne has had second thoughts.

Though the coachman is one of the plan's loose ends, he wants him alive for the moment. If things start to go wrong the eavesdropping coachman may yet be of some further use to him.

"Tell this to the king," Donne urges Norfolk. "Then the king will see that murder is done, by Cromwell men, and in Thomas Cromwell's own name!"

*

Miriam Draper steps down from the coach, and orders both driver and footman to stay with the conveyance. The docks around Gravesend are a rough and ready place to stop, and not somewhere you would leave a coach unguarded. She pulls her cloak tight about herself, and makes for the grim looking quayside, where a most unbecoming sight greets her.

The Happy Wanderer is little more

than a battered hulk, and the two remaining masts are hung with tattered shrouds, rather than full sails. The figurehead beneath the bowsprit is scoured clean of paint, and the hull shows signs of patching, where enemy cannon balls have struck home. A short, barrel like fellow with matted hair and beard guards the gangplank, and he stands to attention as she approaches the forlorn looking ship.

"Mistress Draper?" the man says, and he draws himself up to attention. "It's me, Ben Glover. You made me purser to the fleet."

"Master Glover," Miriam says, and nods recognition of the man, despite the ravages of time, and adventure. "I pray God you are well, and glad to be home in England again?"

"That I am, mistress," he says. "Though the fleet is now but one ship, and she so battered as to be virtually un-sea-worthy. We are back from the savage New Found Land shores, and it is as if we are back from the very pits of Hell."

"Mistress Miriam!" Miriam looks up the gangplank to see a tall black man coming towards her. "I sent word the moment we touched back upon English soil."

"Master Ibrahim," Miriam says, most sternly. "Where are my ships? Where are my treasures, and where are my people?"

"Come aboard, madam," the man who once fooled Henry into thinking him to be the Prince of Abyssinia offers, "and I will explain it all to you."

"You took five ships with you," Miriam says. "One, the Great Harry, found its way home last year, but what of the rest?"

"Come, take wine with me," Ibrahim says. "I did as I was commanded, and built a fort in the New Found Land. Only it was not new found. The natives of that place, who call themselves the *Mahican*, numbered in their thousands."

Miriam is up the plank, and makes her way to the poop deck, where the captain's cabin is maintained. There are a few crew on deck, and they all look at her appreciatively. It has been a long time since they have seen a white woman, and they are still a little shy of the trappings of civilisation.

"Wine, my dear lady?" Ibrahim pours out two glasses. "Just a week out, and we were hit by a great storm. The sea and sky became one, and the day was as black as the night. My fleet was scattered, and that is when we lost the great Harry," he explains.

"They reached Funchal harbour, in Madeira, and finally found their way back to England," Miriam told him. "The ship survived, more by luck than your fine seamanship, sir."

"For this, I am glad," Ibrahim says, honestly. "It means another three hundred lives were spared."

"Tell me of what happened, after the storm had passed."

"I pressed on, until we came to the Florida coast. The Spanish were not welcoming to us, and made war-like gestures to us, so I turned north. We sailed up the coast for two weeks, until we came to where the New Found Land was shown on the copy of my Cabot map. I then had my men build a stockade from sturdy tree trunks, and raised the king's pennant. I named the stockade 'Fort Henry', in the hope that it would please His Majesty and make him amenable to our adventure."

"Then how comes it that you are back, without the riches I expected? What about the furs, and the timber?"

"I set the men into clearing the land," Ibrahim tells her. "At the end of the second week, some natives turned up, begging for food. I set them to work, and fed them. They seemed grateful, and worked harder than my own sailors. We soon had several log cabins within the palisade, and Fort Henry was becoming a village.The next week, another hundred Mahicans came to me. These fellows offered to hunt furs for us, and I accepted. In return, I gave them a few trinkets, and a couple of barrels of watered down ale."

"It sounds like Master More's Utopia," Miriam says. "What went wrong, Ibrahim?"

"They brought us furs. Hundreds of pelts, prepared and ready for shipping, and some few nuggets of silver made for a most goodly start. Then their chief, a big, bronze coloured fellow, suggested he might trap more furs with muskets."

"So, you armed him and his men?"

"No, I did not," Ibrahim replies. "I sent out men to join his hunters. Two of my muskets to every hundred of his warriors. The chief must have had them watch my men, for they soon understood how to load a musket. Then, one day, the hunters failed to return, and I had lost a dozen muskets, and as many men."

"You never found them?"

"Yes, a few days later," Ibrahim says, and sucks in his breath at the memory. "They had been tortured and mutilated. I led my force back to the fort, but it was already under attack. We fought our way back inside, but the end was clear. The chief, a man called Metacusa, was a wily fellow, and he knew how to lay a siege. With over two hundred muskets inside the fort, and a couple of cannon from the ships, he was never going to break in, without losing hundreds of his men. It seemed like a stalemate, but he knew the lie of the land, and I did not."

"Go on."

"He surrounded us, and contented himself with sudden raids against the walls. We lost no men, and killed a few of his. We had plenty of supplies with us, and much more on the ships. I still had four moored in the bay. One night, the natives rowed out in their small canoes, and attacked them. The watch was roused, and we were able to repulse them, but not before one of the ships was fired."

"Did it not occur to you that an orderly withdrawal might be the best course of action?" Miriam asks. "There were so many women and children to consider."

"Of course it did, My Lady." Ibrahim is thin, drawn and exhausted, but he is at the vital part of his story, and presses on to the end. "I decided to retreat two weeks into the siege, when the wells inside the fort dried up. Metacusa must have found the source of the springs, and dammed them with rocks or felled trees. Without water, I knew we could not last another week. I chose sixty of the best men I had, and set out for the ships in the bay. I intended bringing them close in to shore, then evacuating my people."

"What went wrong?" Miriam knows most of this from Chapuys, but needs to hear it from the man himself. She is surprised at his honesty, and the humility in his voice.

"Metacusa must have guessed my intentions." Ibrahim can scarcely go on. "As soon as we slipped away from the fort, he called his war bands together, and launched an attack. We ran back from the headland, but the natives were already over the palisades. The muskets fired, and the pair of cannons roared, but once. I saw scores of natives fall, but the second wave gained the walls, and the fighting was hand to hand. I could only stand, and watch, until it was all over. I knew they would come for the ships next, so I led my men back to the sea, and we boarded the Happy Wanderer. She was the most seaworthy. With so few men, I could not save the other ships. I took their guards aboard, and we set sail. I headed down the coast."

"The Spanish came across your Chief Metacusa," Miriam says. "They found the burnt out fort, the abandoned ships, and the dead. There were no survivors."

"I took one of the women to wife," Ibrahim says, softly. "She was with child. I should have gone back."

"And died?" Miriam places a soft hand over his. "That you survived, and returned is a miracle, Ibrahim."

"At least, I am not empty handed, my dear Miriam" Ibrahim tells her. "We came across a lone Spanish treasure ship on our return trip. We must have looked a sorry sight, with our ragged sails, for the captain altered course, and tried to take us as a prize. My lads fought well. We managed to cut across her, and take her wind. As the ship sailed across our starboard side, we were able to give her a broadside. Though she had twenty cannon to our twelve, we outgunned them, and brought down her mainsail. She was dead in the water then, and we were able to board her. The Spaniards fought well enough, but my lads bested them."

"Then I have a prize ship to sell?" Miriam asks.

"Regrettably not," Ibrahim says. "She was crammed to the gunnels with treasure, but, during the fight, she had taken a couple of cannon shots low down on the water line. We salvaged what we could, before she shipped too much water and sank. I dare say there is over twenty thousand pounds worth of treasure below decks. Your king shall have his portion, and Master Cromwell will be pleased with his share, no doubt."

"Tom Cromwell is in the Tower." Miriam tells him.

"How can this be?"

"He made a mistake," Miriam tells him. "The Duke of Norfolk used it to bring him down.

"Then we must surely do whatever we can for him," Ibrahim replies. "Do you have a plan, madam?"

"Oh, I am sure there are plans a plenty," Miriam says, "but I cannot see how Master Tom can escape this time."

"Have faith, Mistress Miriam," Ibrahim says. "Have faith!"

*

"Mortimer, Lord of the Marches, escaped from this place, my friend." Eustace Chapuys has been spirited into the Tower by Robin Crabtree, and finds his old friend, Cromwell in a contemplative mood. "They say he found a secret way out, and fled to France."

"Lord Mortimer was in the prime of his life," Cromwell responds. "His barber and a bishop conspired to help him. They squeezed him down the privy chute, all slick with turds, and he dropped into the moat. Then a boat was rowed to him, and that was that. I would not like to have been the rower on that occasion!"

"Then there is some hope, Thomas." The little Savoyard ambassador smiles wanly, and gazes about the chamber where Anne Boleyn spent her final days.

"They bricked up the privy," Thomas Cromwell says, "but I fear my girth would have been my undoing. Roger Mortimer was a much thinner fellow, I hear, and a decidedly good swimmer."

"The king is coming back from Arundel to Westminster by river," Eustace Chapuys persists. "His royal barge will be here on the morrow's tide. Your truest friends are awaiting his return. Rafe Sadler will acquaint him with all that has happened, and Norfolk will be kicked back to his kennel, like the cur that he is."

"Ah, you think the king will save me." Thomas Cromwell is on the point of explaining the truth of the matter to his old friend, but decides not to bother. He knows Henry better that he knew his own wife and children, and he thinks he understands the man better than any other man alive. "I am touched by your sincere belief in me, Eustace. What if I am guilty?"

"Guilty of what?" Chapuys demands to know.

"Does it matter?" Cromwell replies, with a broad smile. "Do you recall Sir Francis Weston and William Brereton?"

"Of course I do," Eustace Chapuys replies. "They were Anne Boleyn's lovers."

"They were nothing of the sort,"

Cromwell tells him. "Nor was poor old Norris. I doubt that any of them had even so much as touched the woman."

"Then they were all innocent?" Chapuys asks, appalled at the unasked for revelation.

"Of swiving the Queen of England… yes." Tom Cromwell is enjoying himself now. His arrest seems to have freed him from having to keep all of England's secrets. "Though they were guilty of many other things. Sir Francis and Brereton came to kill me in the night, and Norris helped ruin Cardinal Wolsey. So, I killed them all."

"Then the charges against Anne Boleyn were…"

"False." Cromwell sees the little Savoyard's face change colour. "Though I think she did sleep with her brother. Either way, she was a threat to Austin Friars, and had to be put away. I would have settled for a nice convent for her, but she was too stubborn. She sent men to kill me, and so sealed her own fate."

"Then Henry was well paid out for his sins," Chapuys replies. "He should never have divorced Queen Katherine."

"Then England would have had no heir," Cromwell explains to the ambassador. "With Henry dead, Mary would claim the throne."

"Rightly."

"Tell the great march lords that, and see what happens," Tom Cromwell says. "Harry Percy, Cumberland, Suffolk and Norfolk would all have wanted their own choice on the throne. Imagine it, man. Four great armies, fighting to put their own monarch on the throne. Mary, Henry Fitzroy, or even old Norfolk himself. Then King James would be there, hoping to pick up the pieces. He has some claim to the English throne, through his mother… who is King Henry's much loved sister."

"This is all 'what might have been', my friend," Eustace Chapuys reminds him. "Henry has a legitimate son, and Edward will rule wisely over this kingdom. The king knows you to be his most capable minister, and he will not abandon you over so paltry a misunderstanding." Thomas Cromwell looks about him, at the four grey stone walls, and smiles at the sheer persistence of Chapuys's defence of him.

"I have been arrested, and brought through Traitor's Gate, my friend," he says. "Pray tell me, from your certain knowledge, how many men have made this dark journey, and survived to speak of it afterwards?"

"Mortimer," Chapuys insists.

"Bugger Mortimer," Tom Cromwell says. "If Henry wishes to save me, he must come here and speak with me. Only then can he honestly say he has heard the evidence, and wishes to rescind the arrest."

"Then he will come," the ambassador concludes. "He is, in his heart, a thoroughly decent fellow… and he *will* come."

"Will he?" Thomas Cromwell is not nearly so hopeful about how things will unfold, and foresees stormy times ahead. "And even if he does come here to see me, and then he asks me if I am guilty of tricking him into marrying Anne of Cleves, what am I to say in reply? Yes, sire, I am guilty as charged. I did it for England, and not for you. You do not matter a jot, other than that you happen to have Tudor blood in your veins."

"Help him break the marriage then," Chapuys says to his friend. "Then he will be able to take you back, for he has an excuse."

"Perhaps I do not wish to be taken back, old friend," Tom Cromwell says, with sudden insight. "Perhaps I do not wish to swim in these murky waters any more. I am sick unto death of the Duke of Norfolk. One day, somehow or other, he will have his way… so why not now?"

"Because this country will be the poorer for your passing," Chapuys insists. "You have built a new church for England, made the navy great, and kept the king's treasury full of gold, despite his financial profligacy."

"True enough, I suppose. Let me sit back now, and see if Tom Howard and his gang of mediocre cronies can do any better than a poor blacksmith's son." Thomas Cromwell is yet to come to terms with how sudden his downfall has come to him, and he cannot see the way ahead just at the moment. "How long will it be before they come for me?"

"Sir John Russell's order should give us a week or two," the ambassador tells his friend. "Perhaps even more."

"I am glad the fellow has remained loyal," Tom Cromwell says, "but I said some very harsh words to him. Pray let him know that I now know the truth of it, and that I do sincerely thank him for all of his help."

"I most certainly shall." Eustace Chapuys sees that Tom Cromwell is in danger of slipping into a morass of self pity, and decides that the time is right to give him some welcome news. "Your blackamoor is back from the New World."

"Ibrahim has returned to us?" Thomas Cromwell smiles, and asks after the circumstances.

"He made harbour with one ship, the Happy Wanderer, full of Spanish gold," Eustace Chapuys says. "I must complain to the king, of course, but Henry will, no doubt, take his cut and ignore me."

"Then miracles can still come about," Cromwell mutters. "If God can look kindly on such a rogue, he can spare me a thought also."

"Amen," Eustace Chapuys says, and he crosses himself.

"Amen, indeed," Thomas Cromwell says, and then he laughs at a sudden, deliciously wicked thought. "Thanks be that He is an Englishman!"

~end~

Afterword

When you consider the number of dubious events that Thomas Cromwell, 1st Earl of Essex, was involved in, it is surprising that so minor a thing as a marital dispute should conspire to end his glittering political career.

Historians, whether professional or enthusiastic amateur, tend to agree on little that happened in the golden years of Tudor England. In this case, however, they seem to speak with a single voice. The career of Cromwell came to an end because of the mistake he made in arranging the king's marriage to Anne of Cleves.

What little written testimony there is seems to point to Anne being plain, rather than ugly, and her figure is described favourably by the French ambassador of the time. It seems that the fault, if there was one, lay with the king, rather than the lady. Henry made it quite clear to several of his ministers that he was unable to fulfil his marital duties, and quite clearly blamed Anne of Cleves for his own shortcomings.

From subsequent events, it is clear that Henry, true to form, fell into the familiar pattern of listening to whispering campaigns, and rather than follow his own judgement, deferred to those ministers of more noble birth. The downfall of Thomas

Cromwell is more to do with class than anything else, with well born nobles, such as Thomas Howard, Duke of Norfolk, resenting the commoner for his lowly birth, rather than his abilities.

Despite losing the king's protection, and ending up incarcerated in the Tower of London, Thomas Cromwell was still an important part of events. It was he who helped formulate the plan to rid Henry of his new queen, and many historians believe that he was kept alive for the purpose.

To expect any sort of a reprieve was wishful thinking, for the clever son of a blacksmith had climbed too high, and his star had shone too brightly. Thomas Cromwell had succeeded in changing the face of religion in England, and in breaking the terrible power of a corrupt Roman Catholic church.

Instead of gratitude, he would receive nothing but the cold mercy of a king. Despite falling from grace, Cromwell's legacy would live on, in the persons of those whom he had nurtured, and raised through his Austin Friars days.

Anne Stevens

The next part of Tudor Crimes is: *'Mercy of Kings'* (Book XV)

Thomas Cromwell is in the Tower of London, and all of England holds its breath, waiting to see what will happen next....

§

Other TightCircle Publications

Tudor Crimes by Anne Stevens.
(Volumes I to XV)

The Black Jigsaw by Tessa Dale
The Red Maze by Tessa Dale
The Chinese Puzzle by Tessa Dale

And Angels May Fall by S Teasdale
D I Donna Proud's private life is a mess, her boss is terminally ill, her mother frowns on her chosen profession, and her brother is a doctor. Can it get worse? The answer is yes. The DI is put in charge of a cold murder case, and finds herself pitted against the infamous Grist brothers. She has to break down a wall of fear, and confront a gang lead by the most cold blooded psychopath imaginable.
Kyle Grist is a character plucked from the depths of Hell, and he rules his empire

through terror, and swift violence. DI Donna proud must forge together a team capable of stopping him, whilst still protecting her family... whether they like it or not!

Soul Eater by S Teasdale

DI Donna Proud returns, to investigate a series of bizarre deaths that seem to echo murders from over seventy years before. The killer knows things that have never been revealed about the earlier murders, and seems to have an affinity with a man long dead. Donna knows that it is not possible... but somehow, the Soul Eater is back, and reaping a harvest of death. She must overcome the seemingly supernatural events, and find the truth... before the Soul Eater comes for her!

All are now available through Amazon, as Kindle e-books, or in paperback.

© TightCircle Publications/The Author2018. No part of this book may be sold, reprinted, or electronically transmitted without the written permission of the author, or his/her accredited agents.